Penguin Crime Fiction
*Editor: Julian Symons*
Dressing of Diamond

Nicolas Freeling was born in London in 1927 and
spent his childhood in France. Before taking up
writing he worked for many years in hotels and
restaurants, and from their back doors got to know
a good deal of Europe. When *Love in Amsterdam*,
his first novel, was published in 1962 he stopped
cooking other people's dinners and went back to
Holland. His second and third novels, *Because of
the Cats* and *Gun before Butter*, were published in
1963. They have been published in Penguins, as
well as *Valparaiso*, *The Dresden Green*, *The King
of the Rainy Country*, *Criminal Conversation*,
*Strike Out Where Not Applicable*, *Tsing-Boum*,
*Double-Barrel*, *This Is the Castle*, and *A Long
Silence* (1972). He has also written a straight novel
under a pseudonym. His latest books include
*Dressing of Diamond* (1974) and *What Are the
Bugles Blowing For?* (1975).

Nicolas Freeling

# Dressing of Diamond

Penguin Books

Penguin Books Ltd, Harmondsworth,
Middlesex, England
Penguin Books, 625 Madison Avenue, New York,
New York 10022, U.S.A.
Penguin Books Australia Ltd, Ringwood,
Victoria, Australia
Penguin Books Canada Ltd, 41 Steelcase Road West,
Markham, Ontario, Canada
Penguin Books (N.Z.) Ltd, 182–190 Wairau Road,
Auckland 10, New Zealand

First published in the United States by
Harper & Row, Publishers, Inc., New York, 1974
First published in Great Britain by
Hamish Hamilton 1974
Published by Penguin Books in the United States
by arrangement with Harper & Row, Publishers, Inc.
Published in Penguin Books 1976

Printed in the United States of America by
Offset Paperback Mfrs., Inc., Dallas, Pennsylvania
Set in Linotype Times Roman

'Peace of mind suits me
'As soft white velvet hands become a man,
'As on half-healed wound a dressing –
'– a dressing of diamond.'

*'La quiétude me va comme*
*'Des mains de velours à un homme,*
*'Sur un bobo cicatrisant*
*'Un pansement de diamant.'*

– ALBERTINE SARRAZIN

Albertine Sarrazin, a half-Arab illegitimate child brought up by the Assistance Publique, first adopted and then rejected by a French bourgeois family, was a prostitute at fifteen and engaged in an armed hold-up at sixteen. In prison, where she stayed for precisely half her life, she wrote two best-selling novels which were translated into every European language. Within two years of her release at the age of thirty, she died upon the operating table. While in prison she married Julien Sarrazin, a criminal, who had rescued and sheltered her following a prison-break. At the time of her death, 10 July 1967, she was regarded as one of the most talented and promising of post-war French writers. The scrap of verse above was written in Amiens prison in 1958. She was a friend of the present writer, who never met her. Her memory has been sentimentalized, but she was both a beautiful and a tragic woman.

Colette Delavigne was doing her shopping. She looked at carrots, at little green beans, at Moroccan tomatoes; carefully and without interest. It was a prolongation of the working day that was often a heavy drain upon her resources: her boredom with shopping soured easily and turned to dislike, but she was accustomed to unpleasant chores, and carried this one out after the others, carefully and methodically. The heavy air with its stuffy, slightly sweetish smell, the noise that was like the smell, muffled but metallic with a syrupy note of artificial jollity added by Musak, gave her a faint nauseous headache. She had, even after working hours, enough concentration left to pay no attention to this. She walked with small steps, holding herself upright, guiding her wire trolley in a series of little pushes and controlling it with her finger tips.

She looked at nylon tights; the colours always that little bit wrong, the cut invariably that bit too mean. She had taken hers off and put them in a large envelope, which was misuse of official stationery. She liked to go barelegged in summer, but not only was it felt – strongly – at the office that women should be clothed with dignity: she agreed. Witnesses would be distracted by her bare knees; she would not allow either overheated adolescents or bored but lecherous policemen to regale themselves by hoping to catch a glimpse of her knickers.

From behind (to the supermarket shopper more easily led astray from his purpose) she was an appetising young woman. Calves rather too muscular: it is the case with most young women in France. Feet small with a high instep, in blue leather sandals with cork heels. A plain navy-blue linen frock with a big sailor collar and white piqué edging: no display of sweaty armpit there. French government offices are not air-conditioned. Either the all-too-well constructed nineteenth-century window is open, with the horrible consequences from the street, or one asphyxiates in academic dust. Colette, being the most junior of the examining magistrates, had the noisiest office; she opened or shut her window forty times a day.

She bought three oranges, after feeling them attentively. She did not regard herself as a skilful housewife, but she was accustomed to weighing evidence. She had, besides, been well brought up. If she again took escalopes of veal there would be an outcry. On her way back to the fish counter she took three avocadoes, and once there she took three trout. Annoyingly, she now had to go back for cream. That was conventional thinking. Avocadoes took a lot of oil: so no cream. She decided that there were some bacon rashers left, in which trout could be wrapped, that there were some chives still in her window-box, that she would take fennel for a vegetable, and a pound of apricots for dessert. Colette liked food. That is to say she liked eating, and didn't mind cooking (it was nice to be standing, agreeable to be in movement, interesting to concentrate on a physical activity, and valuable to possess a handicraft). But if not kept in check Bernard easily became English, with a tendency to pornography. As things were it was Bernard's job to buy drinks ('I've quite enough bottles to carry as it is') and cheese ('Supermarket cheese!'). Indulged in these areas of male pride Bernard had learned to accept that he was only allowed potatoes at weekends, in the country.

She waited patiently at the check-out, thinking of nothing at all. Noticing that the other files moved faster than hers did, but they always did. Being rueful about that was self indulgent. The supermarket promoted apathy. One was herded: very well, one was herded. It was enough to try and keep other people's pushful trolleys from bumping one's heels.

She wrote her cheque with the speed of a woman who is accustomed to signing her name at the foot of forms a great many times a day. Colette Delavigne was the 'Children's Judge'. It is not a job given invariably or automatically to the most junior of the examining magistrates (though, regrettably, that is still often the case) but she was a woman and at twenty-seven still one of the youngest judges in France. She wheeled her chariot to the parking lot, content that it did not squeak and that its back wheels seemed willing to follow the front ones. A small thing, but every tiny concession wrung from supermarkets appears as a mighty gift.

Madame Delavigne's car had been the subject of anxious thought. It must not be showy (Bernard had decided) since ostentation would cause legal lips to lengthen. It had to be small enough to manoeuvre easily and park handily, but it must not be a ridiculous-looking object. One had to have a pretty car, to show off a pretty woman. There was also a large and threatening assortment of 'stupid cars' to be avoided.

Impatient with this male servility towards gadgets (who cared, as long as it went?) she had controlled herself while the law got laid down. As though one hadn't enough of that . . . But though she was buying her own car, supported by her own earnings, she allowed Bernard to cast the expert eye. Indeed she wanted him to. She drove a good deal better than he did, but never said so. Nor did she say she wanted to choose her own car. Bernard after all submitted to her judgement in a great many things, and even when secretly convinced he knew better. Even now, after a magisterial summing-up, and when he had pinned the gold medal to the bosom of the Fiat – so suitable – he was not nasty about her suddenly being female and emotional.

'I would really like the little Alfa very much indeed.'

He liked her, of course, to be female and emotional: one cannot make love to a Judge of Instruction, and Bernard enjoyed making love very much. But it was nice of him to swallow his disapproval: he hardly moved a muscle. He didn't walk away and stare out of the showroom window, nor leave loudly unsaid that he thought it a poor choice. He giggled endearingly, and even lent her the extra money to pay for it. To be sure he assumed all the credit when it was a vast success. Even the prissiest of magistrates had not made long disapproving lips. On the contrary, they enjoyed it. Little Madame Delavigne and her very fast car. Buttercup yellow! There were jokes about re-gilding our tarnished blazon. Even Monsieur Zsylotcly, that rather unsympathetic Pole from Béthune, who had been doom-laden for six months ('Little Madame Delavigne will kill herself one of these days') had come gallantly over with a marvel-lous imitation chamois-leather ('Made in Japan, you see') to wipe dead flies off her windscreen. As for the police, who relish pinning parking tickets to magistrates' cars, they revived the charming nineteenth-century verb 'to flirt' and conjugated it down to the imperfect subjunctive, a game which little Madame Delavigne had been known to cheat at.

Colette never left the car outside. Juvenile delinquents were her daily nourishment. The basement garage smelt oddly like a supermarket, of warm metal, synthetically perfumed disinfectant and fermenting vegetables, and was pleasantly dark after the glare of the June sun. She took the lift. Bernard always took the stairs, because of smoking too much. The top-floor flat in the 'Résidence Dampierre' was the most obvious, and it must be admitted the most vulgar, symbol of achievement. Vera Castang, Colette's one close friend, said it had no taste at all. Colette admitted this. But Vera was Czech, and an artist, and alarmingly exacting. She had suffered a lot in her life. She was married to a policeman – not, surely, the easiest of existences. Colette had never suffered. It was a gap in her armoury that frightened her. She was loved by most people, and indulged by all. Vera's finely drawn, almost haggard face disquieted and alarmed her. She admitted, too, the vulgarity of the flat – and was too honest to blame it all on Bernard. Vulgarity, she argued, was inseparable from luxury. The flat was not really very luxurious. The vulgarity was in consequence moderate, and tolerable. Did not Vera agree? Vera didn't but did not at all wish to be offensive to a person she was fond of.

It wasn't even a hideous high tower. There were only six floors of a dullish, child's architecture with timid little balconies. Nor had anyone demolished any pretty buildings: the site had been that of a 'Hatter's Castle' in the most crenellated and curlicued of Victorian Gothic, and nearly all the trees in the garden had been carefully saved. Vera continued to speak of 'Branch Number Six of the Residence Monkey-Puzzle', but Colette refused to be ashamed about it. Bernard made lots of money, selling yoghurt, but he worked very hard. The competition in yoghurt is something fierce.

She dumped her parcels in the kitchen, hung her frock in the dressing-room, pushed everything else into the basket, and pattered into the bathroom, for a shower that would ritually remove the dust of the Palace of Justice. She had not been in court that day: she had been 'instructing'. A judge of instruction, in

10

France, is not allowed to be a member of the tribunal, because of the separation of powers. An exception to this rule is made for the Children's Judge, because it is felt that the trial judge should have the widest possible preliminary knowledge of the circumstances, background and personality of the child concerned. Colette took her work extremely seriously, was severe about the 'secret of instruction', and tried to compartmentalize. A clumsy word, as she was accustomed to say, for an impossible thing. 'But those business men who bring home bulging brief-cases – so very dull.'

While drying herself she noticed that the flat was very still. She opened the bathroom door.

'Rachel? Ra-chel.' The child must be out playing somewhere.

They only had one child, produced in student days in a flush of enthusiasm, which had been a great nuisance but a rather splendid bond with Bernard, who had become a superb nappy-changer and a tremendous expert on baby-food, analysing spinach in the laboratory and in general having a glorious time. He was fond of saying that this had brought him into the yoghurt business, and Rachel, now eight, was official taster to the weird new cocktails, scathing about all those Japanese tangerines. Father and daughter had a relationship so close that it caused Colette problems. Were they too wrapped up in each other? Was she, professionally, and in the search for family equilibrium, too detached and even dry? An only child was in any case in danger of being a nasty brat: the apple of the eye is a bitter fruit to the taste. Correctives, of a suitably charitable and socially-valuable nature, had been sought. Thus, Monsieur and Madame Delavigne were 'godparents' to two orphans who came for frequent weekends and to stay in the holidays. Rachel sent toys to, sewed for, and devoted pocket money to Vietnamese babies. She accompanied Colette to crèches and was approved of by various local Reverend Mothers. Madame Delavigne had often a gnawing feeling that it wasn't enough. But damn it, it was a troublesome equation to solve.

A judge of instruction is 'named' to a post for a period of three years initially. There are interims and vacations and temporary postings, and situations to be arranged in a flexible spirit, but when one's first real post is that of Children's Judge in a proper city, when one's husband works in that city in a business administration, and when it is important to soothe and reassure various elderly and chalky male bosoms who can be sniffy about pretty young women using the magistrates' lavatory, one takes pains not to go perambulating a monumental maternal stomach around the Palace in the middle of what is still a probationary period.

'I'll be thirty,' said Colette, 'and that's quite a reasonable moment to have another baby. And Rachel will be ten. A nice elder sister, and it doesn't matter whether it's a boy or a girl. Out of the jealous stage. And female instincts brought to the fore when they're still climbing trees.'

'As long as you have one then,' said Vera, who hadn't any, and hated it.

Colette put on a housecoat and flowed tranquilly to the kitchen, stopping to put on a record. But once in the kitchen, doubts assailed her. Rachel would have come home and had her 'goûter'. There were no crumbs on the table. That was one thing, but at that age they are perpetually thirsty and there was no dirty glass. Now there was one rule which was firm as iron and that was the instruction that before Rachel went off anywhere she should report it. No note was on the table saying 'Gone to Nathalie'.

Now that was downright naughty, and she was angry. She looked in the child's bedroom – no clothes changed. The swimming-bath was the likeliest, but her bathing dress was hanging on the balcony from yesterday. Colette frowned.

In the living-room, surely, there would be a school bag flung down, surest sign of all. There wasn't. Colette sat down, picked up the phone, and called Nathalie's mama; Véronique, whose mama had just come home; and Jackie, whose mama was still out. Jackie, a wicked boy with a huge smooth mop of wonderful silky black hair whom Bernard denounced as 'a sexy beast', was very suave on the phone; he had lovely manners.

'No, Madame. We haven't seen her, Madame; she wasn't playing with us. Oh yes, Madame, she was at school but she left a different way. No, I mean we left a different way. Sorry, Madame. Shall we look, round the quarter I mean, and tell her to go straight home? And I'll phone you, shall I? It's no trouble at all, Madame.'

Rachel's bicycle, which she seldom took to school, was neatly parked. Neither the concierge, who had clipped the hedge that afternoon, nor his wife, whose Danièle was a lot older, went to a different school, and was sagely doing her homework, but who kept an eye on the little ones, had seen Rachel that afternoon.

This was getting ominous. It was now a quarter to seven, and inflexible rule number two was that whatever the circumstances and wherever she might be Rachel would be home by seven, and do her homework, despite shrieks of 'I haven't any, truly', before dinner at eight.

Bernard would be home any moment. Irritably, Colette wrapped the trout in bacon, cleaned the fennel, made vinaigrette for the avocadoes, and decided to eat the apricots as they were without bothering to make tart crust.

Seven. No Rachel. No Bernard either. Colette raced into the dressing-room, threw on trousers and a shirt, bursting a button and jerking viciously at her bra, slammed into the lift, reversed the car out with a screech, and drove very fast to the swimming-bath, the school, Jackie's house, Nathalie's house – and drew blank everywhere. Seven thirty; home again, tired now, trembling rather, aware that she had driven dangerously. Still no Rachel. Still no Bernard. His phone rang unanswered – he had left and so had everyone else, of course, long ago. Well, he was an adult. Rachel was eight.

'Baba,' called Colette jerkily. 'Baba,' running stupidly into the bedroom.

She put her hand on the telephone to call Police-Secours, mastered herself, for one cannot create a flap just because a child is half an hour late, wiped her nose with a paper tissue, and heard Bernard's familiar Citroën noise on the gravel. She forced herself to wait for him.

Bernard was a stocky man, who in another ten years would have trouble keeping his weight down because his body was slightly too big for his limbs. His neck was short as well as his arms, so that his collars always looked too tight and his sleeves too long: buying shirts for him was always a problem. But he had a fine intelligent head, and his short square hands were sensitive and beautifully shaped. His nose sprang straight from between his eyebrows, and he had large, faintly prominent eyes: with the massive jaw and the short neck this gave him something of a strangled expression which, along with a certain open, candid look, led hasty or unwise people to believe that he was a bit of a stupid fellow. A great mistake.

He was singing to himself, 'Bom-bum-bom-bum', when he opened the door and saw Colette, screwed up and restless, in the middle of the room; very straight, her feet slightly apart.

'Who are you looking for a fight with?' pleasantly. 'Hey, what's wrong?'

'Rachel hasn't come home.'

'Nathalie doubtless – that odious Jackie, more likely.'

'I've been everywhere – all around the quarter.'

'Turn that music off . . . Aren't you getting yourself worked up? – it's a fine evening, and it's not even eight yet.'

'Her bike's here – her school bag isn't. The concierge – nobody's seen her. She hasn't been home at all – that's nearly four hours. Don't say the swimming-pool: I looked first thing. She didn't change – she hasn't been here at all. Sorry, I hadn't realized it was still playing. Bernard, I'm worried.'

'Yes, I can see. Well – mustn't lose our heads. Look, I'll get us both a drink. Give ourselves time to think.'

Docile, she sat down, drank some of the whisky he pushed in her hand, felt sure she had already had time to think – too much. It hadn't really sunk through to him yet. In a little while she would be telling him to sit down quietly while she brought him a drink. Getting at the truth of a tale, disentangling irrelevance, feeling with her fingertips for tiny twisted golden grains of precision in a sandhill of idleness, laziness, incompetence, malice, gossip, boredom, the wish to be interesting, the hunger for excitement – wasn't that what she did all day? This was just a momentary paralysis; the stunned second, the invariable disbelief that it should be oneself, not Mrs, Miss or Mr A. N. Other, that notable all-round sportsman, tax evader, and victim of criminals.

'My dearest girl . . .' said Bernard. 'Now – you've been to the school. To all her friends . . . in the little park? Round the back of the tennis courts? . . . I'd better ring Jackie's father . . . Now she may have found a new friend. Someone who lives further away. She may have mistaken the way home, or not even know it. And be too timid to ask. Come, we don't know everyone in

14

her age-group – even in her own class . . . Some people are very irresponsible – let the children play outside till all hours.'

'It's almost eight. Everybody's eating by now.'

'But you know how she is – obstinate little thing. "Shall I take you home dear – do you know your own way? Oh that's good because I haven't the car. All right dear, trot off" – and if she was the other side of the boulevard – where those streets all look the same . . . Take a wrong turning and she's heading back towards the town without realizing. Nobody pays any heed and she's too shy to speak to a stranger.'

'You're creating a whole fantasy,' said Colette irritably. 'No mother would allow a little girl of eight to go home across the boulevard with all that traffic. She'd either bring the child back, or ring up – at the least, if she'd no car and no phone she'd see that the child crossed the road safely. Rachel's not a perfect fool. Shy, yes – but she knows her name, her address, her phone number, she can tell the time, she knows how to come in out of the rain. You're speaking of a child of five: Rachel's not a baby.'

The phone rang; Bernard threw himself sideways on the sofa.

'Yes? Oh, Monsieur Sillières – good evening . . . ah, Jackie told you. You haven't seen her? . . . no no, not real anxiety of course, but it is eight. A shadow of disquiet, don't you know? . . . yes of course. Of course . . . that's very kind, and friendly of you. Bye . . . Why does one pretend that one isn't worried? Sillières says he's been up and down both streets and talked to Véronique's father, and he knows Jackie is a pest and capable of locking her in the garden shed or what not, but that in the pinch, when it gets serious, Jackie would admit anything wicked, and anyway he can tell when Jackie's lying, and he realizes now that it's serious. Jackie, I mean . . . sorry, I'm rambling.'

'No, I understand.'

'Well,' unhappily, 'better face it, I suppose, I'd better ring the hospitals.'

Colette, very slowly, got up and poured herself another drink, and fussed a long time over taking a cigarette, patting softly at Bernard's jacket pockets, while a quiet voice, carefully reined in, said 'Casualty department, please' three times, to the University Hospital, the Surgical Polyclinic, and the Saint Bar-

bara Centre. She did not stop him when he left his hand a moment on the receiver-rest and then dialled Police-Secours.

'Give me the chief, please . . . Bernard Delavigne . . . Madame Delavigne, the judge . . . a little girl . . . height . . . colour hair . . . eyes . . . frock . . . shoes . . . red school bag . . . my number is seventy-four eighty-four ninety-four . . . yes please, the centre out to the city limits. Yes of course I realize it'll take some time . . . I'm going to have another drink.'

'Yes. But it will have to do now for both of us.'

'I realize that, thank you.' It was the first sign of tension Bernard had given. 'We'd be well advised to eat something.'

'I'll go and cook. I'm sorry – you realize that up to now I just wasn't capable.'

'Of course I do. But there's nothing we can do for some time. They say they've two radio vans and all the available motor-bikes, and they'll alert all the district posts, but we must wait two hours. We must eat, of course, and bear in mind that she may just stroll in at any given second. Having twisted her ankle, or dropped her shoe in the pond or had her bag snatched away by nasty teasing boys . . . children can be so foul to one another.'

'Yes,' said Colette tiredly, 'but why didn't she dump her bag here? It's heavy – what would she be carrying it around for?'

'There's nothing more we can do for the moment.'

'Yes there is. Henri.'

'Man? – or policeman?'

'Both.'

'Isn't that a bit – sort of premature? P.J., I mean?'

Henri Castang, Vera's husband, was an officer in the Police Judiciaire. A borderline friend – but a friend, yes; not just an acquaintance. Bernard rubbed his face with both hands.

'I don't mind if you don't.' Colette from the doorway looked at him. She stood quietly; her hand fiddled with the door-knob.

'I think it sensible,' she said at last. 'So does the judge. Put it simply – it's a friend at court. Would you rather I called him?'

'No. Go and do your cooking.'

The phone rang a long time.

'Castang,' said a neutral voice, professionally cleaned of fatigue or irritability.

Fiddling aimlessly in the kitchen – try as she might she could not concentrate; she took the trout out to clean them, got a knife, and then looked for them idiotically all over the place, even in the sink, for a very long time before realizing that she had put them back in the fridge – she could hear the pattern of Bernard's voice, knowing the way he stabbed at the air with his cigarette to emphasize, head on one side to keep the phone cradled, absurdly beloved and familiar. She felt too drained and stupified to cook: knives would jump at her and cut her, pots leap off the stove to burn her. She hovered vaguely in the doorway.

'He'll be round straight away.'

'Oh. Good.' How stupid it did sound. As though it was a plumber for a leaking pipe. 'Do you really want to eat?'

'Not in the slightest.'

'I don't feel up to it.'

'Have we some tomato juice? Henri likes it.'

'I suppose so.' She made an effort. 'Yes, we have. Do us good, you mean. Vitamins or something.'

'Mustn't drink,' said Bernard portentously.

'No. I don't believe there are any vitamins in tinned tomato juice.'

'No but it's sort of thick. Stabilizes . . .'

These valuable dietetic observations were put a stop to at last by Castang arriving. Nobody ever believed that the police had now arrived. He didn't even look the part, not properly, being on the small size for a cop, and wiry rather than stocky. A round Mediterranean head, and coarse black hair, the sort which goes grey early, as his was, here and there, though he was not much over thirty. A slightly Slav face, not pronounced but as though it were a germ, as Colette said, picked up from his wife. Some Roman legionary in the past, from Daçia or Scythia. He was quite a good policeman though, even if he did look more like an extra in Ben Hur. He was an O.P.A., or adjunct officer of police, a clumsy piece of bureaucratic nomenclature, in the S.R.P.J., or regional service of police judiciaire, which is another. The conservative French, still addicted to ancient francs, mostly called him Inspector. Much as everyone still talks of the Avenue du Bois.

Castang, coming in, sitting down, drinking tomato juice, being explained to, looked as usual like a former steeplechase jockey who has got too thick set for the job. Lined leathery face, tweed jackets with lots of pockets, always full of police rubbish which Vera complained about, sharp mobile birdy eyes, a tendency to waistcoats, tough scarred hands, tight whipcord trousers like breeches, that the horsehair wouldn't stick to, and always beautfully polished shoes. When one visited him, said Colette, he was always cutting his finger nails or polishing his shoes, or both. Oh yes, said Vera resignedly: cleanliness fanatic.

He was already making notes, in a quick practised way, black felt-tip, picking up the disjointed scraps of gabble.

'O.K.,' he said at last. 'Want to let me talk for a bit?' It wasn't meant to be sarcastic; just a professional way of clearing the ground. 'Good, right to call me, though I'm not in the act yet officially and can't be till a formal complaint is laid. Just here as a friend, but will react as a cop: that's the way you want it, I think.'

Colette and Bernard both nodded, both somehow vastly relieved already, both far too scared and amateurish and confused; the business man happy with another business man, the judge happy with the familiar, solid, well-polished machinery.

'For a start; can't yet write off some stupid little muddle or misunderstanding; still the likeliest. Children do wander off and do silly things and lose their sense of time, and we've got to let the cops have another hour to get co-ordinated reports. But let's take into account the worst that can happen: those are our fears, we face them. So we have the P.J. here and the way it argues is this, as Colette knows well. Assuming a crime: the child's alive or the child is dead. I have to say that, as you realize, whatever the effort it costs. But I say straight away that it's by far the most remote, and that we have no reason at all to jump at imaginary horrors. And quite frankly I'm not going to, because there's no evidence whatever, as well as the strong statistical unlikelihood. But we can start building hypotheses of crime, and nine-tenths of that we can leave aside or take as said, because you both know it all, we've discussed it in this room, it's our daily shop – it's the sudden impact of the personal and the subjective that throws us off. So it's my job to remind you that these things are more often stupidly aggressive than violently psychopathic. Psychopath enough to do it, and stupid enough

18

not to see how quickly it will point to him. I'm not for a second trying to tranquillize you. It's exactly what Richard or any cop of experience will say – the overwhelming majority are crude and easy, and need no more than a day's work.'

'I've never had a kidnapping,' muttered Colette vaguely.

'No, dear friend, because they're pretty rare, thank heaven. Tremendously publicized when they do occur – and that's a problem we'll look at in a minute – so the public is saturated and thinks vaguely they occur all the time, and they don't. But whether you've had one or not you can both see that the instruction may be difficult, but the police work is generally simple, because either you have the classic type of the unbalanced girl with an overwhelming need to possess a baby and the typical psychopathic incapacity to resist gratifying desire, with indifference to the notion of a criminal act or its consequences, or you have the frustrated embittered individual with a grievance, generally of low intelligence, who wishes you to suffer pain, indignity and deprivation because that's what he feels himself.'

'They will have their hearts' content, then,' said Bernard softly.

Castang disregarded this. He wasn't there as emotional consoler.

'Colette, of course,' he went on smoothly, 'arouses a good deal of fear in the families of her clients, hence resentment, rancour, even hatred sometimes. And it's an obvious inference, since she's the children's judge, that somebody might want to strike back at her that way.'

'One doesn't think of it – one can't, of course.'

'Conceivable, too, that it could be a child's crime. What – let's just think – have you had in this last year which was grave enough to need instructing?'

'Well – there was the child who made the imaginary confession. The two who threw their playmate in the river. And the one who loosened the wheel nuts of a car. And of course the children who set the school on fire at the time when there was a perfect epidemic of it.'

'Caused,' Bernard put in dryly, 'by the publicity given to the first case.'

'Good point and I'm coming back to it. But you do see, Colette, that there are a heap of people who'll have to be looked at.'

'They scarcely ever show resentment, poor things,' she said. 'They have great difficulty understanding and actually convincing themselves that their children could have done such things. But it's true that apart from instructions I've judged a lot of violent vandalism and delinquency.'

'You see,' easily, 'the terrifying shadow of the really disturbed person begins already to recede. All those horrible ideas of rape and murder fading into nightmare land.'

'You're trying to make us feel better,' said Bernard jerkily.

'Isn't that my job?' asked Castang throwing his hands out. 'I'm not trying to bullshit a herd of scared peasants. I'm giving facts to an intelligent and widely educated pair of bourgeois parents.'

'Selling,' said Bernard. 'Bits of facts. Carefully selected.' Castang took his time about answering.

'As a business man, and experienced, and knowing the world, and moreover pretty bright, you don't have a very high opinion of the police, and I don't contribute much to bettering it. There's a goodish share of laziness and incompetence; a lot of bureaucratic inertia and apathy. And some cops are downright bad – stupid brutal oafs with ideas about keeping the niggers down. And corrupt, of course – all those commissaires taking kickbacks from brothels. Favouritism too, naturally: a complaint from you, a prominent local business man, with moreover a wife in the magistracy, will make them all bend over backwards even if you didn't have a friend in the organization, whereas a complaint from the poor gets short shrift. And all that too we've talked about in this room. There's one thing though you haven't experienced yet and that is how good they can be.'

'Otherwise,' said Colette rather sharply, 'you could hardly expect Henri to stay in his job, and you'd be surprised at my doing mine.'

'Please disregard what I said and believe I'm ashamed of it.'

'You don't have to be, all that much. You're a very worried man and you want to hit out at somebody, and what you said was quite true. I'd like you now to think of something I said a few minutes ago, which is publicity.'

'Yes,' said Bernard painfully.

'I'm just sitting here talking,' said Castang, 'because it's still a bit premature to ask the cops for phase two. If we give that sort of instruction it means mobilizing, since they'd comb out all the bits of waste ground, all the building sites, uh, so on.'

'The rivers,' said Bernard coldly.

'Yes; and a lot of other places. Getting all the police authorities informed and co-ordinated, alerting all the authorities. And the P.J. too, me and all the others, by a formal complaint against X. Colette is a judge of course and can give us orders, but that's not even needed: a phone-call to Richard will do it. It means too that that's headlines in tomorrow's paper. Journalists here straight away, a television crew – and all the sight-seers.'

Bernard had closed his eyes.

'Yes,' said Castang, 'we pay a lot of lip-service to the freedom of the press. There's an aspect of extreme morbidity and cruelty.'

'Is there any way of stopping it at all?' between gripped teeth.

'Yes there is, but it's got to be done at the very start, and what's more it doesn't have to be corrupt, putting in the hush and all that. It can be concluded quite legitimately that this won't serve the interest of justice, and I think,' drawling it a bit, 'that in your position, yours and Colette's that is, the Procureur de la République might give the necessary authority. There are three drawbacks, or dangers, or what do you call them.'

'That you cut yourself off from possible help,' said Colette.

'One – self-evident. A colossal heap of worthless stuff comes in but there's always the chance of something genuine, and if it comes down to needles in haystacks one needs all the eyes one can get, including the silly, the loony, and even the morbid and malicious. Two: that it might backlash, because it's not easy to keep this kind of inquiry discreet, it imposes several difficult limitations on procedure, there are invariably a lot of people in the know and a leak is at all times possible. And if you try to keep something from the press they're apt to be vengeful.'

'You mean Watergating.'

'Right, and that's number three as corollary – it's easily concluded that an effort is being made to cover something up, for personal or political consideration; I'm not spelling it out.'

'Which would mean,' said Colette slowly and clearly, 'that you'd lose your job, that I'd lose my career, that Henri, marked as a friend of ours, would at best get transferred with his promotion broken, and that our lives would be ruined. Including Vera's.'

'God,' said Bernard.

'Hey,' said Castang, 'easy. Colette, forgive me, you're drama-tizing. Listen, we're friends, you've trusted me. You aren't in anything like that sort of situation. No crime or even mis-demeanour can be attributed to you, there's no malpractice or attempt to interfere with justice – it isn't even your decision.'

'No?' said Bernard hotly, 'whose then? Not my child, no?'

'No,' bluntly. 'Proc's.'

'The independence of a magistrate . . .' hastily and angrily. 'My wife is a judge. Sworn to interpret without fear or favour. I know this much law. The Public Prosecutor represents the State, we the People, blah blah. He can't put any pressure on a judge – separation of powers.'

'Darling,' said Colette softly.

'What?' snappish.

'Easy. I think I see what Henri's getting at.'

'Quite right, it's all true,' said Castang. 'But pity the poor policeman. Ground between millstones. Proc decides whether grounds for a charge exist and lays it: we-the-people. Instructs us to pursue an investigation. He finds a case; that's to say we do and tell him so. He then passes the case to the examining magistrate, who from that moment is the sole authority over us. I know this is all stale cake, but the point is that here is – assuming the existence of a crime, or just a complaint – a magis-trate involved. Proc's going to think about the dignity of the magistracy, and the independence of the judicature, and all the rest of it, and he decides – only he decides – how to go about procedure. And I don't need to tell you how that crowd stick together. He can decide whether to pull the curtain down on this affair, and whether he does depends maybe a great deal on what you say to him. And how you say it.'

'As a judge,' said Colette in a dry factual tone, 'I can of course launch a police action myself, and a judicial procedure. I can't,' more dryly still, 'instruct my own case.'

'I, on the other hand,' said Bernard with acridity, 'am the head of the family. I presume I have some say.'

'You're wounding me unnecessarily,' remarked Colette gently.

He made a palpable effort.

'Look, Henri, I've been waiting too for the doorbell to go and the phone to ring. It hasn't. I've let time pass. It is now my job to set every possible human agency to work to find her. The legal arguments don't interest me. I lodge a complaint against X and how do I go about that?'

'You've done it. I register it.' Castang the drill-sergeant. 'I'm an officer of police but not an officer of justice. You need a commissaire for that. So I ring Commissaire Richard. He might be at home. Or alternatively, and I think it'd be wiser, Colette rings the Proc – or you do if you so wish. And ask his advice. Because just ringing the police and telling them to get their tail uncurled from underneath their arse is equivalent to inviting the newshawks; they'll be here in half an hour. I might suggest too that first you give the municipal police a chance to tell you whether they've found her, or any trace of her, before you take this grave step.'

'You haven't a daughter,' said Bernard in a voice soaked in bitterness.

Castang's face stayed controlled, like the White House spokesman at a press conference.

Colette got up, walked across the room, and made a business out of tinkle-tinkle with the ice cubes and getting everyone a clean ashtray. She wanted to give the flicker of unspoken hostility between the two men a moment to subside, and to make an opportunity to show herself that she was in command of her movements, her voice, her ideas. As well as to gain a minute of time, anyhow; anywhere. Bernard was too reasonable a person – and too nice – ever to persecute her with immature resentments about her being a magistrate while he was only a sort of glorified yoghurt salesman. But he wasn't 'himself' just now.

'Henri.'

'Yes?'

'Sorry – I was trying to think. We have to try and reflect . . . before we can decide what is the best thing to do. I know that we've no evidence at all, so you can't postulate. But just on the premises of Rachel's being a sensible child really, on the whole, and not often doing silly things – what does your experience tell you is the likeliest thing to have happened? I don't think either Bernard or I are looking just for reassurance. I think we've both

23

got a good grip of reality. Even with nothing to go on, no fact to situate – can you arrive at any sort of outline?'

'Yes, there are a few general guide-lines one could take, even I think with some confidence, in the lack of anything to disprove them. First consider the quarter in general. It's virtually all clear, modern, open. The children play in full view. There are no heavy groups of old trees, no close shrubberies, hardly any old buildings. Precious little concealment. On a clear summer evening with people strolling everywhere – it doesn't make a pattern for the kind of thing we'd dread. That type of individual is frightened, furtive – they look for more cover; they look for flight and concealment. Then consider Rachel's nature and training. She might not always come straight home if she was in a group of friends absorbed in a game, but she wouldn't just wander off. Even seeing something fascinating wouldn't hold her up for any length of time. Also she's a prudent, sensible child as well as timid. Falling in the pond or losing a shoe – she'd find ways quickly enough of getting in touch with you. Road accidents we've eliminated – no, I think we have to consider a crime all right. I think someone has stolen her. It doesn't mean necessarily anything personal, though in your particular circumstances there might perhaps be more likelihood of some distorted notion of vengeance. I'd be inclined to discount that at present. There are, sadly, many people who hunt for easy ways to make money. The ones of lowest intelligence find that pretty hard, by definition. Some think of kidnapping a child, and an only child of wealthy parents is the most obvious. A highly neurotic variation on snatching handbags. It's a difficult thing to do because if you just seize a child and bundle it into a car and drive off fast it's virtually certain there'll be several witnesses. What other way is there? Some fairly elaborate intricate trap, baited with something really tempting and I don't mean just a lolly. One would be inclined to postulate either a gang of rather dull-witted little bandits, or someone pretty bright but likewise highly psychotic – shouldn't be hard to trace.'

'And how would one go about it – the tracing?'

'You mean if we'd Richard here?' smiling a little. 'Because it's not a job for the private detective. I'm pretty sure he'd start looking along the route back from school straight away. Not just for the classic dropped bag or bust button though that too, naturally, but for any little deviation from the normal pattern of things: strange car parked in an odd place; anyone seen hanging about with apparently nothing to do, some unfamiliar figure pushing an ice-cream barrow or playing the organ, anything. And a house-to-house: the we-have-some-reason-to-believe routine. And back here I rather think he'd like the telephone tapped. Which is of course illegal.' It was the first time Castang had risked any sort of joke. 'Have to be with your knowledge and consent. Because it's evident enough that whoever, be it just a demand to stand-and-deliver, or a dotty gloat about I know a secret, and you'd give a lot to know it too, wouldn't you now, will try and poke you, and pretty quick. At that moment we'd want to be there, on the spot and able to intervene as well as listen. Because of course all these people are very prudish about the police getting to know, and they're apt to think up tricky gags about telling you where to drop money by the milestone on the deserted country road and so on.'

'And are we supposed to go to work normally, behave as though nothing had happened?'

'Oh, then I dare say we'd like to tap the office phones too.'

Colette managed something vaguely like a smile.

'I don't somehow think the senior judge would much care for a tap in the Palace of Justice.'

'No; I think you'd prefer to take a day off. But the phone will ring – and soon: these people are mostly talkative.'

'Does a man have to stay here?'

'It's preferable. One can link the line to anywhere. But apart from being able to advise you or if need be instruct you, rapidly, there might be people hanging around the house. I realize it's a horrible invasion of privacy. But we can put a chap in the cellar – choose a quiet elderly one with experience.'

Colette had been making a deliberate effort to disentangle herself emotionally. This wasn't her; this was some other mother in the same lamentable situation. She didn't know Castang. He was the policeman who had been sent to take down details, after her first anxious call to the police. She quite liked the look of him. It was reassuring. Seemed a competent man. No – better. Able; an able man.

Bernard had been very quiet and still. His business training made him a good listener. He had followed, with what one might call a certain deference, the queries posed by the judge of instruction. Now he entered the conversation without elbowing into it.

'How long will this take?'

'If you'll allow me to phone Richard – half an hour to an hour. He's quite possibly at home, or he mostly leaves word where he can be found. At the worst, in a hurry, I can get Lassalle. The material we'd want isn't complicated. When there's no occasion for furtive concealment' – a thin grin – 'it takes no time to install. For the rest, I don't know what Richard would see fit to order, tonight that is. He'd like perhaps to hear first what the urban police have to say or suggest.'

'I don't want that phone occupied,' said Bernard tightly. 'Not even for five minutes.'

'I understand that – I can call on an outside line. There won't be any palaver – not when he hears who it is. Take advantage of that bourgeois favouritism – with Richard there isn't all that much of it. Simply that Madame Delavigne can give him a direct order.'

'Very handy for me,' said Colette bitterly. 'Bernard darling, I'm thinking about this – this appalling flood of publicity which would burst over our heads. Truly – before you come to any decision, before we ask Henri to do whatever must be done, and I think we have to agree that one of these outlines cannot be too far away from the reality – I'll have to ask the Procureur for his opinion and advice, and take him into our confidence – and I think his experience may be valuable too.'

Bernard looked at her dully for a moment, as though not understanding, before pulling himself together.

'If you wish, I suppose so. It seems like tossing a penny. No – I don't want to sound fatalistic. All the decisions are bad. This must be the best.'

Colette put her palms over her eyes; screwed them to and fro. She drew her fingertips over her face, as though to be sure it was still there and unchanged. She stood up.

'I'll just throw something else on. Something a little more – respectable,' with an ironic emphasis.

'You're taking the car? Drive carefully. Think of the family.' Colette smiled at him, turned, went out rapidly.

The two men looked at each other, looked, as though by a silly

26

coincidence, together at the telephone, looked away again. There was an embarrassed silence.

'How's Vera?' Bernard asked, making an effort.

'Childless.'

'I'm sorry, you know.'

'I'm sorrier. I know, I mean, what it's like, because of experience – but I can never really get there, never know. Imagination just won't carry that far.'

They looked at each other again, this time understanding each other.

'How about a real drink?' suggested Bernard, diffident.

'I won't say no. But let's have something to eat. And put a lot of water with it.'

They crunched a packet of peanuts. They felt hungry then, and plundered two boxes of salt biscuits. Then they had a glass of milk.

'How's the house going?' asked Castang.

Colette and Bernard had a piece of land out in the country, and a shack on it, which they were building on to.

'Bloody awful builders,' said Bernard, and became animated. Two men can talk about the iniquities-of-the-builders for an indeterminate length of time.

*

Colette had stuck the car in hurriedly, nose first, and had to back up the ramp, which forced her to be careful. On the dark, silent street she drove slowly, with exaggerated care at the intersections, dreading the sight of another car. Was anyone there, under the trees? Was she being watched? Was she being followed? Even the sight of a man walking a dog struck terror into her. Another man, turning automatically to quiz at the glimpse of a pretty young woman alone in a sports car and driving so slowly, made her sweat. She rubbed her arm irritably against her side. She turned on to the boulevard. The traffic went faster – much too fast. It was reassuring to be passed by people who did not know her, cared nothing about her, rushing blithely to their pleasures or tensely to their preoccupations, but unaware of her wound.

The Procureur de la République lived in an old quarter of ugly, solid, bourgeois villas from the second half of the nineteenth century, lumpy things in large gardens overgrown with laurels and laburnums. The curving streets twisted into one another, all bearing annoyingly similar names of Roman emperors. Diocletian, Gratian, Valerian – this was a maze. On the left here, surely, with an oval brass plate? No – she must be in the wrong street. She had been here half a dozen times, and thought – felt sure – it was the second on the left after turning off the boulevard. But had she taken the wrong turn? The quiet streets were lined with large old chestnuts trees, all now in full leaf, hiding the ugly villas. With a hysterical giggle Colette decided she was Barberina, losing her pin at the beginning of the last act of *Figaro* – under the chestnut trees. L'ho perduta! Prelude to a lot of dramas.

Suddenly, and with a horrible, heart-wrenching shock, Colette realized that she was, indeed, being followed. An ordinary dark saloon car was creeping down the roadway only two or three metres behind her. Her throat filled as though she were trying to swallow a tennis ball. The car, even at that low speed, lurched dangerously as her front wheel mounted the pavement. Colette grabbed with both hands, at her steering wheel and at her bag lying on the seat beside her. She braked and came to rest in the gutter, huddled and frozen as a rabbit catching sight of a stoat. The dark car came creeping up into the gutter directly behind her: she watched it in her rear-view mirror, clutching her bag fiercely, paralysed with fear. A hoarse, soft voice came from the lowered window.

'Petite Madame.'

In an instant all her frozen muscles unblocked. This was no sinister, horrible kidnapper such as she imagined, creeping up to asphyxiate her with ether or leaping to grab and stun her with a little rubber club. This was just one of those horrible, yes, but familiar – odiously familiar to women driving in a city at night – tomcats who prowl in cars.

'Petite Madame – lost; lonely! Sweet girl, darling girl – bored! Likes an adventure – loves it!' Colette was no longer rigid: she was scrabbling in her bag. It served some purpose at last, that object.

Bernard had wanted her to have it – oily smelly thing, heavy and awkward in a bag. And it had been the Proc – irony – who had authorized it.

'You are a young woman. People do not hesitate to attempt putting pressures of all kinds upon a judge, if they think they see any opening. A young woman can be in a vulnerable position – you drive about in your little car – there are some who would not hesitate to take advantage if they could – I approve of your husband's initiative.'

She had never had occasion – till now outside his house. Her fingers opened the chamois-leather envelope, made for one of those immense, bulky pairs of sun-glasses. It was an ordinary police pistol, a 7·65 'Saint-Étienne', given her by Commissaire Richard, and it had been Richard himself, tall and silver-haired like a Nobel Prize winner, so difficult to imagine with a gun, who had taken her to the police shooting range to teach her.

'Relax. Feet apart. Much like a bow and arrow. Point the front foot. Back foot square. Solidly balanced. You need not be afraid of it. Nasty thing, yes; snake – but a tame snake. The snake knows you, is not frightened of you – the snake only strikes when frightened. Head up. Now, arm up.'

The door behind her was opening. Get out of the car, you fool!

'Champagne in the fridge,' came the soft hoarse wheedle. 'And a nice record on the player.' She stood leaning against the car, her left forearm on the roof. She did not 'see' the man at all. She would be incapable of giving a description, of the face, even the height or weight. The tomcat sidled, rubbing itself along the bonnet of its own car. God! – isn't it possible to do things without guns?

'Darling – shall I drive yours?' God – only a metre away. Instead of advancing her front foot she dragged back the left leg in an instinctive recoil – but she was in a shooting stance. The street-lamp, on the far side of the street, shed a soft oily glitter on the pistol barrel. In the same second she realized that she had not loaded the gun. There were bullets in the magazine but none in the chamber. But the cat did not know that. It recoiled, seemed to crush itself against the radiator of its own car.

'Hey! Careful with that thing.'

Colette's left hand felt the soft tremble of the motor which she had not turned off, vibrating the roof gently. The mechanical heart-beat put courage into her.

'Come nearer and I'll shoot you,' she said.

It stood still.

'Now go. Go, or I'll shoot the car.'

It sidled back, uncertain whether it was being bluffed but frightened enough to not try. Colette took her left hand off the dusty metal, planted her front foot firmly on the pavement, snapped the action of the pistol, pointed it fiercely at the radiator.

'Go. Run.' It ran.

Suddenly feeling all-competent, unfumbling, perfectly cool, she pressed the button releasing the magazine and dropped it on the driving seat. She couldn't recall whether or not the horrid thing would now fire. It didn't matter; she snapped it again. Just as it had been when Richard showed her, the bullet in the chamber was ejected: just as he had done she caught the coppery glitter deftly in her left hand. She got back in the car, put the pistol together, laid it on the seat beside her, threw the car in gear. The car gave an awkward jerk. She'd put it in third instead of first. She corrected, accelerated.

She recognized the Proc's house at once. It was twenty metres further. Under the oval plate was a polished brass bell-push, Colette looked back up the road. Nothing to be seen. The outside light clicked on, a comforting flood. The gate latch clicked. She walked up the path, glancing back to see that the light reached her own car. The Proc himself suddenly appeared on the porch.

'Why – Madame Delavigne. Pleasant surprise.'

'Monsieur Besson – I'm sorry – but there's one of those disagreeable men who follow one at night. I chased him off but he's down the street.'

'Is there indeed? Well, we'll soon settle him. Come in, my dear: ah, I see – he gave you a fright.' He reached for the telephone on the hall table.

'Besson here – Procureur de la République, Rue Gratian. Wake up, man. I want a car patrol, and smartish. There's a loiterer here, and I want him pegged. Come on man, get your thumb out of your bum.' Colette had never heard the Proc talking to policemen in quite this tone of voice. He put the phone down and said, 'I'll cook his goose,' in a high-treason tone, more familiar, even though instead of his robe he was clothed in a Chinese dressing-gown. From the umbrella stand he selected a thick stick.

'Now Madame, if you'll just show me. No need for fear while I'm with you.'

Oh my Gawd, thought Colette. I left the gun in full view on the car seat. But he was already marching along the pavement. She grabbed it and stuffed it guiltily in her bag, almost getting caught when he turned round accusingly – force of habit – and went 'Ha?' with his stick at the dark car. He stood guard over it in a gleeful way that she felt a bit embarrassed about: wasn't this a bit vengeful in the representative of society? She was almost ready to wish the horrid man would get away, and feeling that this was not quite proper in a judge, when another dark saloon car appeared in the light, this one with two uniformed policemen in it, who jumped out and made rather an ostenta-tious business of saluting.

'Loitering and prowling,' said Monsieur Besson. 'There's his car – I dare say that'll provide a few further offences. He'll be hanging about in the quarter. Legitimate suspicion, conduct prejudicial – take him down and charge him : I'm preferring the complaints myself and I want an example made.'

'Sir,' said one.

'Easy,' said the other, already writing down the car number.

'We'll make this gentleman regret his nocturnal lecheries.' It sounded rather like an ecclesiastical court in the Middle Ages: Proc seemed already to be weighing the respective deterrent value of the stocks and the ducking-stool. 'My dear Madame Delavigne, I am so very sorry. Right, officers, that's all.' More salutes, and a wave of the stick.

'Now,' he was saying two minutes later over glasses of port, 'to what do I owe this unexpected pleasure?' And Colette was making a great effort to be lucid and simple, bothered by the sensation of unreality. And what if Rachel was by now home and in bed, having been taken for a ride in the country or some-thing and got a flat tyre; she might have left a note where it had been blown into a corner by a draught, or told the concierge and it slipped his memory, or tried to ring up but the phone was out of order ...

Proc's dressing-gown and slippers added to the unreality. And this ridiculous, humiliating adventure, which somehow had been so much more humiliating to herself than to a probably lonely

31

and certainly unhappy little man. She had over-reacted wildly. There was nothing but bitterness for her in the prospect of policemen turning from the obsequious to the bullying, with a sanctimonious telling-off in the police-court to follow, with a fine of a few hundred francs and a don't-let-it-happen again. Far worse things lay in store for herself.

An unreal sense too about this room: Proc's study, part of the downstairs suite of rooms where she had been three times, for his annual garden-party for the Palace of Justice and the Bar, and for a couple of his celebrated dinner-parties ... Everything then was tidied, and a great deal cleared away, because he wasn't leaving his valuable pieces of Nevers and Rouen faïence around to be used as ashtrays or knocked over! Or even pinched, lawyers being notoriously given to every imaginable vice and frailty ...

The garden-party had been bad enough, for it had been showery weather, and decidedly chilly in this awful house. The agonies beforehand over what she could possibly wear for a summer party in bad weather had been nothing to the reality: women milling about upstairs looking for the lavatory – which was always occupied – and a fearful squash downstairs where Proc, in front of the big carved mahogany sideboard, dispensed hospitality and little jokes while keeping an eye on the hired waiters and seeing that people circulated properly instead of agglomerating into ghastly little cliques giggling in corners.

Not even these agonies could equal the horror of a winter dinner-party, where it was most important that Colette, the junior magistrate present, absolutely foot-of-the-table down where the fish 'got turned over', should not be better dressed than the other ladies present. One couldn't be worse-dressed ...

Frightful lurid snips of flash-back were punctuating her hapless narrative – Bernard's sarcastic and highly obscene witticisms in their dressing-room at home, while she dashed about in her knickers trying on one impossible garment after another: Bernard's hypocrite face when introduced to Madame Proc, a full blown peony in red taffeta: Bernard at table, rather red too (legal Burgundy, and a dinner jacket that had got too tight for him) being polite to a lady in beige tulle, his rather globular eyes fixed upon her amazing expanse of bosom (one of Colette's major problems had been 'how much tit to show?' But she need not have worried). And Bernard's partner, a lady in clinging silks much tighter than his jacket, whose stays were dreadfully in evidence. And herself, uncomfortably aware that Madame Proc was aware that Proc was looking down her frock . . .

He wasn't being in the least like that now. He listened in silence and at the end said, 'Dear me; you have been in the wars,' in an absolutely neutral voice, and poured her a second glass of port, which she took gratefully: she had a slight feeling that it would be nice to get just a tiny bit drunk.

The fact was, simply, that she had never seen him like this before. This was no stiff pedantic elderly magistrate, being pompous at the dinner-table or making rather too much of an offensive but not very criminal kerb-crawler (though she did realize that he had acted in understandable irritation, some of it towards herself for involving him, as well as a feeling that his home and his hospitality had been damaged and smeared). Nor was it the professional, often kindly, sometimes unexpectedly large-minded, but severe and rigid man she knew well enough, both in his room and in court, at the Palace. This was just a quiet, kindly gentleman in latish middle-age, of vast experience and secure in the possession of great powers and much responsibility, paternally listening to an unhappy young woman begging desperately for help, and considering how best to give it. She had come to the end of the tale, which despite herself she had made too complicated, and was stumbling a good deal over the 'publicity' aspect.

'Yes,' said Monsieur Besson after listening in perfectly controlled patience and not interrupting once, or posing any question whatever, 'that is very clear. And – may I say it? – my appreciation of your character and abilities, already high, is confirmed. Now, Madame, I want you to place yourself in my hands.'

'I am, I think.'

'Good. Now give me your telephone number . . . Monsieur Delavigne – good evening; Besson here. My dear friend, my sympathy is superfluous and any words I could add, even, quite worthless. I say no more than to remark that nothing – nothing – will be left undone. Now if you would have the extreme kindness to pass me Castang . . . Castang? – Besson here. Nothing so far? Very well; I'll have Richard with you shortly. Meanwhile you have my mandate to act at discretion: observe the greatest compatible prudence. I'll waste no further time; you'll want that phone free. Let's say I'll reinforce you as soon as may be with a technician, and I'll leave it to you to put Richard in the detailed picture: pray give my compliments to Monsieur Delavigne and explain that my precipitance is the measure of my activity.'

He was already dialling the familiar number of urban police headquarters. 'Procureur – give me the night commissaire. Raynal? – Besson. You had a report of a missing child, a little girl named Rachel Delavigne. Just summarize the action reports for me, please ... Very well. Now pay close heed, please. I want that action doubled. I'll be ringing Richard myself. I want the fullest and most energetic action taken not only as regards your own sphere but the closest liaison ... yes, yes, all that. I want you to ring me in the morning, and after you've given Commissaire Fabre a closely reasoned account of the night's work I want him to ring me: I'll be at my desk at eight. By the way, you'll have a man brought in, in all likelihood. A nocturnal prowler here in my own street. Charge him – yes, keep him for the night.'

'No,' interrupted Colette too shrilly. 'No, please, Monsieur Besson, no. I beg of you.'

'One moment, Raynal. Correct that. You need prefer no charge. Unless there's a motoring offence – we'll let that stand as mandatory. But the lady who is the subject of this aggression, which personally I regard as intolerable, would prefer not to insist and so be it. But I rely upon you to wash this sad individual's head for him – understood? And Raynal, a final detail, but in my view, and note this well, of maximal weight. I take it you have the usual printer's devil hanging around for his morning edition? No press coverage on this matter. Don't be imbecile, man, the child, of course; the other matter is trivial. Not just the automatic suppression of names where a child is concerned, but the whole thing; yes, that's right, prejudicial to subsequent judicial enquiry; this is a P.J. matter and must be absolutely uncompromised. You will take formal note that I will hold you personally responsible for press leakage, and I expect a disciplined body to behave in disciplined fashion: is that clear? You will repeat those instructions to Commissaire Fabre, and he will confirm them in a communication to myself as soon as he is at his desk tomorrow morning. Is that clear? Perfectly clear? Now go to it. I want every piece of waste ground swept, and I want every individual whose movements are not accounted for interrogated, and I say this with the utmost gravity and solemnity. That's all, Raynal.'

Colette shivered. But she had put herself in his hands.

'Are you chilled, my child? Forgive me – my daughter is your age. I do not wish to sound unduly patronizing. Forgive me again – I act towards you as I would to a child of my own. I have, you know, too – perhaps I have never mentioned it – grandchildren. My dear girl – forget, an instant, hierarchy. Forget that I am the representative of the state and the citizen – what after all is more to us than a child? Any child. Try to believe me. Forget that you are a magistrate and part of what I like to believe is in some senses my family. Try to give me credence when I say that as much would not be too much were it the most dispossessed and wretched of immigrant labourers ... Madame Richard? Dear Madame, Besson here, I crave your forgiveness, may I have your good man? Ah, Richard; sorry to disturb your repose. I'm ringing you from home: Madame Delavigne is with me. A child has disappeared. Raynal is of course carrying out the usual verifications, but there are certain aspects leading us to attach what may be a criminal significance ... yes ... yes ... the fact is that it is her own child ... That's as may be seen. For the present, I feel strongly that we should act with delicacy, and I have decided after deliberation that any publicity would not, at least until we can see round this more clearly, serve our cause.'

Richard's voice was soft, and did not clatter in the amplifier, but Colette noticed wryly that the Procureur had the earpiece cupped in his hand and pressed close to his head. That might be the habit of discretion – or was Richard in danger of saying something that might be hurtful? She was in any case making no effort to overhear; her mind was far off, examining the faintly preposterous spectacle of a procureur in a dressing-gown. His Missis had been careful not to put in an appearance; whether from discretion, or because she had taken off her stays and wasn't putting them on again for the Queen, Colette could not guess. A ludicrous vision of this magisterial pair of conjoints in their hymeneal couch imposed itself – with lurid details – on her inflamed imagination: she felt slightly ashamed of herself. Mention of her own name jerked her back to reality, none too soon.

'Madame Delavigne very sensibly called Castang, who as you know is on friendly terms with the family, to add his advice to whatever assistance he could give, and quite rightly he urged her to come straight to me. He's there still, as I gather. His view of the matter is that we'd do well to put in a listening post, which is logical, but naturally he can't move until you've made your dispositions: however, since I am in possession of the facts – sadly meagre alas so far, unless Raynal turns something up and I've instructed him to keep me in touch – you have a free hand and we've lost no time. I think myself justified in the circumstances in asking you to see for yourself. Yes, and Castang would seem the right man to take over the conduct of a preliminary enquiry, since Monsieur Delavigne feels very properly that it would be premature to lay a formal complaint before the possibilities of simple mischance are exhausted ... Quite so, and in that event I will ask Monsieur Savornin to take charge of the dossier, being our senior judge. Pending which, Richard – as unobtrusive as we can; I may count upon you. Till tomorrow, then ...'

'You are kindness personified,' said Colette formally.

'Kindness?' said Monsieur Besson, looking a the word as though it were evidence, turning it over and frowning at it, weighing it. 'Kindness is no more than courtesy; an attribute of charity, a virtue we endeavour to practise without always succeeding. You showed it, if I may be forgiven the personal nature of the remark, in asking me not to pursue your aggressor of a few minutes ago. I have unworthier levers – my two small grandchildren, who will inherit as it sometimes seems to us a world in which charity is a notion to excite derision. But we must preserve them, and try to arm them. My dear Madame, are you really able to drive your little car? Should I not ask Monsieur Richard to pass by and convey you?'

'I'll manage,' considerably embarrassed by these flowery proposals. He was being, perhaps, a little too paternal, bending over her with a scrap too much solicitude and a faint flavour of port. 'I am very touched, you know,' awkwardly.

'We shall hope to remove your apprehensions with the utmost

celerity,' sailing magisterially out to the hall. 'Did you have gloves?' somehow conveying a hint of disapproval that a lady should go out without gloves, even nowadays. 'Good night, my dear. Drive carefully. I shall not be expecting to see you at the Palais – or perhaps I should, confident as I am in a fortunate deliverance. All well? Got your keys? Good. I shall not turn out the light until I see you safely embarked.'

Talking to Proc was a bit like eating cream cake: nice, but one quickly had enough.

Tides of energy and excitement had come up in her in a feverish surge, filling her with wild illusions, leaving her flat and nauseated and lined with lead like some expensive coffin. The last of these, at its height while she felt so buoyed with help and understanding as to be convinced that she would return and find Rachel drinking cocoa on the hearthrug with an excited tale of magic carpets, had gone out with a rush in the chilling realization that the old man, while undoubtedly a kind old man with veins of gentleness in his severity, was also a slightly sexy old beast, who got a wee bit excited by young women coming to him with pathetic tales. Much too gentlemanly as well as too professional to allow little imps to wink at her, but there had been a flicker in the eye there for a second.

The tide went out so terrifyingly fast that she fumbled with the keys in the ignition, had to grip herself, looked firmly into her rear-view mirror – noting bleakly that the dark car had vanished – and pulled her gear lever too abruptly back into second – her right foot was incapable of accelerating . . . The car slackened and crawled, and wavered uncertainly to a stop before the end of the street. Her face was corpse-cold and clammy: she pushed her driving-door open, leaned out, and was violently sick in one frantic jet into the gutter. Rejection phenomenon, came her silly thought. Someone else's heart has been grafted into me. She leaned her forehead on the rim of her driving wheel, letting her whole body go limp as string, vaguely hoping there was no one in the street, above all no kind person to come offering sympathy or brandy, not caring a damn if there was, not even if it were another over-excited little satyr with notions of dragging her out and raping her: she felt vaguely that that would be quite nice, and would be a pleasant distraction. It would be happening

37

anyway to someone altogether different, not herself at all, and she would only be floating about somewhere as a half-heartedly interested spectator.

Just let her get rid of the lead first. Lead had a vile taste in the mouth: another crisis wrung her belly into a spasm and she retched miserably, finding nothing to be sick with but a little lead-poisoned saliva. She scrabbled in her bag for a little flat flask of eau-de-Cologne which ought to be there for when Madame the Judge got a bit grimy, physically and sometimes mentally, on long hot dragging afternoons in the Palais. She kept on finding nothing but that beastly gun at her fingertips, stupidly unable to find the other compartment in the nasty slithery silk lining of her bag. Found it at last, tried to unscrew it to the right, jammed it tight, nearly could not unscrew it at all, managed it at last, spilt a palmful on to her dirty smelly hand, feeling half of it soak through her cotton blouse, smeared the rest across her face, gulped gratefully at the evaporation of the alcohol. The stain upon her blouse was pleasantly cool to her skin. She rubbed at her stomach in a circular movement to evaporate the moisture and dissipate the stain. This seemed to do her good, vaguely. I'm in shock, she thought: I'm doing all sorts of silly things. She decided she couldn't care less if the whole street were full of gaping silent voyeurs, rested her head on the back rest, pushed her body slackly forward clear of the wheel, unbuttoned the blouse, threw the last drops of eau-de-Cologne on her hand and rubbed it again in slow circles over the pit of her stomach.

Really, Madame the Judge, such ideas to be getting, and on the street in front of Proc's house.

Her mind zigzagged aimlessly. Bernard had been driving her home from that last absurd winter dinner-party. It had been very cold, the car icy, with condensation from their twin breaths forming a mist on the windscreen because the heater had not had time to take effect. She had been huddled up, very yawning and soggy, in her fur jacket, leaning forward to wipe the windscreen with her hanky. Bernard, rather drunk, driving erratically, inflamed by heaven knew what but presumably the brandy on the top of galloping frustration induced by all the beige flesh above beige tulle and lilac lace and petunia satin, had become thoroughly irresponsible and had been driving with his

hand shoved persistently between her knees and hitching villain-
ously at her skirt-hem.

'Oh you,' half between a yawn and a giggle, 'do watch your
driving, you're lurching all over the place, you shouldn't be
driving at all, you're pie-eyed.'

'So're you,' slurringly sniggering – the cold burst of frosty air
had suddenly made him much drunker, for he had really been
perfectly behaved all evening – too much so – and breathing
again all over the windscreen. 'Oh damn the stupid thing; never
mind, I'll warm you, chilly wife, hell, those old bastards have
been leering down your frock all evening: my turn.'

'Bernard, keep your eyes on the road. Now Bernard, stop it,
you're bursting my poppers.' He had driven into the garage far
too fast, with a loud squawk from the brakes, heaved her out
like a sack, pushed her into the lift, scrambled her ludicrously
along the passage, puffing like a walrus in the mating season.

'How do you know what walruses do in the mating season?'
asked Bernard querulously, trying to force the latchkey in upside down.

'I seem to be getting shown,' she muttered, muffled from being flumped upside down into a lot of sofa cushions.

Colette straightened up with a jerk, threw the little empty
bottle back in her bag, took a deep breath of the summer night
through the open window, turned the ignition key and accelerated firmly, moving her gears in her accustomed rapid snap,
quite clear-headed now and stomach settled, but twitching with
a need to get home fast and get this over with. Remnants of control allowed her to put the car away instead of leaving it anyhow outside on the gravel, which would only attract attention.
The lift was at the bottom, heaven be thanked. She opened the
doors as quietly as she could, paid no heed to the voices from
the living-room, unable to care whether Richard had yet arrived
or not, and tore into the bathroom, where she threw her clothes
into a heap, made love to herself in a nervous frenzy, and collapsed with her tension snapped at last on the floor. She dragged
herself under the shower, made it very hot, and then made it
rather cold to get her blocked circulation running: even on
this warm evening her feet and hands were icy. She felt a great
deal better, and spent ten minutes on artificial aids towards a
majestic entrance of the mistress of the house into the living-

room, where there were at present gathered three policemen – the atmosphere was almost that of a party, for Bernard was doing his hospitality act, with a great show of lighthearted indifference to the whistling bullets. This was no Mitty performance: she was familiar with it. All that neurotic gaiety was no more than a pathetic determination that his private life should have nothing to do with strangers. She had seen him in moments of extreme fatigue, kneeling on the floor with his head in her lap so that she could massage the back of his neck, spring up to answer the telephone with an Anyone-for-tennis voice that filled her with pity and affection. It would wear off, she decided now: they've only just come.

Commissaire Richard, the chief of the Regional Service of the P.J. and Castang's immediate superior, was a tall handsome man who gave an impression of extreme calm. He had always the healthy look of a man who has slept well: his fine silvery hair never got ruffled and he never raised his voice. Neither Colette nor Bernard knew him at all well – Bernard, in fact, had never met him before, and Colette, who saw a good deal of him and thought she knew him well enough, was surprised now to realize that she knew nothing really about him – nothing of any use. That he was good at his job. That his department was run with a meticulous attention to detail, for he was very conscientious and reliable. That his subordinates liked him and trusted him, because when things went wrong he did not try to shuffle the blame on to underlings but took it himself. Seeing him now for the first time in her own living-room, in casual slacks and a cotton shirt with flowers on it, he was an entirely new person and the shock was small but real.

He held his hand out with the usual small but attractive smile and the usual polite murmur.

'Good evening, Madame Delavigne.' He didn't kiss her hand or anything or try to be the least gushing. 'We were just discussing tapping your telephone.' The police 'technician' stood politely in the background, being unobtrusive, accustomed to being unwelcome, ready even to be treated with hostility and wearing a mask of complete indifference which he would not change whatever happened: a man who has heard everything, and seen most. Even if he had a listening post in my bathroom, she thought, he would not show any emotion or raise his eyes off the carpet. As Castang had promised, an oldish man with greying hair. She went over to shake hands with him.

'I'm sorry to drag you out at this time of night,' she said politely. He smiled slightly but said nothing. Whether he was on or off duty, it mattered so little.

'I was just wondering' – Bernard bubbling irrepressibly, like a glass of champagne that second poured out – 'which article of the Penal Code it is that reproves electronic eavesdropping.'

'Good heavens, I've no idea,' said Colette, momentarily taken aback, since she 'knew her code' as well as most.

'Article 368,' answered Richard, playing up effortlessly, 'invasion of privacy. A felony,' with precision, 'punishable with two to twelve months' imprisonment and a fine of up to fifty thousand francs.'

'Coo,' said Castang, shaking his hand loosely from the wrist in the gesture meaning 'Direct Hit' – 'Hark at maestro.'

'I had it just the other day – the photographer who caught the princess without her bra. "The material used shall be confiscated." '

'So,' said Bernard with a gust of laughter. 'I'll have you all in jail.'

'There's a final paragraph,' imperturbably, 'stating that if carried out in the sight and knowledge of the parties it shall be deemed to be with their consent.'

'I bet the photographer tried that,' said Bernard.

'He did,' placidly, 'but he didn't get away with it.'

'So no private showing to regale us with?'

'Alas, I never even got to see them myself. Royal Highness's large private detective sergeant fairly tore them out of my hands.'

Colette was touched. Richard understood perfectly that these vulgarities were not characteristic of Bernard. For Henri, who knows us better, it is easier. She admired Richard's patience.

'Today we have a collection of other articles, familiar to Madame.'

'Three forty-one and five, fifty-four and five,' said Colette, not showing off. They were indeed familiar to her; odiously so.

'Sequestration and child-stealing.'

'The withholding of a minor,' she mimicked bitterly, 'from its properly constituted guardians.'

'And it's a felony,' said Bernard with sarcastic emphasis.

'No,' said Richard flatly, 'it's a crime.'

'I'm glad to hear it.'

'It's one of the gravest crimes in the code, Monsieur Delavigne. The kidnapping of a child under fifteen, where fraud or violence has been used, whether or not a ransom is demanded, carries a sentence of criminal reclusion in perpetuity. And I spare you the small print.'

'You really know them by heart.'

'This is one of the few which stops me sleeping at night.'

'And me,' fiercely. 'And me.'

'I don't want to eat into your reserves of patience, Monsieur Delavigne, because you will need them before tonight is over. But the three of us here – we are going to give our utmost. Not quote you bits of the code, or show you how much we know by heart. We are not bureaucrats. We are men like you. Right, Johnny,' not wanting Bernard to be ashamed and to present excuses, 'let's get this little job done.'

The grey-haired man opened a shabby suitcase with an ordinary electrician's toolkit.

'I take it you've a cellar, Madame? If you have a chair for me, I'll be out of your way, and the intrusion on your privacy will be kept to the minimum. I can't hear your movements or your conversation – I can only hear the voices when the phone is lifted.' He was fixing a small gadget under the instrument's base plate. 'It doesn't show, but you know it's there.'

'Ingenious,' muttered Bernard, 'but listen, if you're down in the cellar – that's three floors, and where are you going to lead the wires?'

'Middle ages, Monsieur, don't be offended. This isn't a microphone, and we don't need any wires. It's a tiny transmitter. It would hear everything you said, but as I explained we put in this little interrupter linked to the phone receiver-set, so that it will only function when the phone is lifted. There are no wires. Down in the basement I can listen with a headset. I can if need be record the conversation simultaneously on tape. I have, too, my own transmitter, and I can alert the operator at our office at the P.J. and in a matter of seconds I can if need be alert the Commissaire here, or if he wants any other officer in the neighbourhood, in a car, say, or wherever the Commissaire wants to place a man, in a radius up to a kilometre.'

'We don't have anything as sophisticated as the C.I.A.,' murmured Castang, 'but we're up to average Watergate standards.'

Bernard threw himself down on the sofa, and made a helpless gesture with his arms.

'No, you're not impotent,' said Richard. 'On the contrary, you have a very difficult and delicate task. On the instructions of the Procureur, we are going to work this with a complete absence of publicity. That takes away several of our conventional methods of approach, as for example the copying and distributing of photographs. We do have the advantage that Castang, who is going to take the heaviest load in this inquiry, knows your child and is familiar with her. I don't know her at all and I want your family album, so that I can get to know as much of her as I can. That for a start. But what I meant was that if we are to profit at all by this absence of publicity, we have to be certain that your movements arouse no curiosity. For example, several of your neighbours and the child's friends already know, unless I'm much mistaken, that she's missing. You can cover that: it shouldn't be too hard to construct a tale of misunderstanding, or perhaps since she won't be at school a tale of some slight accident which would mean that her absence was not remarked: a sprained ankle or something. Now if you show anxiety and disquiet to the world, above all if you shut yourself up here with the phone, you do yourself no good, but above all you do your cause no good. The moment there's any gossip, and all alterations in familiar patterns cause gossip, the press will be smelling a rat. Indeed this is a very risky thing we're trying. It isn't often that it's successful. It's a deception, and that's never a good start to a police inquiry. However, in the circumstances we can control it, but only if you – for example – put in an appearance at your office and put a face on things. If your daughter is laid up with a sprained ankle, it's normal that Madame and yourself take some time off to stay with her, since it is a child of eight. One of you can always be here at home – I suggest that you spend the afternoon here. The effort will help you too.

'That leaves us. As Johnny remarked he can link to a car,

which we'll use as a sort of mobile headquarters close by. We want to be able to slip in and out unremarked, so I'll ask to borrow your keys to have them copied, and you can count on me to give you a very close account of everything we do and learn, daily.

'Lastly I'd like you to think, right now, of anything in your own life or work that might give us a lead. Obviously enough, Madame's profession brings her into contact with a wide range of unbalanced persons, and there's a strong likelihood that here is where we will find the author of this attempt. The presumption is clear enough; an individual, possibly a parent or relation of a minor implicated in some affair judged or instructed by Madame, is trying to revenge himself upon society, and chooses to strike back at society as personified by yourselves and your children. It seems plain that the Procureur thinks something of the sort to be likely, because otherwise it is very unlikely that he would authorize this silence; it runs against the generally accepted convention, which is that police inquiries should be conducted in public and the usual liberties of the press unimpeded.'

'Come, come,' said Bernard, 'all sorts of hanky-panky never comes to light and well you know it.'

Richard smiled.

'It's not only more difficult than you think to keep things dark, and much more rare than the public supposes, but the reasons are generally good. I've known affairs, yes, where scandals involving high functionaries were hushed up in what has sometimes seemed a corrupt way, but there was nearly always also a good deal to be said for handling them discreetly. Here the matter is clearer: not only is a minor involved, which is the classic exception to the rule that justice be done in public, but it is possible that the whole thing has bearing on some matter still under instruction or not yet judged. The serenity and impartiality of justice may be menaced. There may be no ransom demanded in terms of money, but there might be a demand for an exchange of hostages, perhaps – the liberty of some imprisoned person. This is all pure hypothesis of course, but we'd do well to think about it.'

'I have thought about it,' said Bernard, 'and I have also some experience of the problems involved in being married to a magistrate.'

'All my long lecture,' said Richard gently, and not at all pedantically, 'was meant as no more than an objective viewpoint. If you can bring yourself to think objectively, it will very greatly help you – and us.'

'But you started by asking whether anybody had cause for grievance against myself.'

'I agree that it sounds unlikely. But I've got to keep an open mind – you'll agree that it would be foolish to conclude anything, since we know nothing. That the attack is directed towards Madame in her capacity as a magistrates is no more than the first field of inquiry, the one presenting itself first – possibly also the easiest. A large field?' His eyes went round to Colette, who had been sitting small and unimportant in the corner of the sofa.

'I don't know at all,' she said sadly. 'Nothing obvious; I mean there've been no menaces, beyond the usual collection of abusive, dotty and anonymous letters. My dossiers are all in order, I think. My clerk knows them all of course. As for looking at them – I've no idea. I'm completely confused and bewildered. The secret of the instruction . . . you'll have to ask the Procureur – there are ways and means – one has to ask the first president, the senior judge of the Appeal Court – I just can't bring the procedure to mind – he designates another magistrate . . . oh God . . .'

'Easy darling.'

'You're much better at this than I am. No, don't touch me, darling; I just need a moment. I'm sorry, Commissaire, I'm not a magistrate at all this evening, just a shocked and frightened woman. I've never known it in practice, but of course there's a procedure; the Procureur General, I think, can designate an officer of judicial police, and that would be you I suppose, to inquire into the background, or it may not be necessary: if I'm still officially instructing a dossier I can perhaps ask you to enlarge the scope of inquiry into the backgrounds – oh, I just don't know, I'm sorry. Even a judge has to be allowed an emotional upheaval sometimes.'

'Don't trouble yourself. I suggest that you try to come to work tomorrow afternoon, if Monsieur Delavigne can arrange to get away.'

'Of course I can.'

'And of course I will,' said Colette firmly, pulling herself together.

'And we'll have something worked out by then.'

'It's a complicated existence,' she said, smiling, determined to show her control. 'Article 67 of the code – you know, the judging of a minor – has twenty pages of close print to itself just in the little handbook.'

'I've never counted them,' said Richard smiling. 'The one after all we know best is 224.'

'Which is?' glad to have the tension broken.

'You tell them, Castang.'

'Outrage or insult to an agent of the public order,' happily. 'And punishable, I'm delighted to say, with fifteen to sixty days' jug or a fine up to three thousand, or both, if you happen to call a cop a cow's skin in a moment of exasperation after crashing your car.' All four laughed. Even grey-haired Johnny, silent in his corner with a glass of tonic hardly touched, condescended to smile.

The telephone rang.

There was instant silence. Richard signed to Bernard, and picked up the spare earpiece at the same moment.

Bernard swallowed, wetted his lips, picked up the phone, and said 'Delavigne,' in a creditably neutral tone.

'Commissaire Raynal, Urban Police. Nothing to report, sir, I'm afraid.'

'I see. Well, I must thank you. I suppose that is bad news, or isn't it?'

'It's neither good nor bad, sir. We haven't found your little girl, so that I'm afraid I can't allay your anxiety as yet on that point, but on the other hand we've found nothing that points to any criminal matter, and that if I may say so is good even if it's a negative good. So I want to ask you to keep your courage up, sir, and to tell you that we aren't abandoning this search. We'll now make slightly different dispositions, and widen the scope of our inquiries, and look at things in a bit more detail too.'

'Can you tell me a little more about this detail?'

'Well, sir, we put through a request to the commandant of the gendarmerie for the districts outside the city limits, and we ask for the help of the auxiliary police corps, which gives us considerably more men, and we verify any matter that seems to us at all obscure, and – well, briefly, we cover it all again more thoroughly and a bit more slowly – you'll appreciate, sir, that we haven't had time yet for more than routine checks.'

Richard signalled with the spare earpiece, gave it to Bernard, and took the phone over.

'Richard here, Raynal. The Proc's been on to you, has he? Yes, we're co-ordinating, naturally. I've been waiting to hear from you to set a prelim afoot, and I'll be beginning as of now; I've Castang here with me. Yes. Yes. Proc no doubt will be wanting Fabre and myself first thing, so if you'd have it all written up for when he gets in? I've nothing to say yet of course, apart from the obvious inferences: we'll be going over the ground here at dawn. Right then, old son. And there's a blanket on this, as of course you're aware. What have you given the press?'

'Well, we can't disguise our activity of course,' came Raynal's voice, thin and dry. 'The local people are aware what's going on; they weren't born yesterday. So I've authorized a bald paragraph, using the Proc's formal interdiction to release any details whatsoever. They'll be on to you too, no doubt.'

'No doubt. I wish them joy.'

'O.K. then. You'll say to Monsieur Delavigne I'll ring him in the morning? About seven. Sleep well.'

Richard put the phone back carefully.

'And now I'll be saying the same to you. Do you want a phone by your bed? Johnny will put one in for you. And if you can find means, Madame, to tuck him up for the night. I'll have you relieved, of course, Johnny, in the morning. We'll be going now, because we can't do you any further good here yet awhile. Johnny, you'll give me your buzzer and I'll put it under my pillow. Monsieur Delavigne – sleep! Go to your office exactly as usual. We'll find means to communicate with you if anything at all happens, and I'll arrange to slip in at lunchtime anyhow. Madame – I'm not going to concern myself in matters affecting the judicature, but I want to assure you that means can be found which will save you all pain and worry where the legal aspects interlock with your personal affairs. So good night to you both. Come on, Castang.'

'Good night, and thank you,' said Bernard.

'Good night,' said Colette, desolately, like a nervous child seeing the night-light blown out.

'Good night,' said Castang, being the colourless subordinate, and stopped. 'And Bernard – count on me, huh?'

'That thanks for the nice party?' Bernard summoning a grin.

'My turn for hospitality. Vera will want to make it a thanksgiving. We'll get Rachel back, you know, and quick. I won't say anything to Vera yet.'

'Yes, do,' said Colette. 'I want to be able to turn to her.'

'It's understood,' said Castang. 'See you.'

\*

The two men sat in Richard's car, which had been parked around the corner.

'Tactics,' said Richard mildly, lighting one of his thin, knotty Brazilian cigars.

'Not much doubt in your mind?' offered Castang.

'Not a great deal. Failing Raynal turning something up, we'll assume a snatch, without any speculation on the whose and whys: it'll be the hows which interest us first. The legal end you leave to me, as is evident. She was in a stew, of course, but in fact to get her dossiers over the last year combed out won't be a difficult affair. Safe bet Proc is turning wheels right now and that I'll be answerable to old Jeremiah, since he's senior judge, in the morning. And he's too experienced to fuss, thank God.'

'The legal end,' said Castang disgustedly. 'While you're all rollicking about in the small print and the ticklish definitions I'm being regaled with the gossip of the neighbours. 'Just have a look at her flaunting with her new pram, and how does she afford that on her husband's salary?' That come to think of it would be easy because the good women wouldn't have missed a trick, whereas in a quarter like this a good half of the female population is out of work.'

'Be out there,' said Richard, 'in time for the children going to school. They tack along in groups, and what puzzles me is how anyone could isolate the child, even for a minute or two. There may be some activity, a building site or whatnot, which interests them so that they stand and stare.'

'I can't question the children or it'll be out in no time.'

'Try,' said Richard unhelpfully, 'to find a way of getting round that difficulty.'

'You two gentlemen in some trouble?' inquired a voice, polite but nosy. Neither of them had seen the cruising station-wagon.

'Er – no.'

'You live around here?'

'We were at a party,' said Richard blandly.

'Been drinking a little bit perhaps? You wouldn't mind showing me your papers?'

Knows his job, thought Castang. Body turned a little to the right, disguising the fact he's got his right hand on his gun. Richard flipped open his little leather folder, holding it to the light.

'Sorry, sir, didn't recognize you. There's a little girl . . .'

'Correct and I don't want it advertised. No no, you were quite right – take a good look at parked cars. Anything on any of your reports?'

'Not so far.'

'I'll be having a word with your commissaire in the morning. I don't want any obtrusive controlling by day: this area will be sensitive.'

'Understood.' The station-wagon rolled off, quietly.

'We'll have to do a bit better than the sprained ankle,' said Richard, 'this sort of thing's bound to be noticed.'

'Man with wildly rolling eyes who chased a little girl so that she fell and sprained her ankle.'

'Something along those lines. That might not be a bad approach, let's say, to a school head. I'll see about tightening that up with Raynal. We've got to account for the buzz of activity.'

'And to account for me,' said Castang.

'You can have the little van with Post Office markings. And young Marcel with overalls.'

'Tells everyone with eyes to see that the phones are being tapped.'

'There's that. Surveyor – no, too fussy, and ties you down. I dislike these pretences anyhow. Nothing at all – by far the best and most plausible. You are simply yourself, inquiring into a vague report of children being molested. Which makes a reasonable press release. I give you Marcel, and a plain car. Park on the square, which is central, I'll know where to find you, and it's close enough to the house. Beyond that I leave it to you: I'll be along at lunchtime but with any luck there'll be phone-calls by then.'

'We hope.'

'How well do you know this couple?' suddenly.

'Very little really. Madame Delavigne is a friend of my wife's.'

'That much I'd gathered.'

'I've been in the house three or four times – you know, drinks, supper, and they've been to us maybe a bit more often, since as you know Vera doesn't like to go out much. We weren't ever very formal. Since the girls are pally, it doesn't mean much when she suddenly says "Henri" instead of "Monsieur" – no more than that when she's at home she likes to lay the "Madame la Juge" business aside for a while.'

'Yes, I see. And him?'

'Well, as you saw, he suffers a bit from a slight wish to compensate – she's a magistrate and he's a glorified yoghurt salesman, huh? He knows all about it and doesn't go about with a chip on his shoulder. But he seeks little ways, naturally. So he reads a lot – novels, poetry, you know – and he buys modern pictures. Vera likes him a lot, says he has a good eye. And it comes out as you may have noticed in the slightly exaggerated devotion to the child – he's mad on her, and one understands why.'

'He faithful to her?'

'I wouldn't know. He doesn't sleep with Vera,' grinning.

'A drama around the child – it might be a trick of his?' gazing off into the distance through the windscreen.

'A tricky mind,' said Castang carefully, 'and some suppressed jealousy. But if it were a trick – the clever thing was to call me?'

'Unless,' carefully, 'the trick would be to discredit you. Listen Castang – don't be vexed. You've never caught yourself with your hand on her knee, by any chance?'

Castang laughed.

'You don't know Vera very well. And perhaps, with respect, come to that you don't know me all that well. I can see, yes, given a certain set of circumstances, it would be thought clever, using the child to bring his wife back into line. Throwing total discredit upon her if he wanted – not to speak of me. Isn't it all a bit too fancy though?'

'Since you tell me it is, it is,' said Richard mildly. 'As long as we have taken the possibility into account. To guard against complacency. Just that kind of tricky fake has been attempted by that sort of man. Let's both get some sleep while we can.'

Castang rode home through the summer night that was still tainted with petrol fumes which lingered under the heavy foliage of the chestnut trees. Belated cars were still whisking along the main road, and when they finally trickled to a stop it would be the turn of the big lorries rolling in all night to bring the town its supplies. Police eyes would be watching the markets and the abattoirs, the loading platforms and railway sidings, the rubbish dumps and breakers' yards, the garbage collections – and the cemeteries. Those for cars as well as humans, and for the quite incredible amount of throw-aways our wasteful generation amasses so cheerfully. A city this size: that is a lot of work. Sorting out the discards in a great mound of evil-smelling waste – it formed by far the greatest body of police work. Garbage miners we are, thought Castang cheerfully. And paper miners, naturally, in this delightful country where the written word is sacred and which devotes so much ingenuity to writing everything down on as many different bits of paper as can be invented. Pauvre France! Salt is surely simpler!

Being 'condemned to the salt-mine' was a joke so old that one had long ago extracted and refined all the humorous remarks, surely, that could be made upon the subject. The tunnels were worn smooth, discoloured and dulled by the extreme familiarity of daily usage. It took a sudden jolt of this sort to make one look again. A crime which was one of the few that still had the power to shock, to galvanize apathetic policemen who have seen too many of the grimy little oddities of human behaviour. One slogged drearily away at the rock-face with so little idea beyond 'another cubic metre metre to shift before knocking-off time' that one had small concern for the beauty or originality of the crystals. Get them out, shove them on the conveyor belt, cart them up to the surface where they will be pounded and refined and weighed and numbered and packaged. One's dull, mole-like eye saw so little.

Suppose Richard had been right? Not of course where he was concerned – assuming that a magistrate who happened to be a brilliant and attractive young woman were to choose a playmate, she would hardly plump for a dim police official with his shabby respectability, his blunt, brutalized perceptions, his mean little ambitions and still meaner little cautions. Richard might say that stranger things had happened, but not to Castang they hadn't!

Colette – hm, to be sure. He knew very little about her. But Vera knew a good deal, and Vera was a perceptive person, who saw a great deal that his rigid, professionalized, narrow tunnel of a mind could not grasp. He had, he supposed, a certain virtue in that he tried to struggle against apathetic indifference, not just to accept the rock-face and the pickaxe with brutish passivity. He did try to see things a scrap larger, to try to see the pattern and the meaning in it all. But Vera went further, for she was a light-bringer, who illuminated what she looked at. She had shining, brightly burnished qualities. Virtues, one could call them. She was, for instance, the most utterly unselfish human being he had ever encountered.

They lived in a flat which was beyond their means, in a 'good' bourgeois street nearer the town centre, good because quiet, with plane-trees along the disused towing-path of an abandoned canal whose grassy bank the municipality had been to some pains to tidy and embellish. Here they had a small second-floor residence in a tall, narrow nineteenth-century town house whose solid construction had resisted alteration well enough for it to be an awkward flat, but more soundproof than most. The tall, well-proportioned windows gave a nice view on the weedy old waterway: this had been of great value to Vera, itself alone worth the rent they had to pay.

Castang found her reading in bed. She did not always sit up to await his return – which would anyway have been unreasonable and nearly impossible – but she tried, and sometimes succeeded. She was pleased to see him. She put down her book and smiled brilliantly at the dusty, vaguely grumpy figure sitting down to take its shoes off, unbuckle its gunbelt, get rid of all the junk a cop carries around in its pockets. A tired cop taking his gun off is something like a middle-aged woman 'getting out of her stays'. He heaves a sigh, and scratches the tickle, and rubs his stomach with pleasure.

Patience was her foremost attribute. No: a stronger word was needed, but Castang had not found anything better than an old biblical word standing for an early-Christian sort of virtue: fortitude. The young woman – she was only twenty-eight – had suffered a lot already in her life, and had been enriched by it instead of being impoverished. There was nothing sour or mean about Vera, and Castang, who saw a good deal of sourness and meanness in his everyday existence, was daily reminded of how lucky he was, and made little acts of thanksgiving.

She was not even really pretty. Exotic, to be sure, with a bell of fair hair over strongly-marked Slav features. In certain lights remarkably, even startlingly beautiful. She had too, or had had formerly, a beautiful body with unusual harmony: her carriage was stiff now, her walk hesitant and limping. Up to a few months ago, indeed, she had not been able to walk. As a young girl she had been a gymnast, full of promise, on the national team. After coming to France she had helped train the girls of the local club until one day a neglect of precautions and an unlucky fall had left her with damaged vertebrae. Traumatic paraplegia: she had been stuck in a wheeled chair for two years. She had made herself walk again at last by sheer perseverance; courage allied to strength of character.

True, a gymnast is a disciplined person. She had also some talent for graphic art, having several strongly-marked Czech characteristics, besides her cheekbones. Drawing is also a severe discipline. Briefly, Vera since early childhood had learned more from life than just the satisfaction of animal needs.

It stood her in good stead as a cop's wife. She had no experience of love affairs, for Castang was the only man she had known, let alone run away with, let alone slept with, let alone married. She was pursued by terrors when he was out at work in a job which she knew – and felt – to be at best harsh and ungrateful, at worst ignoble and treacherous, nearly always laborious, and liable to become painful and dangerous without any warning. She was one of those persons, and they are fairly rare, whose vivid imagination magnifies pain and danger but who refuse to be cast down by quaking terrors and who meet their nightmares head-on.

To Castang, the unimaginative policeman, this called for a continual effort. He had perpetually to be on tip-toe to keep hold of Vera. He had learned occasionally to anticipate her, but more often to tag on behind, and to be humble without being humiliated. Some of her fortitude had rubbed off on him.

It had made him a useful tool in the hands of his superiors. He was, on the whole, a pretty fair policeman; scrupulous, observant and patient. A brightish lad, who had had no trouble passing his baccalauréat (though it had taken a good deal of doggedness getting through law courses), he had passed the police-officers' entry examination enough above average to give him a fair start. But marrying a political refugee (who is always a nuisance to the constituted authorities) hadn't done him any good. He wasn't quite accommodating enough. In the salt-mine he shouldered his pickaxe sturdily, he did his work to the satisfaction of most, he was preparing his commissaire's examination and would probably pass it. If he wasn't unlucky, and watched where he put his feet, he had a good chance, seniority aiding, of finishing his career as a biggish fish in a middling pond. But he knew pretty well that he would never be anything but a centurion. It wasn't likely that he would ever be, like Richard, the chief of a criminal brigade in an important town, because otherwise he would have known enough not to marry Vera. To get out of the salt-mine, and have a job on the surface, and walk round with the word 'engineer' printed upon the plastic plaque clipped to your breast pocket, on a shirt that has no sweat stains, you need to be a bit of a politician.

But in his generally dismal tunnel he had discovered the branch of which Stendhal speaks in a famous metaphor: the bare branch which left overnight in the salt-mines covers itself in glittering crystals and becomes an object of delight, and amazement. The name of this branch was Vera.

She had slid down in bed, so that her face framed in a crumpled pillow was square and heavy, with a double chin over the book propped on her chest. She was studying him as usual while he went through the conventional movements of undressing and padding into the bathroom to brush his teeth. Saying nothing as usual. She never did say anything very much. What on earth did she see? He was an ordinary-looking person.

'Anything you want to talk about?' she asked at last. Anything, that is to say, neither too boring nor too technical. She knew after all that he had been to see Bernard Delavigne, having been there when the phone rang: 'Give them my love', she had said, the way one does. He got into bed, gave the pillow a whack to make it fluff up, wound the alarm-clock, setting it gloomily for four: pity the poor detective.

'What we hope won't be a horrible story with a bad ending – Rachel is missing.'

'Oh God!'

'Yes, right in the bowels. Nothing to tell you though; I've got to be up at dawn, which is sort of early. Just the obvious checking-up so far, and the beginnings of a routine inquiry. I have to trot around the quarter at first light; see if there's any cigar-ash or something. But we're pretty helpless,' turning out the light 'until they get a phone-call, which is what we pray for.'

'So Colette lies waiting for a call.'

'Bernard too, poor bugger. Much less well equipped for waiting. You know how centred he is upon that child. It must torment one worse than any other crime. Not just the physical vulnerability of a child but the breakdown in security and stability which a child needs so desperately.'

In fact, Castang said none of this. Telling Vera this horrible tale at midnight – what was the good of that? She would simply lie awake all night living through it. He had – all by himself – quite enough imagination to know what the child's parents went through.

'Oh,' grunting vaguely, 'Bernard was in a flap about something at the office. Handy reference book, the Police Judiciaire, knowing its penal code by heart. Pick its brains in return for a drink or two. Hadn't asked you, because "the men had to talk business". But Colette was asking for you. She's not very well, it seems, and is staying at home tomorrow, and if you could get over to cheer her up, she said, she'd be grateful.'

'Um,' said Vera vaguely. She could drive a car. An ordinary one was difficult because of the clutch, since her left leg was poor at obeying the orders given it, but an automatic gearbox solved that, and except in vile weather Castang took his bicycle to go to work. The 'um' was only a symbol in an equation involving washing-machines, shopping – Vera hated supermarkets – and a half-finished drawing.

'I'd like to; I haven't seen her in a month.'

Castang turned the light out.

'Got to be up at the crack of dawn, damn it. A place Richard wants me to look at by early light, before there are a lot of people about.'

'Why didn't you get back earlier?'

'You know what a gasbag Bernard is. Lot of fussy hospitality to excuse himself taking up one's time.'

Vera was not hurt at not having been invited. She liked Bernard, but with a large dilution of indifference: she thought him a selfish person. Richard's bright ideas, thought Castang vaguely . . . Now if Bernard fancied Vera, and if I chose to be a tiny bit complaisant, seeing that Colette is a judge of instruction, and a friend at court is a powerful aid to an ambitious cop . . . thinking myself vastly cunning . . . Bernard quietly takes the child and hides it out with some obscure granny. He need make no scenario, lay no elaborate false trail. All he has to do is say nothing, produce a convincing show of anguish – oh yes, it could be done. It would be the work of a thoroughly sociopathic personality, but that was incidental. Having dug a pit into which several magistrates and the whole of the local police apparatus have tumbled, the mine can be exploded: you produce the child, explaining that you had removed it from moral contamination and staged this little comedy in order to demonstrate, beyond all possibility of hushing up the scandal, the iniquity of persons in public life unworthily holding positions of great trust and honour.

And if such a plot existed, thought Castang, pursuing the theory to its logical conclusion, the plotter wouldn't even risk very much. A sociopathic personality might be so far gone as not to count the consequences to himself, or to imagine that none existed. The laying of misleading information, outrage to magistrate, contempt of court. And who knew but that with a clever lawyer and in the enormous blaze of publicity, and the extreme discredit into which you had managed to put both police and judge, you could, he rather thought, expect to get away with a good deal by playing the string of the betrayed husband and the devoted father protecting the family honour.

Who said I wasn't imaginative? thought Castang.

'Bernard drives himself too hard,' said Vera sleepily. He realized with a start that all this monstrous fantasy had taken about ten seconds.

'All that business of keeping up with Colette and not being just a banal cheesemonger.'

'Uh,' said Castang, burrowing into his pillow to get comfortable.

'Sleep well,' Vera's book, forgotten, fell on the floor with a crash as she turned over.

\*

He tried to cut his alarm off in a split second so as not to wake her, getting out of bed quietly with no flump or flinging back of covers. But while he was shaving he heard the buzz of the coffee-mill.

'I'm going to give you two eggs,' said Vera, 'or you'll be starving by eight.'

'Why did you get up? – I could easily pick up a crust of bread in a café.'

'What a waste of money,' disapprovingly, 'and anyway why not get up? This way I can get my housework done and I might get over to see Colette, which I'd like to do. I'm simply profiting from the occasion. Are you likely to be back for lunch?'

'Very unlikely,' with a face.

'What's this job you're on?' in a resigned tone.

'Suspected kidnapping.'

'Times,' she said sadly, 'one could almost wish for a clean homicide. And I stay here, doing the dusting.'

Castang bicycled to the office, which took him ten minutes. All was quiet; the duty sergeant was playing cards gloomily in the litter of last night's coffee-cups. There had been no telephone calls during the night, no alerts, no fresh instructions. He got to the municipal police.

'Commissaire Raynal – Castang at P.J. . . . Morning, sir, Castang here. I'm on my way to go over the ground on Monsieur Richard's instructions – anything I ought to know? There's nothing on our teletype but I thought I'd better check with you.'

'We've had a right battering,' said the voice, dried and wearied. 'I've a coop full of identities to check. I've violent drunks, a boy on LSD and three concealed weapons; I've also two affrays and an unlawful wounding, but I've nothing for you, I'm afraid; nothing whatever. The gendarmerie aren't in yet and there are several verifications to make. I'm summarizing any outstanding queries for the Proc and Richard at eight, and meanwhile – you're taking a radio car? Ask Lassalle to check with me around seven thirty. But it's all negative as far as you're concerned.'

Richard had been as good as his word: young Marcel appeared, yawning. 'The garage gave me a 204; I've got it outside the door.' The smallest size Peugeot station-wagon, dark green, no aerial, nothing whatever to distinguish it from ten thousand others.

The Avenue Mozart had been a cart track ten years ago. The main road south from the town led through a valley, linking a row of villages two to three kilometres apart which anyone in the district over the age of forty could recall when they really had been villages, little rustic dorps full of farmyards and dung-hills with a rustic bus to the town once every two hours. Now they were suburbs, with a suburban service every twenty minutes. The main road was linked the whole way by the parking lots of industry and the forecourts of filling stations into one continuous ribbon of concrete, and even the hinterland of fields was filling up steadily with housing estates, so that the still obstinately resisting strips of wheat or maize or vegetables were bordered with ungainly little heaps of broken rooftiles and sodden cement bags left by builders, and the dusty cabbages would have a fine full nutty flavour of car exhaust. The Delavigne 'quarter' had acquired its standing from being situated on the brow of a hill which even Castang could remember covered with vines. The wine had not been of good quality but the ground had sold for a good price, because one had fresh air, and a view. Here and there a few ragged little patches of vines still stood, hemmed in by walls, in little orchards with some rank grass around the edge and perhaps a cherry- or walnut-tree too old to bear fruit, where an obstinate old farmer or two had refused to sell.

The Avenue Mozart, lined with still immature plane-trees, climbed the hill in a gentle oblique slope, leaving the main road a couple of hundred metres before one reached the old village centre, where the original country *mairie* still stood next to the fire station and the old nineteenth-century school on whose wall could still be made out the faded paint saying 'École de Filles' on one side, housing now the overflow of suburban bureaucracy: housing office, labour exchange and social security bureau. The old village fountain still stood, kept because 'picturesque', where horses used to drink under a group of fine lime-trees, on a square now asphalted and car-parked and surrounded by stunted-looking acacias which gave no proper shade in fine weather.

They were early enough for the square still to be empty, so that Marcel could park close in under a real tree which would give them shade: it was going to be another hot day and the later arrivals would find that by lunchtime their little tin perambulators had become scorching sweatboxes reeking of hot metal and cooked plastic upholstery.

Castang looked around. The working day was about to begin, for even suburbanized 'country' is earlier in its habits than the town and most of the men had a trip of nearly half an hour to get to work. The shopkeepers were beginning to open their shutters and sweep their stoops; smells of coffee and bread were beginning to drift across the square; the tobacconist was taking his pile of morning newspapers inside and children were scuttling to the baker; the greengrocer flung out a dustbinful of yellowed rot with a crash and prepared to throw buckets of water over his wooden stall before winding out the faded blue sunblinds. At the corner the proprietor of the Café of the Belle Étoile was grinding up his metal shutters to proclaim with a noisy advertisement that the vanman now unloading meat in front of the butcher's could come and join the two overalled characters who were intending to have a quiet beer before beginning on the garbage-collection round.

'I've had no breakfast yet,' said Marcel meaningly.

Stupid boy, thought Castang, glowing in the possession of an admirable wife.

'Five minutes then, and no more. And pay for it yourself. Get me a paper, first.' He looked about him, stretching his shoulders in the still pale morning sunshine. Yes, there was the new school, a few score paces down the road on the valley side: the usual low block of wide windows with an asphalted playground in front and an ambitious tulip-tree in the middle. From the hillside the children would come down that little alleyway on to the square, crossing the road here where the two-way traffic was split and slowed, with a cop controlling the crossing at the four daily rush-hours. The alleyway led up the hill, steep and crowded with the older buildings of the original village. One could not even see the roofs of the tall blocks of the Avenue Mozart on the brow of the hill from this sharply foreshortened viewpoint, and there were several paths which turned and zig-zagged across the steep hillface. That, certainly, would be the place for him to start.

Marcel came back with a paper; handed it to him, bolted for the Belle Étoile. Castang leaned against the car radiator and unfolded it. Outside it smelt already of sun and dust: the inner pages clung together in a moist, pleasant smell of newsprint which smudged his fingertips. There was only a small para-graph.

'Police last night were alerted by the news of a child missing in an outlying residential quarter of our town. It was at first uncertain whether the child, described as being under ten years of age, might not have wandered off at play while on the way home from school, or have met with some accident in the street or elsewhere. Later in the evening, however, a report that the child had met with an aggressor was contradicted at police head-quarters. 'We know of no aggressor,' our reporter was told by authorities. 'We are making routine verifications of a variety of rumours. These alarms are generally the result of a misunder-standing. We have no reason to suppose the existence of any criminal occurrence. We are, however, looking into an un-substantiated report of a hit-and-run accident.'

'The name and address of the child concerned have been with-held, under the ruling that publication could only cause addi-tional anguish and disquiet to the relatives and would not be in the child's interests. To our reporter's query whether this ruling did not give rise to belief in a criminal attempt Commissaire Raynal, in charge of the unusual activity at regional police headquarters, replied that this was at present an unjustified assumption. 'It is far more probable that as a result of some misunderstanding a momentary confusion exists; I have no more to say about the matter.'

'At the time of going to press no further news had been received. We understand, however, that the inquiry has been enlarged to include the districts outside the city boundary.'

No mention of those gallant officers of the P.J. . . .

'I'll last for a bit now,' said Marcel, chewing noisily in his ear, 'where do we start?'

'Right here,' tapping the radio set.

'Bloody hell. All day?'

'There'll be intervals,' dryly. 'We don't know much about this operation but if we can intervene at all it has to be rapid. Richard has to know where we are, and we have to be able to transmit or receive a message with no loss of time. You can raise me on the clicker,' pointing to the fountain-pen receiver in his breast pocket, the little gadget which tells a department store manager, or an engineer on a site, or a patrolling police-man that he is 'wanted in the office'.

'Richard's carrying one too.' He picked up the handset and pressed the transmitter button. 'Castang here; getting me all right? . . . Good: I'm on the ground. Message for Richard: we're parked on the old market place, by the fountain. Proceeding. Message ends. Put me through to Johnny . . . hallo, old son; sleep well? . . . yes but not enough . . . no messages? Nothing whatever? . . . Nothing here either. I've checked with Raynal – negative all round. You'll be hearing from him on the landline, no doubt . . . yes; yes. I know her enough to know she makes a good cup of coffee. Give her the usual consolations, tell her I'm here. I won't be in there during the course of the morning, unless of course things get hot, but you could say to her that my wife will be along later. She'll understand. Say to Monsieur that nothing prevents him going to work as usual, and of course an approach might be made to him in the office, and to string along, naturally, with any demands made. I'll be in to see him at lunch-time, and so will Richard, no doubt of it. Luigi will be along to relieve you as soon as he gets in.

'That's it: anything to query? Leave it at that then; bye.'

'Where do the parents live?' asked Marcel.

'Up the hill here.'

'Must be pretty rich. Be a ransom demand, wouldn't you think?'

'Maybe,' said Castang briefly. 'But then why hasn't there been one already?'

He walked up the hill. One had no idea of the line taken by the Avenue Mozart from down here, but the 'Résidence Dampierre' was at the brow of the hill, so he took the steepest line. He supposed it was natural to think in terms of a ransom. Between them, Bernard and Colette made a lot of money, and the exterior signs of this prosperity were not lacking. The Dampierre itself, a snobbish building whose front was faced with dressed stone; Bernard's flashy white Citroën; Colette's equally noticeable yellow Alfa. Suppose one assumed nothing more than a gang – for there were generally two or three bright sparks in this kind of act – of the most banal, straight-forwardly greedy little bandits. And that was a perfectly reasonable assumption. No idea whatever of vengeance or hatred, but plain naked extortion.

It made a very simple pattern. They might have no notion that Colette was a judge: what interest would her work hold as long as she brought home the money; handbags full of it? They would have looked for nothing more than a rich young couple with one child. Looking up Bernard in the phone book, perhaps following him to work – but concentrating on no more than a crude snatch followed by an equally crude stand-and-deliver. But – he had just answered this himself – why in that case hang about?

The bank, of course. They wouldn't phone the night before, giving everybody time to get organized and make a plan. By leaving an uncertainty they could perhaps hope that the P.J. were not even in the act, and that nothing had been done beyond the sort of vague search described in the morning paper. So they'd wait till Bernard was at his office, and then make one brief call, giving him as little time as possible to set any countermeasure afoot. 'Go straight to the bank' – it would not be difficult to find out which bank in advance. 'Go straight from the bank to the Prisunic next door. Carry the money in notes in a paper carrierbag, holding this loosely by your side. Walk slowly past the counters, stopping to look at them. That's all.'

It could very easily work, thought Castang grimly. Bandits now, even the crudest, the most amateur, the most juvenile, knew enough not to propose the drop-off on the lonely road, the brown suitcase hidden in the long grass behind the milestone. It was far too easy for the police, first to be staked out waiting for the pick-up, and second to have the famous suitcase stuffed with old newspaper. The Prisunic would be how I'd work it, thought Castang. Plenty of entrances – too many to cover at short notice. At say nine in the morning, enough people to create uncertainty and confusion, but not enough to block all dodging or to jam the passage-ways and exits. Three people needed. One to snatch the bag, stuff it quickly into a plastic carrier such as fifty others were carrying at any given moment. Pass it quickly to number two and melt like lightning into the crowd: very little risk if one wore inconspicuous clothes. Number two walks quite slowly, attracting no attention. Meanwhile number three, by some simple manoeuvre like suddenly screaming 'Pick-pocket' or 'Stop Thief' or spilling a lot of small coins on the floor, distracts everyone. And quite flatly, by the time the con-fusion is sorted out, all three can have easily melted away and joined up at an inconspicuous car in the parking-lot opposite.

The child is now nothing but an embarrassment and must be got rid of. It has been kept, probably doped with sleeping pills, in any flat or studio in the town. It is bundled into the car, driven out here to the village, set suddenly on its feet in any corner, and will simply wander dazedly towards home with no thought of raising an alarm. That would not enter its head; to find Mama would be the notion which would crowd out every other. It would not have been harmed or ill-treated (the one bright spot in this whole unpleasant scenario): why should it? These were not sadists, deranged psychopaths. Money was the one thing that interested them.

The child cannot even give an adequate description at that age. It had had a sack put over its head. Later, perhaps, a young woman who gave it an ice and had dark hair and was wearing jeans. A young man with long curly hair. It got given a cup of cocoa and fell asleep. What more in its bewilderment could a little girl of eight have to tell? It was only in books that kidnap-pers had a handy stammer or a gold tooth, and a flat with a large coloured oleograph on the wall of President Kennedy, or the Pope, or Marilyn Monroe – or hell: what would a child of that age be certain of recognizing which did not exist in ten thous-and dumps? 'There was a lamp with a pink shade, and a tele-vision set, and a packet of cornflakes on the table, and the man smoked Marlboro cigarettes like Uncle Fred.'

With a very slight but sudden shock Castang found himself standing in the Avenue Mozart. And there was the Dampierre fifty metres away across the road. By the simple expedient of following the steepest line he had retraced the path that Rachel followed four times every day, on her way to and from school. Running downhill, it would not be much over five minutes. Ten if the policeman down on the square held the pedestrians up at the crossing to let the traffic get a bit less congested. Going back uphill – ten minimum. Fifteen if one took things easy. A child, dawdling on its way home, maybe twenty. But it was not quite that simple. There was no neat, direct, hollowed out watercourse (a child, like water, flows along the line of least resistance). Rather had the water been split into twenty miserable underground rivulets by the inequality of the terrain and the vagaries of inheritance laws, and trickled downhill now fast, now slow, drop by drop, before collecting again into two or three little brooks on the square below where the main road flowed along the valley and where still further a little river, hopelessly abased now and polluted, wandered with uncertain steps down into the town to join the big river, its ancient pastoral loops crossed and recrossed by the railway line ...

There had been water flowing down. Probably still was. Rusty pumps stood in the corners of overgrown gardens: outside one or two of the oldest houses still stood worn stone washtanks with the water siphoned up a pipe and lipping over the slimy greenish edge into a storm drain. But there was no direct path. The child, at three different points, could have taken two or even three ways. At the bottom, where the hill was steepest, lay still a thickly-caked mass of the village houses from the seventeenth century, encrusted along the edge of the square and up the slope, solidly built upon their deeply dug cellars in heavy blind grey stonework. There were four narrow alleyways leading up the hill, more or less parallel, wide enough – just – for a car to pass, so that they were all one way streets, two up and two down. Double, even triple lines of unchanged houses with high-walled narrow gardens, steep-pitched cobbled yards and outbuildings, with the dark dank streets going up more or less straight between, three roughly modernized in much-patched irregular macadam with tall weeds growing at the corners, one still the slippery uneven cobbles of the early nineteenth century.

But a hundred metres up the slope a newer road, cut perhaps fifty years ago, crossed obliquely. This road – the Rampe Notre

Dame – crowned the steepest part of the slope, and had been discovered back around nineteen-thirty by townspeople who wished to invest in a little country air and what then had been a pretty countrified view, for 'pavilions' – pretentious tiny villas with tiny gardens – clung like leeches to the sides of the stony outcrop which farmers had sold off cheap as too awkward to be of much use.

The slope grew easier above this, for which Castang, a bit puffed, was grateful, but the pathway was still crooked, making three corners in as many minutes to skirt what had been patches of vines until it popped out, surprising one, upon the bland concrete modernity of the Avenue Mozart, engineered in a long gentle slant back towards the town.

Having completed his topography he began to work slowly down again with an eye to the details. From the boulevard down to the top of the Rampe was patchwork. The building speculators, since this ground had become so valuable, had had to wait for obstinate old peasants to die before wedging ever-more expensive constructions into ever-smaller and more awkward scraps of waste land. Even now they were having to wait for a few minutely morselled and parcelled corners of nettle or thistle where some avaricious old biddy, aware she was sitting on a goldmine, was holding out for a better offer. Or wasn't having a high wall run up a bare two metres from her window . . . Castang had stopped, because he had found a likely-looking spot. A piece of grey house-wall, blinded by peeling grey shutters, looked up and across to a three-cornered bit between two new constructions – and one only a shell, left apparently half-finished and seemingly abandoned, as though the builder had run out of finance. The corner was no more than a rubbish tip, with rank grass growing round a pile of drainpipes, littered with torn remnants of cement sacks and old cigarette packets. Cars had stopped and parked here. Recently? – it was hard to tell on this uneven ground, dry and baked by a week of sunny June weather. Lovers, or fornicators rather, he thought distastefully noticing a discarded contraceptive. And children have played here too.

Had the trap been here? There were few passers-by, where it was too awkward for all but the residents' cars, too steep for all but a determined pedestrian. In mid-afternoon there could easily be a blank of ten or fifteen minutes' silence and solitude. A child, meandering slowly back from school, could – yes, it was certainly possible – be snatched here and perhaps quickly anaesthetized behind those drainpipes. A rag soaked in ether, which was simply bought in any *droguerie*. An involuntary shudder at the sickly asphyxiation of it; the foul smell – until of course one has had to do with a disintegrating, deliquescent, very dead human being.

A sharp grating creak made Castang turn his head. A shutter had opened. Sunlight pierced the grey barrier, but all it showed was a grey old woman, framed in faded greyish wallpaper and surrounded by fusty greyed bolsters. A biddy airing her stuffy bedchamber for the permissible ten minutes before shutting out all air and light for another regulation twenty-four hours. The biddy regarded him with suspicion.

'Good morning,' said Castang sunnily. 'Your ground?' She cackled, snaggle-toothed.

'Not for sale, young man. And you ain't the first. There's many would like to get their hand on that.' It was exactly as he had thought. A peasant woman still saving candle-ends, although her declining years were nicely featherbedded by the judicious sale of corners that had just been good enough to grow a few artichokes to feed to the pig.

'Police,' he said politely. 'Have you perhaps seen anyone hanging around who had no business here?'

'Ah. They was there last night, poking around with a torch. I seen un.'

'Who?'

'More police. They come up the hill with a car – and how come you don't know that?'

'Plain-clothes,' flashing his medal. 'That was the uniformed branch. We had a complaint,' casually.

'Complaint of what?'

'Oh, a lady had her handbag snatched. You've seen no vagabond or something similar hanging about yesterday afternoon?'

'I lives round the other side,' regretfully. 'I only see here at night. Think nobody sees them. I watches them,' with relish.

'Who?'

'Fuckers,' she said with even more relish. 'The builders parks their cars there. But they're gone. Got no money,' enjoyably.

'Yesterday afternoon,' he offered loosely. 'A lady on foot. Say mid-afternoon, around the time the children get home.'

'The children,' spitefully. 'Brats! I ain't seen,' regretfully.

Castang saw that it was the truth. The biddy lived in the front, facing downhill. Except for her spyglass on the fornicators she had no interest. She might have yelled at children, who would have cat-called bad names. Unable to chase them, she would have abandoned the fight, secure behind the blind wall.

'Rich women,' happily, with a glance of hatred up the hill at the bland white blocks whose roofs showed. 'They don't pass here much. Too lazy. Easier to take the car round. Serve her right.' with gleeful spite. 'Putting the prices up.'

'I'm much obliged.'

'Wouldn't go taking that trouble if it was me, would you now? But I'm only a poor old woman living alone,' inviting pity, anyone's, even his. 'Can't even manage the vegetable garden no more.'

'I've no doubt you manage,' said Castang blandly. Toothless rattlesnake! She gave him a glance of vicious joy.

'Cops!' she said with disdain, and closed the shutter. She had seen nothing. If she had she'd have been all over him. Disappointed, Castang moved away downhill. Before he left he moved over to examine the grey wall. Scratched with a sharp stone, in children's writing, was the legend 'Elise is an old bag.' He agreed.

Nothing more, down to the bottom of the Rampe; nothing but bare roadway and corners overlooked by windows whose grimy net curtains would twitch at the slightest movement. Plenty more women, old and young, hoping it was the bailiff come to repossess their neighbours' hire-purchase telly, but interested even if it were only the South-Western Gas Board.

But where the Rampe gave way to a fork of two alleyways down to the village there was something more interesting, which he hadn't seen on the way up, because the entrance had not only been to his back, but masked by a retreating angle. The courtyard of a farm; hadn't been worked for twenty years or more. The valley land had been given up when the children had decided that industry paid more, as well as being easier: the vines on the hill slope had been neglected even before the ground of the Avenue Mozart had been acquired cheap, and a discouraged, embittered farmer had been glad to take his profit and retire to somewhere deeper in the country, where he perhaps had relatives. For this yard and the buildings lining it had long been dead. The wooden shutter of the hayloft yawned drunkenly on one rotted hinge. Some shopkeeper in the plumbing trade used the shed as an entrepôt for materials he had no room for: a bath and a couple of w.c. blocks stood under the decaying roof, with their protective tape still adhering. A heavily chained and padlocked stable door showed where copper piping and taps – the stuff easier to pinch – was secured, and on the decrepit yard gate was a notice half rust and half chipped enamel saying 'Paul Entreprises Sanitaires. In case of absence apply at shop.' No chickens had scratched the grass-grown cobbles of this yard for a long time. The shutters of the farmhouse itself were never opened, as could be seen from cobwebs. But someone still lived there, for the lock of the door was kept oiled and there were fresh scratches on the weathered wood.

There was room to drive a car in and park it unnoticed. People did, because there were patches of oil. That would be the usual beat-up Citroën van belonging to Entreprises Paul, plainly the sort of plumber who always says he'll come, when called on the phone by anguished housewives with a leak, and turns up six weeks later – if at all . . .

Castang was interested. Nobody overlooked this yard. On one side the Rampe Notre Dame stretched dustily, its protective revetment seven or eight metres high and topped with grimy bushes. On the other was an awkward house, built tall and narrow for bygone days of cheap servants, with a 'For Sale' notice that had been there two years at least because the owner was greedily holding out for too much money. The yard was nowhere overlooked, except perhaps by some ghostlike Miss Havisham out of *Great Expectations*.

Examining the ground, Castang found confirmation of an old widow clinging on still in the farmhouse. A fresh rabbit dropping lodged between two cobbles. And two more, under a decidedly shop-soiled bidet dumped barely clear of a leaky drainpipe. No rabbit-hutches and no sign of hay. Some antique biddy even more decrepit than Elise, who probably lived in one room, along with the rabbits for company. But it was another likely bit of ground, better in fact than the other. Nobody opened a window to ask what he wanted, and when he knocked on the door nobody answered. Hm. Castang walked slowly down the alley and back to the car. Marcel was in his shirtsleeves doing a crossword. There had been no calls and no messages. The sun was already hot.

'My turn for a quick visit to the pub,' said Castang. But he did not aim for the big café in the square, its bright star now attracting a dozen customers, but for a decrepit little pub on the shady side, between the two alleyways, with a forlorn look of having given up trying. The Café de la Liberté. Liberty Bar, thought Castang, with a faint twitch of the nose. Hands in pockets, looking like a loitering stable-boy, he strolled over to Liberty Bar.

Just as he thought; a place that had given up trying. Nobody came here but a few villagers, who gathered to shut out the twentieth century and wrap themselves in the musty curtains of the old days. A poky little café with half a dozen decrepit tables covered in smelly unchanged cloths, an old zinc counter, the legally obligatory rack of lemonades and syrups which nobody touched and some dusty apéritifs made by firms which had gone out of business in 1950. Even the man who came shuffling out to serve him was deaf, though a sharp look seemed to say that he pretended to be deafer than he was.

'A white wine,' said Castang.

'Glass or chopine?'

'Chopine.' The jug was of a pretty old pattern. Even the glass was more shapely and fragile than 'modern' pub supply. There was one customer. Castang carried his supplies over to this table, because the customer was looking at him with a remarkably spry eye. The funny thing was that he was no peasant. A 'bourgeois' but a bourgeois from a bygone age. He wore a Panama straw hat of peculiar shape, like Monsieur Brun in the Marius pictures, and a kind of tropical suit whose cream colour had darkened to that of stale camembert cheese. Perhaps he lived alone, because he had been breakfasting: a large coffee-cup stood amidst the crumbs of a croissant. A little glass brimming with some colourless alcohol stood untouched before him. He did not look dilapidated or drunken: he was washed and shaved. He could be anything from sixty-five to eighty. He had the perfect immobility of all retired men who sit long hours in cafés.

'You don't mind?' asked Castang politely.

'Not at all; like company.' The lips hardly moved but the voice was as spry as the eyes. 'Passing through?'

'In a sense.'

'Not selling anything.'

'How do you know?' amused, and pleased, because if this old boy liked playing detective he had come to the right shop.

'Bigger café over the road. More animated. More commerce … Cleaner, too,' as an afterthought. 'Dirty old man that,' with a glance at the bar. 'His white wine's more honest, though. No thanks, I don't smoke – no, I don't drink.' Dry cackle. 'This here is my kicker. Lasts me till sundown.'

'Algiers – or Saigon?'

'Hanoi. You want me to talk, I'll talk. But you aren't interested in Hanoi. You're a cop.'

'Right, but where does it show?'

'I've seen more. What are you interested in?'

'This old part of the village, going up the hillside.'

'What's happened there?'

'Oh a woman from up on the boulevard going down to the shops – had her bag snatched.'

The old man chuckled.

'Do better than that. You're senior – it shows. Handbag! Not even the boys in blue would stir off their arse for that. Not the child that was attacked, no?'

'Shrewd.'

'Not shrewd, and stop trying to flatter. Just experienced. Been a civil servant,' tasting his drink, 'a long time.'

A shrill yell echoed in the alley. Feet pattered outside the grimy window. The children were going to school.

'You don't notice them, sitting here every morning?'

'Why would I notice them? My son was killed at Cao Bang. My daughter lives in Narbonne, doesn't want to know me. I've no interest in children.'

'Who still lives in the farm at the top of the road?'

'Old Léon. Dotty old bastard.'

'Dotty what way?'

'Got a lawsuit going against the mayor for over twenty

years. Bloodthirsty bastard too. Sleeps with his shotgun. Lets it off at anything that moves.' There was a sudden gush of nostalgia. 'When I was a boy here the hill was full of birds. Nothing now – sterile. Léon shot them all. The boys in blue are terrified of him. Come to deliver a summons, get a charge of number five in the seat of their pants.'

'No rabbits left?'

'Here?' with incredulity.

'Tame ones maybe. The old villagers keep them. Like Elise.'

'Elise? You've been getting around. Poisonous old cow. The rabbit would bite her, and die of it. What's this obsession with rabbits?'

'Just wondered. The old villagers do keep them. I thought I saw one.'

'Remarkable. Wouldn't let them out. Too many cars – too many boys.'

'Old Léon there all the time?'

'Never there at all. Spends his days at the tribunal, presenting petitions to get the Minister of Justice impeached. Or at lawyers' offices. Or at the notary's, changing his will.'

Vera would like that. A French version of Dickens's Miss Flite, a figure from Balzac. But it didn't sound helpful, except that he was 'never there'.

'You know all the villagers?'

'Not many left, now. But they come here, yes. You mean I hear all the gossip? Would know if anyone were liable to attack a child or such? No, I wouldn't. I'd know if anybody's seen or heard something, yes, and I have to disappoint you. And I spend time in the other café too,' dryly, 'so don't waste yours there. But if there's somebody mental floating about – no, I wouldn't know. Nor would you. Because I've been a civil servant all my life, and I've never seen anything to lead me to believe the human race is worth a snap of the fingers.'

He drank off his 'kicker'.

'Let the bomb fall, my boy, let the bomb fall.'

'I've given you another confidence to keep to yourself,' said Castang, finishing his wine.

'It's safe. But let me tell you – you're in the wrong job. Look at me. What do you think my pension's worth? Where would I be, hey? – if I hadn't taken a hell of a lot of bribes? And

71

those, mostly, invested in stuff that's worthless, now. If I hadn't had the fortune to have a bit in Shell – where would I be now? What's a child more or less? I've seen so many die.'

'A man has to have something to hold to. Otherwise he'd never be able to hang on. One has to persevere.'

'For the good of the state?'

'No, for oneself. Not to give in. What good, otherwise, to be a man?'

'You're a goddy. Say the rosary, ring the angelus at twelve. Like the white fathers in Hanoi. A salvationist, heaven help you.'

'What else is there – once you no longer believe in humans?' He banged on the counter, brought the shuffly man out, got separated from a couple of francs. What did that poor old sod believe in, then? That it 'would last his time'? It never has. That's why we cling to the memory of our youth, when the army knew how to fight, and even the footballers gave all they had. Now they just think of the press conference they'll give, after the fight. But he believes in keeping his wine honest, because that's all he's got. I'm much the same.

'Think forward my boy,' said the old colonial hand, sitting there chuckling over his empty glass and his empty coffee cup. 'Think forward to when you're my age.'

Castang smiled, but went out angry.

A depression. He stood in the sunlight, and shook it off. He went back up the hill. The bare sunny yard and the abandoned sanitary appliances grinned at him like old discoloured bone, or the teeth of a retired civil servant. The blind shutters of old Léon's house disquieted him now that he could picture a red-eyed little man, hopping about like a rabbit, aimlessly, scribbling away by the light of a paraffin lamp, because the electricity had been cut off, at a long memorandum concerning procedural faults during the hearing in the Court of Civil Appeals.

Now look, put a stop to that.

Weren't there any young women in this god-forgotten neighbourhood? He ran one to earth, finally, in one of the gimcrack modern blocks near the top, her absurd tiny balcony full of children's underclothes on washing lines. Worm's-eye view. But it gave a steer to another worm.

Another depressing performance, because a young, active, pretty woman with three small children who kept her on the trot, I-can-tell-you, was only pleased to have someone to grumble to. Handbag snatched? – they'd be welcome to mine; there's never anything in it. Those bloody shops down there, they'd pinch the salt out of your cabbage. Walk down? – yes, and up too, dragging the shopping on a trolley. I've never seen anything. Oh yes, I know Elise – complains all the time about the children. Old Léon? No, never laid eyes on him. I know that farmyard but I've never noticed it particularly. I don't know anyone round here. The villagers – of course not. Interested in nothing but money. The rich women on the boulevard? That toffee-nosed they wouldn't give you the time of day. I'm from the town. Thought it would be nice out here, healthier for the children. But these flats are far too small. And expensive – one does nothing but run after the payments. The school? – it's all right I suppose. Modern and that. They think up a lot of stuff to occupy the little ones, but the children do no work, it's not like when we were at school. But at least it's quiet here. The elder children are all these motorbike maniacs, you'd never believe it, even the girls. They roar up and down the boulevard. Don't come up the alley much. Safe? Where is safe, now? But no, I've never known anything bad, not yet, no, no dirty old loonies talking to the children or showing themselves, and if there was I'd soon settle his hash I can tell you. We don't go out at night; where is there to go to? The telly, not that it's any bloody use. I'd like to go out but the man comes back dead tired from work, and one can't afford it anyway and who's to look after the children? God knows why we do it, it's a thankless existence. But oh well, that's the way of the world. Do your job, hope for something better, sometime even if sometime's never. Next year – there's always a next year. Isn't that what the Jews say? – on their big feasts don't they drink to 'next year in Jerusalem'? And never losing faith all those years. What'll we drink to, hey?

'Thanks, not in working hours,' said Castang austerely, making a getaway, since plainly this good woman was convinced that he had just dropped in to cheer her up.

He worked his way back downhill again. None of the variations in the route – leading for example to 'Jackie's house' a little further down the avenue – showed any possibility of ambush. Anyway, on all the evidence Rachel had been alone and had not accompanied 'Jackie's gang'. There were those two nooks. For there must have been a car, and there must have been a good deal of hanging about. Perhaps several days had been needed before a moment came when Rachel, even making four trips a day, had passed alone and out of sight and earshot of another child or a casually passing adult. And in the morning, both early and just before midday, there were workmen passing, housewives shopping, windows open everywhere to air bedclothes and shake out dusters. Whereas on a hot, sleepy mid-afternoon . . .

Back down in the village the Établissements Paul were easily found, and a noisy clattering woman in a shop full of ironmongery handed him over to a vague, greyed man like an old badger in his workshop, with a perpetual ragged cigarette burning wispily under a ragged grey moustache and his glasses pushed up on his forehead, giving him a perplexed look, as though he could never quite remember what job it was he was supposed to be doing. Castang felt he now knew all there was to know about Mr Paul.

'Look, I'm a police officer; I just dropped in. We've had some trouble up the hill over the other side, woman had a bag snatched and some vague reports of vagabonds hanging about. Now I notice you've got materials stored there in a pretty casual way. Gate all rotted, no proper lock – you ever had any trouble up there? – clochards sleeping there or anything?'

Mr Paul, from long practice with his frustrated customers, was vague and evasive about everything. Well yes, they did have some stuff up there but it was mostly junk. A few baths and such were padlocked in the shed. He didn't go up there much; maybe once a week. At night it was safe as the bank. Old Léon was opposite: it was well known he never slept but prowled about with his gun looking for rats or whatnot: the old bastard would shoot at anything that moved. And who'd go in by day to pinch a bidet? People did park vans or cars there sometimes because there was no room on the road below and no parking allowed on the Rampe. Rabbits? – nobody up there had rabbits. He had some himself, but not up there. Down here.

Did the police think he kept rabbits in his pocket or something?

After this long speech Mr Paul rubbed his scratchy jaw with a greasy hand, degreased himself casually with a handful of plumber's hemp, deftly relit his cigarette from the blowlamp, refreshed himself with a glass of red wine and indicated that the interview was at an end and the police would do better to go out and catch a few criminals instead of wasting all this time. Castang retired sullenly.

But before going back to his base he trudged up the alley and went over the ground again carefully. The dry ground and uneven cobbles told him nothng. There was still nobody about. Nobody took the faintest interest when he picked up four or five rabbit droppings and put them in an envelope. He didn't know what the technical squad would have to say, but they could tell him, he thought, whether the droppings were as he suspected yesterday's. Which might be interesting. And at least it was a proof that there had been a rabbit, and he hadn't just dreamed it. There was no rabbit now.

He went back to the car and sent Marcel for a cup of coffee and a pee. He had a little talk with the office. Richard had gone to the Palais for a conference with legal and police bigwigs. Nothing had happened and there was no news. Luigi had taken over the phone stake-out from old Johnny. Luigi reported that he was quite happy, with several paperback thrillers Madame Delavigne had lent him. Yes, she did make a good cup of coffee. She was very white and peaky and had hardly slept, but she was quite calm and controlled. She hadn't been out at all. When he had gone to the bathroom he had heard women's voices – a lady had come to call, which was good, stopped Madame roaming nervously around. Monsieur Delavigne had looked like death warmed up, so Johnny said, but had gone to the office at the usual time, saying he'd pretend he had a dose of flu, which looked convincing. He had phoned, to say that the office was perfectly normal, and – in guarded terms – that the mail was in and contained nothing interesting. No office phone-calls either. He was, Luigi thought, putting on a pretty good show. Yes, it was odd that there'd been no news at all. Because everything was now pointing to a criminal attempt and a ransom demand. Perhaps the bandits were waiting to let everyone work up a real sweat and then put in a snap demand at rush-hour, just before the banks closed, when checking cars would be twice as difficult.

Hold your line; there's a call now.

Castang nearly bit his cigarette in two, but the voice, sounding decidedly Hamlet's-Father through several electronic relays, was only Richard's. Everything was in order, there were no problems, he would be over at lunchtime, tell Castang, for a bit of a progress report, and here was the Procureur de la République, who would like to have a word with Madame Delavigne, and since this was a personal word he would be obliged if Luigi would momentarily switch out the relay until that little ting told him that the private conversations were over: thank you.

Castang put the handset down, smoked his cigarette out, waited until Marcel was back; thinking about rabbits. He strolled across the square, busy now with mid-morning activity, and down the fifty metres of side street to the primary 'Groupe Scolaire' – from three-year-olds in the crèche for working mothers to the ten-to-eleven children who next term would be moving across to the secondary school along the road, at the bottom of the Avenue Mozart. The midmorning break was in full swing: already on the square Castang could hear the thin shrill shrieking of playing children, one of the most attractive sounds on earth. As usual it dug into him. Vera, Vera, why have we no children? Even when half paralysed, and against her doctor's head-shakings, she had refused utterly to 'take precautions'. But she'd been trying well before that time, too.

Madame la Directrice was in her office and would be glad to see him, said the concierge. Up the passage, third on the right. She stood up politely to meet him, a thin, pale, slightly faded blonde of fifty in an almond-green jersey two-piece. Smart, bright, gentle, beautifully balanced; a perfect honey. Time for him too to meet a honey: the world, so far this morning, had been sufficiently cranky. What a joy to meet this delightful, nice-smelling woman who understood everything without any laborious explanations, and made brief, sensible remarks.

'Of course I know Madame Delavigne, though I only know her from a couple of meetings: Rachel is a child who gives no trouble. A good judge – if I'm any judge of judges! Naturally, we share the same interests. We've had no professional contact. I have some backward or deprived or difficult children, as who hasn't, but so far we've managed to handle our little delinquency problems without recourse to the courts! A melting-pot like all large schools, and since we have the old village with the modern suburb imposed upon it we're bound to have a few rough edges arising from the different backgrounds. On the whole we're very fortunate. The district is wealthy, the mayor is reasonable – I've had his two daughters and they're both at the secondary now – and we have the added fortune that this is a pilot school approved by the ministry, so that we've two nursery classes in foreign languages, an English and a Spanish, and we're proud of them.

'Rachel – I know her fairly well. She's a reserved child with a good moderate intelligence, no very great imaginative projection, well co-ordinated and well integrated. She plays, soberly and a bit stodgily, with the gang – oh yes, I know all about the awful Jackie; she's a useful brake upon his wilder fantasies. She's very shy and has nice old-fashioned manners, curtseys like a little German girl. Quite plain, and no extravagant vanities. Rather too fussy and meticulous, perhaps a little too much cotton-wooled by her father, but on the whole robust and self-reliant. Certainly not the child to wander off irresponsibly or fall for any crude offers of lollipops . . . I quite agree with you, if there was any trap it would need to be skilful.

'No, we've had no trouble of that sort. We take no responsibility of course outside our gates. That main-road is a perpetual anxiety but the mayor is good about having it properly supervised. Those alleys up the hill – yes, for a child like Rachel – where does she live? At the very top? Ah; I live halfway down, myself. As one gets up there are fewer children, naturally, and those the richest, generally picked up by car. She'd make her way alone quite frequently, the more as she is a solitary child, who stands and gazes at things and takes her time absorbing them . . .

'I quite agree, and of course publicity wouldn't do us any good either – I'll have a word with her form mistress at lunch. There'll be no drama. The sprained ankle will do very well for a few days. We'll add a few words to the children about exhibitionists and so on, though it's not a problem around here.

Not so many little girls nowadays worrying about father's big hairy dangly thing. The town children take it for granted, and the country children are all used to the cock jumping on the hen. Among the little ones there's any amount of male vanity and boys brandishing their zizi in the lavs, and once that stage passes the natural modesty of the pre-teen years gives them a good protection.

'Not at all, Monsieur Castang, a pleasure. And a pain, of course. I'll say a prayer. We won't dramatize. I've no doubt you'll have found Rachel in a very few hours, and I hope Madame Delavigne will agree that unless there's been physical maltreatment – which God forbid – sending her straight back to us with the minimum of disturbance in her patterns will help the trauma heal the quicker. Children need patterns, you know. Above all, they need to know where they stand. Even a certain coarseness, a slight brutality, is preferable to well-meant wavering and shilly-shally. Good-bye, Monsieur Castang.'

A disciplined woman, as well as a sensible one. She had hesitated ever so slightly before her final phrase – but no, she wasn't going to meddle in police business. Neither morbid curiosity nor emotional displays of self-indulgent sympathy entered into this woman's patterns. He made his way out, through a faint, comforting, rather pleasant smell of small children's pipi into the hot, dusty, still air, and a world inhabited by Pauls and Marcels and imbeciles. And mayors.

Castang called on the mayor, and the local police, and the local secretary of the Federation of Parents. He learned nothing new. By a quarter to twelve – telling Marcel his lunch-break did not begin before twelve, or end after two, and to leave the car where it was – he was following 'Jackie's gang' at a discreet distance up the hill. Jackie had pocketed some chalk, and stopped before three admirers to draw a face on Elise's wall, add two swastikas and the slogan 'Heil Hitlerin', and swagger on home. Castang walked quietly in at the garage entrance of the Résidence Dampierre just before the business men got home and found Colette and Vera having a calm, respectable, bourgeois Campari-orange before lunch. Thanks, he'd like a big Suze with lots of ice, and might he have a wash? Yes, he did think poor old Luigi would like a pastis, and he'd bring it down with pleasure.

'Great hypocrite,' said Vera when he got back.

'It was much better that you heard it direct from Colette.'

'Sorry,' said Colette, 'I must go for a pee. Damn it, I think I've been every ten minutes, ever since breakfast. No, I haven't taken any pills of any sort whatsoever. I did weaken around mid-morning, but Vera stopped me. She's been marvellous,' with tears brimming hatefully, 'and Monsieur Besson rang up very kindly, and so did the senior judge, and everybody's so kind, and you've worked like stink all morning, Henri, and Bernard's being absolutely controlled and utterly perfect – and God – why don't I hear – where is my child?' And rushed head downward for the lavatory.

'Don't give me any more,' said Vera. 'Just give me some more ice to stretch what I have. She hasn't broken down a second, all morning.

'You're out working, at least,' Vera went on. 'You move around, you talk to people. While the women have to find their own devices. They shop, they cook, they iron, they do some washing, they do the little jobs that the cleaning woman has dodged or forgotten – and they carry on a dialogue with themselves. I'm used, of course, to feeling helpless, whereas she's accustomed to getting things done; to giving orders and seeing them punctiliously executed.'

Colette came back with her eyes carefully painted.

'I suppose I've sent a lot of people to prison one way or another. The law prescribes, such and such, one is there to ad-minister it. There is no particular case of conscience. One ex-amines each instance with care, naturally, to decide whether such a one will benefit from course *a* or course *b* in the pretty restricted range available. It can happen quite often that one de-cides with no hesitation that prison is the best choice. But after only one morning's prison I shall never feel quite the same.'

She had fine eyes. She was looking at Castang with them, but not seeing him.

'I recall a seminar given in the magistrates' school, on psy-chiatry. The mark of mental health, said the good man, is the ability to repress our knowledge of the world's cruelty. Yes yes, we all nod, it's obvious, the usual illustrations; animals tearing one another to pieces, abattoirs, going on to prisons and capital punishment. Followed by group discussion; yes, prisons, dreadful places, very bad, the young criminal is corrupted and so forth, and of course all the little students have read Albertine Sarrazin between all the doses of Hans Gross, and there's an outcry about homosexuality and the lavatory bucket, sitting there eating the ghastly noodles while some girl is pissing a metre away. The man pulled us up straight off. Read it more carefully, he said, and quoted a letter, a remarkable letter in answer to a boy asking her opinion on capital punishment. Three main points. First, it's infinitely better than life imprisonment. We fell on that, of course : just shows how bad prisons are, etcetera. Second, it's a chance to finish well a life begun badly, a life that has been nothing but dirt and savagery. Another point one cannot, as a student, understand. Thirdly, quoting Sarrazin directly, "I have learned to accept this as I accepted all the rest" – a lesson we evidently had to learn too. Finishing conversationally, the herr professor told us that when a patient walked into his office saying the world was too grim to bear, he treated him as a sick man . . .

'The patient was right, of course, and saw life clearly. But he was ill in the immunological sense, having lost certain basic defences – or if you like the illusions that keep us sane . . . Now, boys and girls, chew on that.'

'In other words, thank God for the opportunity to exteriorize – or is it externalize?' Vera's French, sometimes shaky.

'It's the old thing,' said Castang. 'The police are callous. But all the arguments are emotional.'

'They are, aren't they?' said Colette dryly. 'What happens if I'm called upon to judge the kidnapper of a child? I suppose I ought to be thanking God for sending me this unusual opportunity of enriching my experience.'

The door opened, and Bernard and Richard came in, laughing heartily together. Hell, thought Castang, a clever bastard that Richard. Not only makes a good entrance but at just the right moment. And plainly he's a lot better at this than I am.

'Time for a drink,' said Richard calmly, kissing all the girls' hands in his carefully aseptic thirty-centimetres-away manner. 'After which I make a small progress report and Castang and I go for lunch and plot.'

'And I go home,' said Vera.

'Certainly not, you're staying for lunch,' said Bernard firmly, 'I've seen nothing of you yet.'

'We were just talking about Albertine Sarrazin.'

'Albertine,' said Richard, 'delightful girl. No, I never knew her but she's a mine of home truths. In the provinces, she says somewhere, the judge, the President, the Proc, the director of the prison and the principal Commissaire are all cousins and in the clan. *"Maqués ensemble"* is her vivid expression. Perfectly true: I've been at the Palais all morning conspiring. I won't go into details, Madame, you'll hear them all this afternoon. But to be serious, my report is briefly this – go easy with that whisky – we're inclined to treat this as an attack. We don't know yet what sort of attack, so we're being wholesale. All available resources of the magistrature, the P.J., the prison authorities, everything down to *"assistantes sociales"*. We're looking at every affair judged or instructed by Madame in the last two years, linked to mental homes, prison releases, provisional liberty, psychopathic anything – the lot. We're largely agreed that this is where the answer will be found.'

'Somewhat academic,' said Bernard mildly.

'Somewhat academic,' agreed Richard. 'You mean what are we doing to get your child back promptly? I haven't had a chance to talk to Castang yet: that'll be over the steak and chips in a few minutes. It's my main difficulty, to keep police procedure away from juridical entanglements without the one losing sight of the other. So we won't sit here chatting amiably, but we drink and run: come on, Castang.'

'So there's still nothing – bar talk,' said Bernard pathetically. Like a child whose birthday is on December the twenty-fourth and who has had only one present.

'I don't want you to give me time. I grudge every second of it. But time is what I must have. It isn't the serenity of the law. It's a matter of verifying factual detail. We keep the listening post, because we're convinced it will bear fruit. We keep what is vaguely termed a consort watch on your home and on yourselves, and we wait: we must wait; we've no choice. So, to work.' Richard gave Vera an official smile. 'I'll let you have him back by this evening, Madame – I hope!'

'Well,' said Bernard solidly, 'what's for dinner, so I know

what wine to get out of the cellar? By the way has anybody taken a drink down to the slave of the phone?'

'I did,' said Castang. 'We'll be seeing you.'

'We eat down in the village,' he said to Richard, crossing the road. 'I've got the child's route, and I may as well tell you that even if we do a house-to-house we'll be lucky to get any witness. As you'll see for yourself. I want you to look at two points. Both are possibles. Neither shows any indications on the ground, though if you agree I'd like the technicians to go over both. I've one piece of totally unconnected evidence which I'd like the lab to look at this afternoon.'

'Which is?'

'Shit,' said Castang succinctly. 'Rabbit-shit.'

'We'd every other kind already,' muttered Richard. 'Ah,' with a passing look at the nook opposite Elise. 'I'll hear what you have, first.' and 'Ah' again, at old Léon's courtyard. There was still no sign of that worthy. Was he making rabbit stew, inside, or was he content with a sandwich, in some strange corridor of the Palais de Justice? A man with a grievance against the law . . . It had nothing to do with a judge of instruction, who is not concerned with civil cases. But in the tortuous, obscured mind of an elderly countryman? Can't go too fast, thought Castang, reserving his fire for the twelve franc fifty 'fixed menu' of the Hôtel de la Poste on the square.

'Rabbits,' said Richard thoughtfully, unfolding his napkin.

'Raw salad and the steak-and-chips,' said both men together.

'And to drink, gentlemen?'

'Carafe of Beaujolais and a bottle of Vittel,' still together. They were accustomed to 'business lunches' together.

'Rabbits,' said Richard again. 'It would be clever.'

'To entrap a child,' prodding about. The usual raw carrots, red cabbage, green peppers, tomatoes, cucumber, and a dab of mushrooms in the middle, 'Greek style'. The usual, in short. Police vitamins.

'I remember reading,' said Richard, tearing a bit of bread in half, 'an interesting footnote on the Boston Strangler.' Glug glug went the Vittel water, which was Évian, but no matter. 'You recall perhaps? – after a series of sadistic murders the problem was to persuade either young or old women living alone – hey, leave me some carrots – that however determined

82

they were never to open their door to a stranger it was in fact a very simple thing to gain entry, even with a police lock on a top-to-bottom bar. Red cabbage and tomatoes – you've noticed? – look horrible on the same plate?'

'Close your eyes.'

'Exactly. The trick is to get the woman to open the door herself, thereby nullifying all the bolts and bars. Now you – too much pepper in these mushrooms – as an experienced policeman, how would you go about that?'

'I'd put on overalls and I'd say "Plumber, Missis".' Castang was thinking of the Établissements Paul. 'Most women are so happy to just get a plumber they don't stop to think of where he came from.'

'Not bad. In fact very good, because that was exactly how it was done. But I was thinking of a demonstration made by a police officer at a conference, which so frightened the girl secretaries present that they were paralysed,' spitting out a lemon pip.

'Well tell me – I may want to try it myself some day.'

'You mew like a kitten. A lost and frightened kitten.' Richard demonstrated, causing the people at the next table, tucking into spaghetti, to look at him with horror, a rather repulsive performance when busy eating spaghetti.

'Jesus.'

'Now rabbits . . . it's even better in a way. Trouble is, if it's a real rabbit, it leaves traces. These traces you have found. I think we'll have a talk to this old Léon. I say,' plaintively, 'talk about false fillet.'

*Faux-filet* is the French translation of a naughty kind of sirloin steak, with all its gristle left on to make it look bigger. The chips were not greasy – that is an English rather than a French fault – but there was a large quantity of hard, tough, twisted fragments.

'If you can't eat you can always drink,' said Castang cheerfully, filling his mouth with bread and pouring out an ominously purplish Algerian Beaujolais. 'It's our fault – the smell of steak and chips, the sight of a menu, our extreme hunger – we salivate like Pavlov's dogs when the bell goes. Irresistible – exactly like the kitten.'

'Yes, the blood runs cold. So easy, so discreet, so incredibly simple. That case – terribly simple, a poor type. They put the whole resources of the city into it. War room, computers, the entire police, the F.B.I., Boston and Harvard Universities, all the brains: it's a classic in police procedure. Only a few years ago. If I eat any more salad I'll turn into a rabbit myself. Turned up some extraordinary things. The fellow himself had a gag of measuring girls – 'you'd make a good model'. Believe it or not there were girls who ran to change into tights – there were girls who stripped naked!'

'You'd never get away with that now.'

'I'm none too sure. Listen, they turned up a suspect, used to ring girls up. I'm Doctor so-and-so, I met you at a party, I was struck by your intelligence, can I come round and continue the discussion? You won't believe it but he bedded hundreds. And do you know what he turned out to be? – a pickles salesman!'

Instead of being asphyxiated by a good meal Richard was excited by a bad one. He pushed his plate away, filled the wine-glass up with water, and pointed a finger.

'Fiction. But good. Psychopath wants to kidnap a pretty student. Stops her on deserted street and says, "I've just run over a dog. It doesn't seem badly hurt but it can't move. Come and look." Girl walks over, straight into a rag filled with ether.'

'Yes – I thought of the rag filled with ether. But an old peasant – say – wouldn't operate that way. Like the old one the other day – locked the wife up in the bedroom because she talked all the time – gave her nothing to eat. Cream caramel,' snapped Castang at the waiter, who asked if they had eaten nicely.

'No – it was lousy. And a cup of coffee.'

'Just coffee,' said Richard. 'Yes, we know, you're only the waiter. And I'm only a business man from the town. But *if* I find myself complaining to the tourist board, tell your boss not to be open-mouthed with innocent astonishment.'

Richard sat back, not sprawling but properly fitted into the chair, head upright, his back very straight, the way he did in his own office. He lit one of his cigars, exaggeratedly long thin things from Brazil which looked innocent until one had the imprudence to take one when offered: they kicked like an army mule, therein resembling Richard himself. He too was tall and thin and tightly wrapped; he too looked harmless. He had pale opaque skin which did not tan, regular, quite handsome features, fine thin hair of a distinguished silvery colour worn short and flat. He had a quiet slow voice which he never raised or hurried. His clothes were neat and dull, running to grey suits, cream shirts and dark ties. He never lost his temper or said merde.

Yet he was feared, though it was hard to find out how or why, for he was equable and fair with his staff, and liked by them for never denying or dodging responsibility when things went wrong. He was generally believed to be absolutely honest, and known as meticulous and painstaking. A good administrator and a dangerous policeman. As far as was known he was quite unpolitical, but managed to be on good terms with everyone. Why did one never feel quite at ease with him?

Perhaps because nobody knew him. If he had any friends nobody had ever seen them: he was known to have a wife but nobody had ever laid eyes on her, nor did Richard ever telephone her to say he'd be late for dinner, or complain there were holes in his socks. Even Castang, who as a senior member of the criminal brigade saw as much of him as anyone, felt slightly ill at ease in this distant presence.

'You're not very happy with this old Léon? Very well, run him to earth. See about getting to the bottom of this rabbit affair. And let me know; I'll be in the office. You'll want a search warrant: I'll have a word with the judge. One good thing about old Jeremiah, he leaves one a freeish hand, doesn't tread on one's toes at every step. These young judges who insist upon controlling every step of an inquiry . . . very well Castang; let's hope it turns out this simple.'

*

Bernard and Colette Delavigne were having a better lunch than the two policemen. It had been to both of them a relief, and a pleasant surprise, that there are always so many stupid little details to take one's mind off a larger problem. Thus Colette's cleaning-woman, at best a touchy soul, who had become filled with peculiar suspicions when she had come for the usual two hours' housework. Why was Madame at home? She wasn't sick or anything, was she? The notion had got lodged in the good woman's mind that Colette was checking up on her in some way, and had been difficult to dislodge.

It was quite pleasant to have time to spend for once on cooking. Magistrates' schedules gave her an hour in the morning to get things prepared, but one had now a luxuriously large number of hours. She had had time to work out quite an elaborate and fiddly idea involving the trout which hadn't been eaten the night before – and to get heartily fed up, and wish she hadn't begun – before Vera turned up. The right person to ask aid from. A much less brittle character than herself, with 'moral resources'. She seemed to have built-in shock absorbers: her whole face had stretched and wrenched with pain when Colette had abruptly emptied herself of the whole tale. But she had been so sensible. Not that she'd said anything particularly intelligent; in fact she'd made several remarks which Colette, privately, thought rather silly, but even flat phrases like 'Hard for poor Bernard to learn not to fuss' had been comforting, because Vera, somehow, was too generous and too broad to fuss.

'People show up well, in crises.' It was banal, yes. 'I know that Henri, of course, is much more sensitive than anyone gives him credit for under that tough-cop act he affects, and so do you or you wouldn't have called him. He didn't say a word to me, cunning old devil, but that's a good sign. But I meant Richard, who isn't nearly as dry a stick as he seems – he won't just do all the obvious things. I've known it once or twice before. He's one of those people who can surpass himself; raise his game like a good tennis player: he doesn't operate all on one note, though you'd never believe so to look at him – you know, that air of only caring about keeping his out-basket empty is most deceiving. And that horrible old Besson . . . I don't know him at all except from seeing him in court a couple of times but you said yourself you were astonished at how kind he was to you last night. I'm not astonished a bit really: he's evidently genuinely fond of you and values you. That's very good for him; make him look at his ghastly job in an altogether different light.'

'Very good for me too, you mean?' Colette asked in an angular sort of voice.

'It would be atrocious of me to think of anything so vile,' said Vera, upset at the idea of being so priggish. 'Hell, my hair's awful this morning; I do wish sometimes I had a wig.'

*

They were sitting on the balcony; it was almost like a party. And just the two of them. An anniversary, or something, thought Colette without sarcasm, but a certain tenderness – her poor Bernard, he was taking this awfully hard. Despite much gallantry from him, Vera had refused to stay: had a highly developed sense of making one too many. Men had a pleasant innocence: he was enjoying his dinner, and it was doing him good.

She had made stuffing for the trout, to stretch them a bit, with new vegetables and cream and stale breadcrumbs, and a cream sauce to go with them. She had braised them with a glass of white wine, and added the reduced juice to the sauce: it had come out very good. Bernard was now eating Rachel's trout as well as his own: she had kept this for the slave-of-the-phone, but Castang had said reasonably that the neighbours would think it very odd if they saw her carrying trays down to the cellar, and not to worry about the slave; young Marcel would bring him in dinner and a bottle of beer and in general all that the heart could long for, and she wasn't to worry. She had enjoyed her own trout; she'd remembered chives, and they'd made all the difference. The recipe, oddly, was one of Vera's . . . And Bernard had gone down to the cellar with a drink-for-the-slave, and come back with a nice bottle, a rosé Pinot, beautifully dry and flinty, just right with the cream sauce.

'Say what you like,' said Bernard, polishing his plate with a bit of bread, 'a good meal is a lift to the morale even in the most evil circumstances . . . Raspberry tart!'

'Vera made it. Her pastry is so much nicer than mine and I never can understand why. I do all the same things. I watched her exactly through every detail.'

'Those funny stubby fingers of hers,' said Bernard affectionately. Sidelong glance; was that euphoria, or did Bernard have a small sneaking regard for the Czech, amusing, and sometimes very attractive Madame Castang which secretly overstepped decorum?

'You fancy her, do you?'

'Good God!' said Bernard, shocked. Much too shocked. 'Is there more tart?'

'Yes there is, but it's for tonight, and you're not to go greedily stuffing this afternoon. Stay where you are, I'll make coffee.

Would you like a 'little glass', since you don't need to work this afternoon?'

'No – I'd only fall asleep.'

She brought him his coffee, and one of his small cigars: he beamed like a baby, sitting there very happy in the dappled sunlight through the climbing plants – her cleaning-woman was very good with climbing plants and brought them slips from her own – which guarded the balcony from indiscreet gazers across the street.

At the moment when perfect content was about to descend like, as the French say irreverently, 'the Child Jesus in little velvet shorts' there was a loud noise. The teen-age son of Monsieur Robin, the technical director in the local office of Électricité de France, who lived just below them, was also sunning himself upon the balcony, and improving the climate with a transistor radio. Bernard's day was spoilt.

'One pays a lot of money to have some elementary comforts and even they are denied one. Illiterate bawling drool; might as well live in a council flat if one's going to have that thought-substitute fed into one's digestive tube.'

'He's only a boy.'

'I'll damn well complain to Robin. Some people have no consideration whatever.'

'They don't, do they?' said Colette. 'Let's make a complaint to the police,' in a colourless voice. Glance of fury at this betrayal.

The noise hushed abruptly: another neighbour had made a pained telephone call. Men – doesn't take much to upset them. The row, as Vera remarked, there was this morning when Castang found they were out of shoe-polish! Why are men so inflexible?

'Everyone's windows are open – just think of the weekend. We can be eating behind the shack, without a sound.'

'Except aeroplanes. And the fact that by then it will be raining. And the small detail that our daughter is – God knows where.'

'We'll be laughing at our own fright,' said Colette, unconsciously quoting Vera. 'Behind that pedantic manner Richard is an outstanding police officer. And Henri Castang is a person in whom one doesn't just have confidence but complete un-questioning faith.'

'You're very keen on him all of a sudden,' with a nasty look. 'He's never impressed me particularly with his intelligence – perhaps he has some appeal to woman I don't know about.'

'Bernard please . . . I must change dear, it's time I started thinking about the office. Have a quiet afternoon. If you wanted something to do you might look at the little washstand in the lav; it empties too slowly.'

'Ah yes, and I've got large amounts of paper in my briefcase – oh, I won't be short of work!'

'There's still a cup of coffee in the pot,' said Colette sooth-ingly, whisking into one of the dark frocks suitable to Madame la Juge, 'zip me up, would you?'

Bernard stared gloomily out of the window, determined to master his irritation and perfectly able to do so, but frenzied by female fiddle-faddle. Go and be done with it! Don't hang about powdering your nose. Ordinarily he enjoyed the swift deftness with which she 'put on her face'. But it was not until he heard the motor of the little car reversing up the slope from the garage and saw it swing to accelerate away down the avenue that he felt comfortable again inside his skin.

Odd sensation, being alone inside the flat. Accustomed to the routine of commerce, to beginning early and finishing late, with those immensely long and lavish business lunches in between, it was rare that he got home before Colette, and when the lamp burned late for judges of instruction, as sometimes happened, he had Rachel's company: they nibbled biscuits together, and he made big fizzy drinks that she liked to sip from, and he played long absorbed games with the small supple body perched on the arm of his chair, making knots in her fingers and seeing if she could get her foot into her mouth, while she licked her finger and made comic patterns in his eyebrows, or borrowed his comb to give him new hair styles. He turned away from the window with a sigh, and went back again to undo a series of complicated knots made in the cord of the venetian blind. Well . . .

It was nevertheless agreeable to be alone in the flat. One felt unexpectedly rich, like a schoolboy given a sudden half-holiday.

He poured himself a second cup of coffee and despite previous denials a glass of raspberry alcohol – and was going to steal another piece of the raspberry tart, but scruple overcame him. He carried cup and glass over to the armchair. The living-room was becoming cooler and shaded as the sun moved around to the west; he could lift the blind. The room was trim and neat from the extra housework Colette had done this morning. Better than the hasty rigid tidying that betrayed the hand of the cleaning-woman, who always put dusted objects down in irritatingly just-that-little-bit-wrong positions. The books were not forced too tightly into their shelves, or mathematically aligned, today, but breathing in a warm comfortable rhythm.

It was rare enough to be noticeable. Colette disliked antique furniture – 'I haven't time to look after it myself and one can't trust the women to do it properly' – and had chosen everything here to be modern and labour-saving. He found it all rather lifeless, but he had himself no skill or taste for pottering about with carpentry any more than he had for going fishing: too nervous and impatient. And she was not a *femme d'intérieur* either; she cooked as a duty, sewed as a chore, stuck bunches of flowers in vases the way they were bought and complained that she never had any time left for painting. Thoroughly efficient, yes. Always well dressed and a 'credit': meals were always on time, he always had clean shirts and socks: for any friend or even business acquaintance he could always count on a poised, intelligent, witty and delightful hostess. The 'house' ran like silk. He realized how lucky he was, and was grateful, and did his best to be considerate and unselfish. To buy her frivolous nightdresses and exotic dressing-gowns and new sorts of perfume was easy; to take her out to concerts, which bored him stiff, to tête-à-tête restaurant dinners, which he detested, was harder: to cook a meal when she was kept late an amusement which had palled – but he had acquired techniques.

Bernard picked up a book and prepared to make himself comfortable. His content, painfully won back, was short-lived because he had hardly turned three pages before the doorbell rang. A wild hope that this might be Rachel, or at worst Colette back with hot news, was dashed when he opened: the police again. Despite the hot day Richard was as cool and neat as a slice of ham in aspic.

'Not interrupting?'

'No – no, I'm by myself. Can I offer you something? Coffee?
– a drink?'

'Thanks, I've just had some. Can I have a little talk with you,
Monsieur Delavigne? Completely informal, just between ourselves?'

'Of course. Please sit down. You prefer those cigars of yours?
– these are Cuban . . . What exactly does it mean, a little talk?
A sort of interrogation?'

'All police interviews are interrogatory, by their nature. A
television interviewer, on the other hand, is trying to ask questions whose answers will make a portrait of someone vivid,
alive isn't it so? It's a thing Castang's good at. But I didn't want
to ask him to do this. After all, he's by way of being a friend of
yours. It might have caused some embarrassment to both of you.'

'You're being tactful,' said Bernard.

Richard smiled.

'You want to ask personal questions and you choose this
roundabout way of preparing the ground.'

'Yes, perhaps a little more personal than a television interviewer.'

'Well, I can't object, I suppose. I don't think I've anything to
hide. I don't altogether see how it advances your inquiry – or
mayn't I ask about your inquiry?'

'You may, and I'll answer, because we can be quite straightforward with each other. The inquiry is official, which is to say
we have by now grounds for hypothesis, a criminal complaint
is made against X, the Procureur of the Republic has instructed
the criminal brigade to use all means in its power and all dili-
gence, a dossier has been opened and an instruction begun by
Monsieur Savornin, who is the senior judge of instruction – I
don't really need to tell you all this, because you know through
your wife how the legal machine works. To come down to what
concerns myself, I am as you know the commissaire command-
ing the criminal brigade, and we have an official inquiry, which
concerns yourself. Good, you have every right to know all
about that. It is in a sense three-sided. We have a senior officer
examining and following up all possible physical traces – that's
the affair of our friend Castang, and right now I may tell you
he is busy with some promising material. I don't wish to raise

your hopes unduly; I suspect this may prove inconclusive, but it must be gone into, and it may lead to other useful discoveries.

'Secondly, as you know, due to the particular position occupied by your wife we have afoot a very deep-reaching inquiry into the background of any personage, normal or abnormal, who might be thought to have a sense of grievance against justice, and for juridical reasons this inquiry is being conducted by the legal authorities. This is, by the way, quite usual: all affairs conducted by any magistrate come up regularly for review by the Advocate General.

'And lastly, parallel with the direction and administration of the local P.J. services I like to conduct my own cases. I'm not just an unadulterated bureaucrat. I like to know a little of the human backgrounds to an affair as important as this, and that's what I'm here for. To fill in, if you like, the gaps in my knowledge of the characters and personalities involved – to ask some questions that may strike you as unpleasantly personal and indiscreet upon occasion, and you are of course aware that you have every right to refuse: there is no compulsion whatever upon you. But I cannot deny that it would help me, especially in as difficult an affair as this – a family affair.'

'Smooth speech,' said Bernard. 'Sounds well practised. I know now where I stand.'

'Quite right. Between men. Not even businessmen, telling one another great lies and perfectly aware of it, enjoying themselves. You are lucid, sceptical, suspicious – all of which is good. Tell me lies if you must; I'm used to it. Like a doctor when he asks how many cigarettes a day I smoke – he doubles the answer he gets.'

'It's a psychiatric examination?'

'Something not too unlike. I want to get to know you.'

'Sounds like damned cheek. You want to ask personal questions and I'll put one to you. In what way does this advance your inquiry, as you put it?'

'Your daughter has disappeared, Monsieur Delavigne. After considering what we know we hypothesize a criminal attempt. Kidnapping is one of the gravest crimes there is, equivalent to a murder. At this moment we don't know enough. It becomes important for us to find out all we can about the lives and backgrounds of the persons involved.'

'But good God, man, you're talking as though I had murdered my wife and had fallen under suspicion; it's preposterous.'

'Look at it another way. You're a business man: assume you are going to employ a man in a position of confidence. Before you give him that position you want to know a good deal about him. Not only his curriculum vitae but his character. Things like had he ever had trouble with the law, does he drink, has he been divorced, does he pay his bills, is he thought of by those who know him as a stable and reliable person? Big firms think nothing of getting an inquiry agency to run a neighbourhood check, of asking to meet his wife, of having his handwriting analysed, even of psychological tests. The Americans went as far at one time as to insist on lie-detector tests. All that, it could be claimed, is an abuse of civil liberties and an invasion of privacy. But they still run security checks on everyone considered for employment by a federal agency, and that's a lot of people.'

'I don't understand the allusion – I see no possible parallel.'

'The parallel is in the justification for these actions, which is the security of the state and the safety of the people.'

'But good heavens, man, if I suffer a burglary and as the injured party make a complaint – I'm utterly innocent.'

'That is only an offence against property. We're talking about a crime against the person. Try to understand – innocence has nothing to do with it. If you were in a car accident, even if the other party were openly, self-evidently at fault, in the case of material injury there would be an inquiry into your behaviour. Had you been drinking, were you preoccupied or absent-minded, had you perhaps had a lapse of attention even if not actively negligent? It is our job to make these inquiries. We have to do it thoroughly. A court might demand to use our findings as an element in assigning a share of responsibility – which can amount to a great deal of money. The average person, protected by his insurance company, does not think a great deal about that. He doesn't think about crime either, because the odds are he's never been involved in one. A crime of this sort could lead to something a good deal graver than even large sums of money. It leads to loss of liberty, imprisonment for perhaps many years, and that marks a man's whole life.'

'Well all right, all right,' said Bernard irritably. 'I know all this; I'm married to a judge.'

'Just so,' said Richard curtly, 'and you're accustomed to thinking of it all as an intellectual abstraction. This isn't a game; this is real. So just forget all the detective stories full of bumbling Scotland Yard Inspectors. Forget all the gangster films full of Hollywood Indians getting shot and falling down. Forget the prison movies with a phoney wrench at the emotions when the fellow gets guillotined at the end. This is for real. I'm being patient, Monsieur Delavigne, because you have suffered a very severe blow. Also because you are an intelligent, educated, sophisticated man. Also because you are a prominent citizen married to a magistrate. So I treat you with every possible courtesy and consideration. The poor don't see me that way. They see me with fear and hatred, because I'm a cop, the fellow who can take them by the collar and put them in jug, the enemy. They think there's another law for the rich, because they don't distinguish between the law and the application of the law. The law confers upon me the right and the obligation to put such questions to you as I see fit, if I think that justice will thereby be served.'

'Oh all right,' said Bernard sulkily, 'no need to make a speech. I'm sorry,' with an effort. 'One just doesn't realize. It's true – the police are like road accidents – always happen to other people. All right, go ahead,' wearily. 'Put your questions.'

*

Castang was thinking the same thoughts. One does it every day: one goes through the same motions and it's all routine, all meaningless. One is a cop the way one is a plumber: it's just a job, and the fact of being blunted by the distrust and dislike shown all day makes one more insensitive still. Even now – a kidnapping. Means there's an extra panic on. And lordy, it's the child of a magistrate. Double the panic, because the Proc and the judge are affected and they'll by gum see the screws are turned. And we'd still just shrug and grind on because one does one's job, more or less well, as circumstances permit. Oh sure, sure, it's watch your step, don't fall asleep on this one because these are highly placed people and if you do anything stupid it'll be your neck. It still wouldn't make that much difference, seeing you're a conscientious cop, and vigilant and diligent and blah. Not even that I know Colette and Bernard, or that she's a friend of Vera's: I've been involved before in inquiries concerning people I knew. Hell, one knows a lot of people. But a child . . . a child is altogether different.

Not just in the emotional sense; innocent and vulnerable and all that. A child is special because it is free of human degeneracy. Even the most vicious, brutalized child is not yet defiled: it has a sort of purity. The public has become so apathetic to violence and brutality that it shrugs at a road accident and drives on fast for fear of being bored, for fear of being given forms to fill in, for fear of being deprived of pleasures. When there's a hold-up, nowadays, the witnesses look round sceptically, looking for the television cameras. 'I thought it was for a film.' They can't switch the bloody box on without seeing a lot of oafs brandishing guns and slugging whoever stands in their way, which is all right because it's a baddy. We've seen so many joke policemen that the real ones become a joke too: it's like naked girls; they're just so much dead mutton. So to excite and tickle the public one has to reach out more and more desperately for a devalued exoticism. Getting more and more unreal in the name of realism.

A child is the only human being as yet uncorrupted.

'Old Léon' had proved tiresomely elusive. At the district law court he was well known: oh yes, dotty old man with delusions about justice, he's always around. Haven't seen him today. To the clerks of the local notaries' office he was midway between a standing joke and a dreaded bore. He was a bore or a joke everywhere. Castang wasn't sure it was either that dreary or that funny. He slammed back into the car.

'Palace of Justice,' he told Marcel tonelessly.

The Palais is a really terrible building, and nowhere can the crushing bad taste of the eighteen-eighties be studied to greater advantage. Slab after slab ad infinitum of mouldy travertine – the same that Robert Browning's bishop was worried about, when he ordered his tomb in Saint Praxed's Church – lines the hall, so excellently named *Salle des Pas Perdus* in French. The vast unwieldy double staircase and the soot-caked ceiling, the long claustrophobic passages, the rows of top-heavy oak doors with bare wooden benches outside: it gives the worst possible impression. From the pompous pillared entry, where flimsy yellowed carbons of legal notices, all several years out of date, curl their corners behind a massive iron grille, to the fire-escapes leading to the bare and dusty courtyard, there is not a scrap of art, not even the monstrous *pompier* art of the eighties – unless you count the two immense sphinxes in petrified margarine which guard the bottom of the staircase. And not only is there no art, there isn't a scrap of colour, of greenery, of the sootiest or most depressed of flowers: it is far worse than a graveyard. In all this chilled and congealed grey grease the message 'Abandon Hope' can clearly be seen written.

Castang was so accustomed to it– it was after all only a very little worse than the grim building, which in Napoleonic times had been a military hospital, where the P.J., along with a thousand other municipal administrative departments, was lodged – that he rarely noticed the horror. Perhaps he noticed it today because just before arriving they passed the Hotel of the Préfecture; an elegant eighteenth-century palace, classically simple, light and elegant, in warm red stone, with a fountain sparkling on the lawn and flowers massed upon every balcony. Now if the Ministry of the Interior has money to pay gardeners why has the Ministry of Justice none to buy dynamite?

As for Colette, who worked there daily, she had come to accept it with stoicism, the way a Polar explorer learns to accept the existence of blizzards, or eternal night in the wintertime. She spent a good deal of money on flowers, but as she said, 'It is the fires of heaven must cleanse this place', and it was indeed difficult to see what a human agency could do, short of a few parachute mines. Certainly this much was obvious, that long, excessively flowery and rhetorical speeches about the reform of the magistrature were not going to alter this monument in a hurry.

As usual on a hot sunny June afternoon there was nothing happening at all. The hall had its usual smell and colour of long-dead chrysanthemums and there was not a soul to be seen. In the corridor outside the offices of the judges of instruction there was the usual sediment of hangdog witnesses on benches and a few brisk gendarmes, amazingly smart in pressed summer khakis and polished black belts, with mournful criminals tacking

96

along at the end of handcuff chains. Outside the *grande instance* offices on the floor above an advocate came sidling crabwise along with a stiff neck and gown almost as rusty as his hair. Two more pleaders with waxy complexions and brightly polished shoes were chatting on a bench with piles of paper between them. At the corner two very smartly dressed and highly painted bourgeois women were evidently trying to 'wake the place up a bit'.

'The judge doesn't really seem to understand . . .' went the voice, full of money and assurance, as he passed.

No sign of anybody like old Léon. He went all round the far side, past acres and acres of judges and greffiers to the civil courts: Marcel, working the other direction, came suddenly round a corner and shrugged.

'Try the Parquet,' they both mumbled.

The magnificently named Offices of the Parquet of Monsieur the Procureur de la République were on the top floor; a thing Monsieur Besson complained about more than the need of a coat of paint. 'The serenity of justice implies a certain austerity.' Such had also been the opinion of the sphinxes.

Prowling noiselessly up and down, tacking off at angles to hug the wall, dressed in a Sunday suit with a gold watch-chain in the waistcoat, a little old man crackling with energy and frustration, stopping to rehearse grievances in the window-bay before darting on again – Castang watched him for a moment. The un-co-ordinated movements spelt insanity clearly enough, even if not really certifiable. He nodded to Marcel.

'Monsieur Martin?'

'You don't hurry yourselves, I'm bound to say.'

'We are officers of the Police Judiciaire. We have some questions to put to you.'

'I've got more than a few to put to you.' A fierce look from the light prowling eyes. 'I can only hope you're a bit more conscientious and less frivolous than some of these quill-pushers, because if I don't get some satisfaction around here pretty smart I'll be taking this matter to the Cour des Comptes in Paris, and they'll be combing out a few of these provincial magistrates' wigs for them, I can tell you. Because the waste of public funds in this place . . .'

'Let's sit down. You're Monsieur Léon Martin? And you live at number one, Rampe Notre Dame, Samois les Roses?'

'And let's see your identification, young man, for a start.'

It wasn't easy. The old boy bristled like a hedgehog with procedural points and rights. He knew, apparently, all the codes by heart, from Public Health and Social Aid right through to Criminal Procedure. In order to stop young Marcel giggling, Castang had to get quite hot himself on everything between Article 224 – outrage or insult to an agent of the public order – to Article 230 – threats and menaces addressed to same. The reservations of Article 64, which states that there is no crime or felony when accused is in a state of dementia or constrained by an irresistible force, were of small help to him. The racket at one moment reached such proportions that a variety of typists got sent popping out of the mattressed doors to inquire what the hell was going on, and finally a youngish substitute came bursting out himself.

'Oh it's you, Castang – what the devil are you playing at? . . . You start making scandals here, my friend, and I'll have you down cooling your heels at the Depôt in no time at all. Well if you've got a warrant, Castang, why in heaven's name don't you execute it? . . .

'Any more lip,' exasperated, 'and I'll instruct the officer here to put you in handcuffs. Get him out of here, Castang, or we'll have the Proc out complaining.'

There was a moment when Castang got seriously worried at the old boy's excitement, and Marcel was plainly wondering why he didn't take him downtown for a cell and a psychiatric examination. They got him out at last and slapped him in the car, where Castang explained that by right of the mandate duly signed by Monsieur le Juge, etcetera, they were going to search his house. More legal outcry. They could only do so in the presence of the commissaire and his own legal representatives, and so forth. It all made for a tiring afternoon.

Old Léon lived, and slept, and ate, and washed, in the kitchen. The rest of the farmhouse was strongly Miss Havisham, and the cobwebs had not been disturbed for ten years at least. There was no sign of Rachel anywhere. Nor was there any sign of rabbits. In, on and around an old writing-desk there were papers and letters dealing with half the laws of the Republic, and he had to go through them all. But there was nothing, remotely, to do with any criminal affair, or with Madame Delavigne. And the cellar was full of coal, winebottles, potatoes and broken furniture. Castang felt an acute frustration. Damn it, it had looked promising. Quite apart from physical opportunities and possibilities, a man with this much grievance against 'the law' had an adequate motive. But there was not a shred of evidence.

Now that he had a splendid new grievance, of course, he was stamping about suing all and sundry for false imprisonment and unlawful constraint and arbitrary search and lord knew what all. He was also exceedingly gleeful. Whatever it was the police thought they were doing they now cut a lamentable figure; it was a massive and total victory: Castang cursed his own clumsiness, feeling sure that somewhere at the start he had taken the wrong line. Could he not have cajoled, enticed, enlisted sympathy, gradually coaxed the recalcitrant old bastard into being forthcoming? Perhaps he could; he had tried. But to old Léon he was just another proof of the law's injustice, one more rusty spike in the iron maiden. No use insisting or explaining. He would always be 'Them' who are against 'Us'. It is a daily part of the experience of any policeman, and there's nothing whatever one can do about it. They were, as near as makes no matter, seen off the premises with the shotgun, amid exultant toothless grinning.

'Thought you could come and push me about. Not the first. But I'm still here – and I'll bury the bleeding lot of you.' To the end of his days old Léon would be convinced that this had been one more effort to strip him of his property. He would tell tales in the pub about it, and only the ex-civil servant from Hanoi would add two and two, and hug his silent enjoyment.

'Got our heads washed there,' said Marcel, who had rather enjoyed seeing his superior officer with soap in his eye.

'Yes,' said Castang briefly; 'pity I can't take it out on you.' It is painful to be completely helpless in a situation one might have been able to handle if one had just been a little better collected.

\*

Madame Delavigne – unaware of the drama raging over her head outside the Parquet offices, where old Léon, tired of making complaints about crooked notaries in writing, had come to have it out man to man, and would have too if they hadn't with that typical cowardly brutality put the cops on him, which just showed how frightened they were – Madame Delavigne was working on a similar equation to Castang's. Whatever she did, she reflected sourly, magistrates had a trick of seeing it as a manifestation of oppressed feminism, and were quick to band together against any women's lib nonsense. They see an able and energetic young woman, who carries out her legal functions with competence, and does not pester them with any damned biological functions. When secretaries or typists get a bit emotional about their men and their hip-line it is put tolerantly down to silly girls of inferior intelligence, and faulty upbringing, who stuff themselves with low-fat yoghurt but are too stupid to see that women's magazines are a far more indigestible diet. Little Madame Delavigne does not pester us with untimely displays of knee and bosom, does not spend interminable hours in the lavatory, leaves us mercifully free of boring involvements in her menstruations and fornications and lactations, has a good little head screwed on her shoulders, and still manages to be pleasantly feminine. But now there's a drama about a child throwing the whole place in an uproar: somehow one always knew this would happen. Colette sighed. Liberated women, she suspected, will always be deeply neurotic.

*

Commissaire Richard was in his office. However incompetent the prevention of crime might be the administration had to be kept running. He emptied his pockets of a variety of old envelopes with remarks and reminders scribbled upon them, as well as a good deal of neatly noted agenda, and picked up his phone to get a technician.

'Daniel, find out what you can about this.'

'What is it, rabbit-shit?'

'Unless,' said Richard patiently, 'it's hare, or peacock, or maybe a walrus.'

'You mean what it had for breakfast and whether it ought to have its appendix out?'

'Be witty upstairs.'

The phone rang. Castang at the other end, being toneless about his frustrations with old Léon.

'Very good,' said Richard equally tonelessly. 'We are of course bound to check up on it. I won't say I expected no better. No rabbits, by the way? Mm; we'll see what Daniel has to say about these rabbits. I want you to move over to the cheese factory: I think it's time we knew a little more about Monsieur Delavigne's background. As for the lady, I don't want you to allow your wife's friendships to colour your judgement, but we'll discuss that when you come in this evening – shall we?'

'Understood,' said Castang briefly, and rang off. The Commissaire went on with his paper work. In parallel, his mind dwelt upon little Madame Delavigne. These emancipated women, his inclinations told him, had a built-in tendency to neurosis. That Czech girl of Castang's . . . No fault of her own of course, and none of his. A delightful, interesting and attractive woman. And stable; she didn't throw strains upon her man, not at least such as to diminish his work performance. But it alters him, no doubt of that. Quite a complex situation, and one which will take some careful attention.

It had happened to Richard in the past to find a member of his staff entangled by personal relationships in a criminal investigation. It had even happened to himself, once.

Not his wife, thank goodness. She was, he thanked heaven for it, a comfortable and satisfied woman who was quite content to stay at home and do the housekeeping. Doubtless it was very regressive and reactionary of him, thought Richard dryly, but he was profoundly grateful for the fact. His own tastes did not run to frustrated women. He liked his roses full-blown; large comfortable girls unworried about their hips and unimpressed by the floor needing scrubbing, who weren't ashamed to get down on their knees to it. A woman's body needed that. Cooking, scrubbing, lifting heavy children, plenty of shit and lots of sex, and you had a thoroughly used, contented woman on your hands. And that, thought Richard grinning, will be denounced as 'sexual fascism' by a pile of constipated men who are run by their wives. Hm, little Madame Castang was an artist. And little Madame Delavigne a lawyer, and the two women were friends. And both were very nice girls. Artists. Monsieur Richard liked artists; they were necessary animals. But if he had been an artist the women Rembrandt or Renoir liked would be the ones he would choose to paint. And shall we now join the ladies?

If you started keeping an eye on Castang it would be very quickly noticed, since he is not at all an imbecile and he might anyway be waiting for it laughing. And if you let him see it and let him know that you know he's seeing it that's the kind of thing which might in some circles be thought clever, but in Richard's book wasn't in the least clever, because if you didn't trust people you'd never yourself be trusted. It was that simple. No, trusting Castang is a thing that we will not fall down on. But trusting Madame Delavigne is a different pair of shoes.

Richard rang for his secretary, who was young, Italian, quite voluptuous, and mercifully liberated, with the utmost contempt for notions like being seduced by her boss: her sex life was her affair, and she didn't worry him with it.

'Fausta, my dear, have you any cold mineral water?'

*

Castang had made a stop in the pub too, with the same thought in mind. The big pub this time, since their lavatories had been modernized, and there was a reasonable chance there of a good wash in reasonably civilized circumstances.

He could see easily enough why Bernard was proud of his 'cheese factory'. True, it was nothing but a kind of cardboard box, painted a rather horrible bluish grey and looking as though constructed of packing materials, standing in a relatively quiet side road halfway back towards the town, but it looked smart and neat, with quite a wide strip of mown grass and a screen of poplar-trees. All very hygienic; the refrigerated van being hosed down at the service point had been scrubbed spotless, and a glass panel in the wall on his way to the offices gave a glimpse of pastel green tiles, stainless steel tubing, and girls in bunchy white overalls. And the managing director, a quiet man with very little hair left on top, but a generous distribution on his bare arms and open neck, confirmed the good impression.

'Certainly we're proud of it, but it's the result, you know, of some rigorous self-discipline. We ploughed every penny back for ten years: what would you say when I told you that neither of us took a penny home and that even now we live on salaries no bigger than those of the accountant and the chemist?'

'I'd be impressed and I am interested to hear more.'

'No paperwork, no secrecy, nothing in compartments. This door is open. Anybody, the girls or the drivers, can walk in here if they've a problem and tell me about it. Well, what's your problem?'

'I'd be glad if you'd close the door now, because it's a secret. Personal and confidential.'

'Aha. Well, we've no tapped telephone here.'

Castang forbore to tell him that he was in error.

'Monsieur Delavigne's in some trouble. He's receiving a certain number of unspecified menaces: there's been as yet no overt blackmail demand, and we're in some perplexity as a result, because the threat and the hostility may be aimed at him personally, or perhaps at his wife.'

'Yes – he was looking seedy. Went home at lunch. That it?'

'So I come to you in confidence, and I hope you'll be open with me. I don't wish to pry into your affairs, but I'd like to know whether all is well between you, and whether in your knowledge all is well between Monsieur Delavigne and everybody else.'

The man put his bare arms on the desk, joined his hands loosely, and thought carefully before answering.

'Of course you can smoke. Thanks, I don't. I'll try to be brief. We're very open here, Bernard and I have a good, loose, complex relation. We don't have rigid limits to our responsibilities, though I handle most of the financial details and Bernard does most of the marketing: we interlock on most things, because of overlap. I dare say I don't need to tell you that a business of this sort is very competitive and that a constant effort of imaginative vision is needed – production is dead simple; a question of turning out yoghurt, and maybe the chemist worries about putting avocadoes in it without losing the nice fresh green colour – where the shoe pinches is packaging, distribution – recall we're up against gigantic enterprises like Saint Gervais. So I see Bernard constantly, and of course I know him very well. Now how to answer your questions simply . . .?

'I'm as you see me, in shirtsleeves. You'll find me everywhere,

looking for ways to make the girls' work less monotonous, trying to load a lorry with less waste movements, quite as much as
going over figures with the accountant. I'm totally involved,
this is my entire life – my secretary here is my own wife. Very
humourless and boring you'd find us, solemnly talking about
yoghurt at our own supper table. Now Bernard . . . he runs the
sales staff and talks to buyers. He wears a smart suit and a tie. I
do a lot of travelling – but he goes to the meetings and the lunches. I'm a very outgoing, free-spoken spontaneous personality;
I like to think I'm very uncomplicated. Bernard is too in a way,
and at the same time he has a secret side, closed and sealed off.
There's a lot goes on in his mind I don't know about, whereas
I'm an open book. I am the son of a small farmer, a country
boy. My wife was a country girl. She can make camembert; she
made our first batches of yoghurt in our bathroom. Now Bernard is a city boy, infinitely more sophisticated, and his father
was in textiles – he's a third generation of bourgeois commerce.
I'm a first. There alone is a very considerable difference. I don't
mind telling you that I never read anything but technical literature, don't know anything about music, and my notion of art is
nice pots to put the stuff in. Bernard likes books, novels – Jesus,
*The Count of Monte Cristo*'s good enough for me. So I don't
move in his circle. Above all not in his wife's. I've met her, of
course. She comes to dinner with us twice a year, and we go to
them twice a year, and we all get on well together, and I find
her a very nice, quiet polite girl. Yes? – very simple terms, very
childish, I use to judge her, huh? I'm like that. It's all I know
about her. I'm not her speed. I know nothing about law, save
trying to keep inside it. Ethics and morals and philosophy . . . I
mean I'd bore a woman like that stiff. A magistrate, from a
family of magistrates. *Noblesse de la robe*, as they say; a legal
upper class: her family has it in the blood, where mine were just
Limousin yobboes. What have we in common?'

'Good,' said Castang, 'that's all clear.' It was, too, because he
knew most of it already. Bernard talked about his partner freely
enough. With respect, and affection, and with humour.

'So you know nothing about his home life?'

'Good heavens no. And less about his wife's, if that's what's
bothering you. If on the other hand there was anything that
created troubles here at the office then I would know. I can see

you coming; has Bernard been a naughty boy? Well I'm not going to peddle any stale gossip, it's not my style. I don't allow any malice and backbiting around here; it interferes with the running of the place, and I'd get rid of anybody inclined that way. And my wife keeps an eye on the girls. All right, so I'm puritanical, so I'm old fashioned, so I'm a Jansenist old bastard. But no knickers-down in the store-room around here: out, even if they're good workers, because it just leads to trouble. What they do outside is none of my business and I try to be Christian; pregnant girls make good yoghurt and I'm not asking to see their marriage lines.'

It was all a bit too good to be true.

'One doesn't sack a partner,' gently. 'One wouldn't even sack a good accountant or a good chemist.'

'Sorry, my dear man,' flatly, 'no soap. I'm not gossiping about my partner, or my senior employees. The furthest I'll go is that I know of nothing, repeat nothing, that would would give rise or has ever given rise to any troubles here in the factory, and I know of nothing, I'll underline that for you, nothing, which might have landed anybody here in a blackmail demand. As for Bernard, he's my partner, my junior partner if you like, but his contributions to this enterprise have been and continue to be highly important and exceedingly valuable. He doesn't let me down, I won't let him down, and that's the secret in a nutshell of why we are successful. Sorry, Inspector, I can give you no further help. What goes on outside these doors is not my affair and I know nothing about it. Inside, everybody here reckons with me. You question anybody you want – outside. Here, you'll find me tough. I don't permit you any inquiries, not without a mandate from authority. O.K.? Is it fair, is it clear, is it understood?'

'Yes, but don't get tough. There's no need and it doesn't impress me. I won't try any backstairs politics with you, and I'll take your word that you know how to handle what goes on in your premises. Just don't try to tell me you run a finishing school for young ladies.'

'My dear man,' suddenly very human, 'one has to close one's eyes from time to time, and the hard part is to know when.'

'People being more difficult than yoghurt.'

'I'd rather my job than yours.'

'And oddly, I'd rather mine than yours. Even if it doesn't smell as hygienic.'

The man studied him with his head a little on one side, shrewd-eyed. 'I'd like to get one thing clear,' suddenly. 'You're acting upon a complaint by Monsieur Delavigne in person? You promise me that? Does he know you're here?'

'Not in as many words. He's well aware that a bright light might get poked into all sorts of corners, and he has accepted that.'

'As a man with a singularly boring and unscandalous private life, perhaps I have the right to say that I would have very little enthusiasm for anyone looking at mine.'

'I wouldn't want anybody looking at mine,' said Castang mildly; 'it's a matter of not having too many illusions, or maybe changing the pattern of illusions. As a state official, whose job is investigation, I might feel obliged to keep my life free of scandal, or I might feel that even if subject to scrutiny I could rely upon the solidarity or even complicity of my superiors. Imagine for a second that you were a highly placed official, in let's say an American national-security programme, and you knew that people had turned over every page of your past and were observing – and recording – every detail of your present. Maybe you'd feel that you just didn't care: you might go living a flaming varied sex life in broad daylight knowing perfectly it would never be publicized. How do you imagine the people feel who direct these surveillance operations, knowing that they themselves are under the same examination? Or do you think that whatever they do it will always be covered by higher authority? Permitting themselves every kind of corruption and finagling, telling themselves, and maybe even believing, that it's all in the sacred name of state security and the national interest.'

'You seem to have given the matter some thought. I confess I haven't.'

'I don't suppose it makes much difference. You and I are both condemned to the possibility that at any moment our private life might not exist any more.'

'I would answer that, perhaps, by saying that I am a small business man and as such enjoy no protection in high places. And that you were a relatively minor official, and as such the protection you would enjoy was limited. Everyone knows that

106

corruption, and if necessary protection, exists at higher levels and that if you, for example, discovered a damaging fact about an important personage you would report it to your superiors, knowing perfectly that it would there be smothered. You would be told to forget it.'

'And,' said Castang smoothly, 'you're suggesting that I might forget it officially but pursue it privately, just to round my income out a bit.'

'It's been known,' bleakly. 'There's no reflection upon you, since I think we were both speaking impersonally.'

'And do you think Monsieur Delavigne enjoys protection in high places?'

'Knowing nothing about his private life, Monsieur Castang, I really couldn't say. It is not my business. And if you'll forgive me we'll put an end now to this discussion – personal or impersonal – because I have the peculiarity of business men, which is that they're frequently busy.'

'I'm much obliged to you.'

\*

Richard was initialling reports on his desk.

'Well? Sit down.'

'I saw Delavigne's partner. Interesting man. Huh? What motivates business men, makes them a success – it got quite complex.'

'Come to the point.'

'Maybe there isn't one. Cagey of course, and prickly. Made a big thing out of not knowing anyone's private life and not saying if he did. Is himself a peasant, a farmer's boy worked up out of the ruck by talent and determination. Got the characteristic suspicion and dislike of the bourgeois. Couldn't quite stop himself voicing his feeling that things were different for them. Thus, outside the office, where he says, and I believe him, that there's nothing, he claims he doesn't know what might happen. True up to that point, because he feels that Delavigne, and the wife, are sophisticated people with whom he has little in common. Bernard works hard, produces results, dovetails in well, is good at the smoothie commercial stuff this man feels he hasn't the time or the talent for. There is some buried resentment. Bernard has an easy assured life, and is married to a magistrate, which gives him a free ride all over the shop. When I did a bit of coat-trailing he hinted fairly broadly that if there was a blackmail attempt they'd both know how to cover it up. Anything scandalous would be smoothed out in the old-boy network. One interesting point which might appeal to you – Bernard worked for some years without taking more than a nominal salary, but has a big expensive flat and a country cottage. This fellow's wife is a peasant girl, she works with him as his secretary, they have two children who live back on the farm with the family: themselves they live in a dreary little flat in quite a poor quarter, where they've been ever since they started, and don't entertain. A couple of years ago they bought a piece of land out in the valley, and they're going to build a house, because the business is beginning to pay off. An architect is busy with the plans. It isn't at all grandiose. No secret about any of that; it's common knowledge. Still no phone-calls?'

'Still no phone-calls,' said Richard. 'A peculiar pattern. Nothing comes to light. The Parquet has been checking those dossiers all day, and so far with no result at all. Twenty-four hours, and nothing whatever. There's no sign of the child anywhere. I'm putting a man over on the house, for what good that may do. It begins to look like a sort of torture, a deliberate intention to create pain. Or else,' unwillingly, 'a brown-paper parcel hidden somewhere where it won't turn up for a few days. In which case . . .' Neither man cared to spell it out.

'Go home. We have to try and rethink it all from other angles. Here's your rabbit report. It's meaningless to me, even if it had anything to do with the matter in hand. Go home and knit socks.'

Castang, who had his report to type, cast a sour look.

'And don't think paperwork is any pleasure to me,' said Richard in a flat tired voice, slapping a pile of folders still waiting to be read.

The report was brief, technical, and as unhelpful as Richard suggested.

(a) Yes, this is rabbit.

(b) Adhering dust and grit suggest urban or suburban area. Conclude caged or tame animal, whose owner lives within reach of country district. Analysis shows animal to be nourished on fresh greenstuff as gathered in any field. Trace also of dried material: i.e. hay.

(c) Animal appears healthy and free from parasites.

(d) We're not really experts on rabbits. From the material available the subject seems to be the ordinary domestic species.

(e) The excreta are fresh, dating from between twelve and twenty-four hours. Sun-hardened, but interior moist and undecomposed.

Conclusion: on this amount of evidence, nothing can be put forward with certainty. The best that can be said is that in probability the subject is the ordinary brown short-haired animal, well-nourished and undiseased, which enjoyed a moment of liberty sometime yesterday, and anything more than that is conjecture.

Castang went home.

*

Colette had left the Palace of Justice a little earlier than usual, and her shopping done found herself in the worst of the rush hour. It was very hot: flocks of men in flocks of cars creeping along the dusty grilling roadway glared resentfully at this cool, self-possessed, superior young woman, so elegant and unruffled in her expensive little car. She felt very far from what she looked. A sense of depression invaded and possessed her; she felt terribly vulnerable, as though these hostile and grimacing faces were the masks of wolves.

Ahead of her, a vast lumbering lorry belched smoke at her: the traffic was too dense for her to overtake. As they were turning on to the main road and preparing to speed up a little the lights went amber. The lorry accelerated to try to steal the amber light, and she with it. The light went red a second too early. The air brakes of the monster stopped it dead, and her own bonnet came to a halt an inch from its numberplate. Another lorry behind, thundering up with idiotic excess optimism, braked furiously with a loud inefficient squeal. She glanced up into her mirror and shuddered violently at the sight of the huge radiator grille ready to bite the Alfa's trim little behind off. If his brakes had obeyed a sluggish boot and a dozy brain a second slower she would have been pulverized between the two masses of steel. A thing which had happened a day or two before to a twenty-two-year-old girl in a *deux-chevaux*: it had been in the paper. The sense of vulnerability swept over her and engulfed her. Men, said the psychologists, felt so safe inside their little mobile tin womb, projecting aggression around as though it were a safety-barrier. And a car was so fragile: it took so little to crush one inside in the sort of horrible weld of bright flesh and bright metal – a crumpled kleenex tissue – that she remembered from the 'traffic' seminar at magistrates' school. In the ravine between steel cliffs, held immobile by the red light, she had all too much time in which to recall a shakingly vivid experience.

The introduction had been bad enough. Thin elderly silver-haired law professor accustomed to rule coughing shuffling classrooms, with no need to raise a thin, elderly, academic voice above a dry conversational level, as though he were discussing Aristotle.

'Before these films are shown I want you to think back to what we have come to accept as the limit in human degradation: to wit the photographs and newsreels taken in the death-camps, to which one might add, by way of contrast, the pictures shown to Herr Hitler of the conspirators in July forty-four, strangled with piano wire and left hanging from meathooks, and perhaps the official photographs, released to the glee of numerous millions, of the row of Nazi chiefs left hanging in their turn. To the younger among you that will seem very ancient history.'

'Napalmed Vietnamese children,' interjected a sarcastic student voice, 'are slightly less ancient.'

The professor was unperturbed.

'We are not discussing politics, Monsieur Massillon, and I need only remind you that every generation has its horrors and refer you to the drawings of Goya. Man's cruelty to man is less our theme than man's indifference to man.

'The man who took these films will show them to you himself. I asked him to; I wanted a living link between the camera, which is often indifferent and impersonal, and the audience. I will introduce him very briefly. Herr Ahlers is German, served through the Russian campaign in tanks, became after the war a news-agency photographer and at my age has seen everything two generations of war and disaster have to show. I might add that he has worked in Vietnam and filmed napalmed children there. In the discussion to follow this screening he will answer questions.

'A word now about the films. They cannot be shown to the public without causing hysteria. They were taken for the Police School in Fontainebleau, and will be screened for you by the courtesy of an instructor there. When I saw them I asked for them to be shown to you. Your careers will call upon you to judge life and death: it is even possible, in the present state of the law, that some at least of you may in the course of your functions be called upon to witness the supreme moment prescribed by the criminal code, I mean the death penalty. I have furthermore thought it proper to use these pictures to illustrate the differences between English law and our own. You have learned a good deal about English law, and I have been present at discussions where its superiority in many ways has been advanced. Like most arguments about the biggest and the best these arguments are in general futile. The law is simply different. Evolved over the years in pragmatic style it suits the English very well. We have adopted another system and time has shown that it suits us well. One of the principal differences, as you are aware, is the way judges come into being. As you know the English choose their judges among barristers – pleaders, who are well equipped to weigh the arguments of other pleaders. A good system. Our studies, I might use the word today, are more clinical. We do not want our judges to be like generals who have never seen a shot fired in anger. We are concerned with the study of the human being: today we look at the pathology. These films are the result of the human being at work, inspired by vanity, by unbridled impatience, by aggression born of misery and frustration, by fear, by what you have learned to recognize as paranoia. The springs of crime. It is very easy to commit a crime. As you will now see.'

The light had gone green at last. It had been a long wait.

The German cameraman had been standing patiently with downcast eyes, an elderly stocky man of a faded khaki-grey colour, informally but smartly dressed in a neatly pressed, unfaded khaki safari suit and sandals. Oddly, perhaps cleverly, he chose to disconcert his audience with a low-clowning act, pretending to write on the white screen with an imaginary chalk as though it were a blackboard, dropping his chalk, using the pointer instead, getting frustrated, covering his pretended confusion. He did this well, with rapid supple timing: even priggish students laughed and all relaxed and stopped being bored.

He banged his pointer and poked it at the screen. Nothing happened: he did an angry act of frustration. He was a driver. At last he got a picture. A publicity still of a beautiful shiny new car.

'Cocorico,' he crowed triumphantly. When the laugh died he spoke in French with a clown-German accent.

'*Also meine Damen und Herren,*' the very voice of Chancellor Adenauer, 'we look at dirty pictures.' Appeared a lot of naked bodies in laboriously copulatory attitudes. 'Oh,' hiding his eyes and rubbing his crutch like a chimpanzee, 'bad picture, put to make police laugh. Ah, we make girls laugh. No no, not emotions. Not laugh, not cry, *ce n'est pas à faire pleurer Margot.* So you know me already, I am old man, tank captain Russia, also desert, hot sun, tank go plouf, burned inside, smell bad. A beginning, isn't it. Holding nose. Now more pictures. *Norddeutsche Rundfunk*, we make the reportage world-wide, here nice animals Lake Rudolf, pretty flamingoes, here Alaska pretty Eskimoes, here Bali, pretty naked girl, sorry mistake not Bali, Greek island, naked Mrs Kennedy. Now Vietnam, go very fast, Phantom fighter, that me inside, go too fast to have political opinions. So here, this Vietnam baby all burned, and this soldier-boy from Iowa impaled on bamboo spike. Neither very nice. Here tank run over little boy, any tank, tank got no political opinion either. So now very important cameraman, film everybody, here Mr Nixon laugh, here Mr Brezhnev laugh, both very funny men, very nice, make joke. Here Lyndon, very sad, go to funeral give widow medal. Here English big stateman, Sir Ranthony, he tired, rest James Bond house Jamaica. Here French big statesman, grand Charles, secret army shoot his car, he not impressed, give sack like intendance, all incompetent. All done same camera, I hold up, my baby, old-hand camera fifteen years I got him, but you bored, finish all this boredom, now colour movie very brilliant, you see, you wait a second, here, fine autoroute, very fine shiny car, publicity Mercedes-Benz, I chase. I lean out of window, like to film fine impact like gangster movie. Sorry I miss impact, got fly in my eye. So here after impact, bad imitation hamburger, no good for *bei uns zu hause*, even catsmeat man no want. Here gendarme, blow in mouth to resuscitate but hell, where mouth? Can't find. Here doctor, good surgeon, please cut there with little sharp knife, but little knife no good, better get circular saw. Aha, come *sapeur-pompier*, good idea, oxy-acetylene cutter, no much like, cut metal but first burn meat, smell like tank. All that work, here, this he get out, one hand to put in coffin, small problem for undertaker, coffin much too big, never mind, we fill up with roses.'

The students had by now realized the reason for the clowning.

\*

The light went red too for the Avenue Mozart. Colette was pleased, this time. She felt that while she was on the road, sealed away from telephones and doorbells, it gave time for things to happen. News, and it would be good news. She pictured already the beaming faces; a grubby, excited, dishevelled Rachel.

'Mama, I went on a horse and we galloped.'

'Hallo darling, have you had a happy time?'

A paternal brigadier of gendarmerie, very neat, *cap-à-pie* in his smart khaki summer uniform. And the child's much-loved German uncle, with a delightful ability to clown, and keep little girls amused. Now a bit sheepish and shamefaced at being thoughtless and causing a drama.

'Ach Colette, I sorry, I make you anxious, but everything now O.K., she come with me, we make nice ride, eh Fifille, *on a rigolé ensemble, pas vrai*?'

'No no, it was very irresponsible of you, you clown but we were out of our minds with misery.'

From the sidestreet down to the village a silly boy on a ridiculous little firecracker bike made a dangerous turn right in front of her and accelerated frenetically up the slope.

'Boy take wings here,' said the voice of the kind uncle. 'Bike make like rodeo cow down there, you see, I take zoom lens, there. This distance he fly, so-o-o, and here gendarme measure, he not believe, is seventy metres on wing. Here is boy, very good, all still in one piece, big surprise, how come? We look, he got one-piece leather suit, we find everything inside, nothing missing, even head still in helmet. But better not unzip suit. Put like so in graveyard, because inside, soup. Like making apple

113

sauce, very fast centrifuge mixer, done in a second, so brr-brr and is ready – purée.' And a photograph of the eyes, which finished off one or two budding magistrates for the rest of the day.

'God,' said Colette out loud as she parked her car, 'send us a deliverance.'

'Why does he talk like that?' asked several students.

'International pidgin,' said the world-wise Massillon. 'They talk English and Russian the same way, and they don't even notice what language they're operating in.'

'I think too,' said the professor, 'that he wanted to emphasize the extreme infantilism of mentalities unable to distinguish between the Keystone Kops and a shattered child.'

\*

'Have you brought anything for dinner?' asked Bernard anxiously.

'Dinner, yes, dinner, oh yes I've been to the butcher. Didn't see anything which pleased me. Bought hamburger.'

'Hamburger,' disappointed.

'Yes, very dull I'm afraid. I'm sorry; I know it must have been horrible for you, shut in here all afternoon.'

'I passed away an hour being grilled by Commissaire Richard. Disconcerting individual. One goes to the cinema and the cops are all unsuccessful wrestlers of impenetrable stupidity blowing smoke in the suspects' faces. You're accustomed to them of course; I'm bound to say I found him disconcerting.'

'Don't tease me, Bernard, I need a moment to recover; I had a horrible nightmare in the car. What is she called by day, the nightmare?'

'I've no idea, I'll look in the dictionary,' glad to seize on a distraction. 'Very odd: cauche, old French, and mare from the Dutch, a nocturnal monster. Surely it's just a female horse? Unhelpful, the etymology. Hm, the English is just as bad, says it's an incubus.'

'The pale horse, perhaps, in the Apocalypse. I don't care, she comes by day too and she's diabolical in origin.'

'I see her dark, but with pale blue flame where her breath ought to be. We'll ask Vera, she's the graphic artist. But what about dear old Freud?'

'I'll tell you what Vera would say about dear old Freud,' said Colette, grateful to him, 'she'd say he was a solemn imbecile.'

'What form did it take?' asked Bernard interested.

'I was crushed between two big lorries. Stay with me here in the kitchen. Just talk to me, talk about anything at all.'

'Have we what you'd call a reasonable marriage?' His mind was still running on Commissaire Richard. Colette took her frock off, hung it up, and put on an overall, glad to find her mind running on cold soup again.

'Huh?'

'What is our solidarity worth? – I mean when we are attacked, as we are now – does it weld us closer together, or tend to split us apart? If for example you were one of these liberated women?'

'Am I? I don't have the impression.'

'Well, are you?'

'You mean you don't know?'

'I've occasionally wondered.'

'Wondered what?' the judge's mind exasperated by this vagueness.

'Whether you had lovers, for example.'

'Liberated women don't have lovers. It's unworthy of them. Afraid of being pawns in a sex war, of being denigrated. Very dull for them. And exceedingly boring for everyone else.'

'Well, have you?'

'Odd question for in the kitchen. What would your opinion be?'

'I don't want to sound complacent. I'd say there were a few strong factors against you. You are strongly fastidious. All right, leave that aside for the moment. You come of a family with a long tradition of scruple and integrity.'

'Which I revolt against most obstinately.'

'Very Catholic.'

'Me, or my family?'

'You refused utterly to sleep with me before we were married.'

'What would otherwise be the point of marrying? Concubinage in law confers the same rights.'

'One can't have concubine magistrates,' comically.

'I really can't see why not. Except that concubine is such a ridiculous word.'

'And if you had a lover you'd need to be appallingly discreet. Not one's close friends: one just doesn't choose lovers among really close friends.'

'I can't think of any friends who're that close.' She was beginning to feel cheered. Despite everything, it was somehow comforting that poor Bernard should have felt too the breath of the nightmare. Even the shaft of keen hatred towards that prissy old woman Commissaire Richard came and went in a flash. An irresistible gaiety began to bubble up.

'And not casual acquaintances,' Bernard was saying earnestly. 'I should think the men – the magistrates I mean – choose their mistresses among careful respectable married women, not a rackety nightclub gang.'

'Well, who do you see as suitable?' asked Colette. 'Among the discreetly married men, who can be counted upon not to compromise the magistrature?'

'I don't know who we know,' said Bernard laboriously. 'Henri, perhaps.'

Loud slightly tinny laugh.

'I see. A policeman would only compromise himself. Anything to reinforce this suggestion?'

'I've watched him looking at you sometimes.'

'How does he look at me? Lecherously?'

'Not quite the right word. I don't know. Perhaps concupiscent.'

'A magistrate's word that,' the laugh unforced this time. 'As long as he doesn't start looking possessive. And if you're going to be liberated and start asking questions about my lovers I take it you'll accept that I can do the same.'

'That's reasonable,' said Bernard, sounding downcast. I'll teach us both to have nightmares, thought Colette.

'What are we having to drink?' she asked enjoyably, testing the meat for seasoning. 'I'd like a big serious Bordeaux, since this is an occasion. And does the slave of the phone like his steak underdone?' Bernard trotted off: Colette blanched her tomatoes and threw them in the mixer bowl.

'The slave says he'd love a drink but no food thanks, his wife will be cooking a slashing meal and he wants to do justice to it. The other old one will be here tonight. I asked what he thought about no calls at all and he said in his experience it was odd, but the job stayed the job and whether there were dramatic developments didn't alter the case.'

'There are going to be dramatic developments,' splitting a green pepper and throwing it on the grill.

'That's what I thought so I brought two bottles of Bordeaux.'

'Very sensible.'

'Covers a lot, that word. Shall I make salad?'

'There are still a few chives, and there's walnut oil if you agree but don't overdo it. So you don't mind if I search you a bit in a magisterial way?'

'I dare say,' chopping chives carefully, 'that you don't expect All your subjects to tell All the truth the Whole time. Anyway, isn't it privileged? I've no lawyer present. Abuse of inquisitorial powers vitiates the process. There. Small Suze?' running the cold tap on ice-blocks.

'Large Suze. I'm ready too,' sitting on the sofa and stretching her legs out comfortably. 'Very well. We start with the office, but I think we eliminate that, because dear Jérome is so fussy about sex in the office; there's probably more in the Palace of Justice. I have the utmost difficulty in imagining him and poor Anne in bed together. On the other hand you've always been given to casual approaches to kitchen-maids.'

'There, if I may say so, speaks the young lady from at least four generations of snobbery.'

'I agree, I suppose. I dare say I am a snob, though sleeping with policemen doesn't sound like it. But so are you, you know. You are extremely irritated now and then by my bourgeois ways, and relieve your tensions by bundling secretaries. Not your own, to be fair. Distant ones who act lordly. Still, you're a sensitive and vulnerable person, and you try to form permanent relationships. You need reassurance and you want a woman you can rely on. Is that fair?'

Bernard tinkled his ice-blocks and said nothing.

'To do you justice there's a great deal more in you than a crude need to assert yourself, and you would be very quickly bored by physical satisfaction if that's all there were to it. Bundling a secretary after too much lunch in a moment of irresponsibility is more a revolt against that deadly seriousness Jérome

117

brings to tinfoil lids on pots, more than me; am I right? Your grievances against me are more important, without trying to flatter myself.'

'Go on,' woodenly.

'You are conscientious and meticulous, but it is a strain, because while you bring a strong sense of scruple to work you are still ashamed because you feel a dilettante by comparison with Jérome. Give me a cigarette.'

Bernard was enjoying himself by now. He no longer had that strained, glaring look around the eyes.

'It's not intended to be in the least insulting,' she went on earnestly. 'You were brought up, after all, in a family with a gift for commerce which had got wealthy thereby, and you were full of resentment – lord, I remember you in your Stalinist phase, fulminating, when I knew you first. Fearful porcupine you were about parental indulgence and the easy ride you'd had in childhood, and so uneasy about being *nouveau riche*. Ashamed of your laziness and ashamed of your own facility – oh, the attitudinizing that went on.'

'But I wasn't complacent, I hope.'

'No, but don't be now because you were not at all pleasant; detestable to your own family who were really perfectly inoffensive, and amazingly aggressive to mine, whom you still detest. The grill ought to be hot by now: I'll do the steaks. You can be monstrously egoistic of course, and the combination of indolence and impatience can be very unattractive.'

'I'm going to need the second bottle,' drawing the cork of the first. 'I'm beginning to feel overwhelmed. Is there more?'

'Oh yes, lots. You were very nice to me, horrid conceited little doll that I was. Spontaneous and generous. I found you good-looking, too.'

'Pop-eyed.'

'Well-made eyes. An open and attractive expression. Vile, often, but never mean. And despite your frightful temper seldom rancorous. Shall we go to the table? Yes, in answer to your question I think we have a good marriage. I often think I don't appreciate it as I should.'

'I don't think myself I'm any great catch,' he mumbled with his mouth full.

'Very splendid, this,' draining her glass.

'Palmer. Old firm. Very snobbish.'

'I can't think of anything more snobbish than drinking Palmer out of a Baccarat glass while eating hamburger. I love you very much. Yes, give me more, a lot more, I'm going to get gently drunk on this. Already my tongue is far too loose for a magistrate's. I love you because I'm a great disappointment to you but you rarely show it. You find me rigid and artificial. You loathe my being a judge and you resent the clan intensely; all that tight-knit family of lawyers with Besson at the head. Like Bordeaux growers. Or shippers, who are if anything even worse. Little provincial aristocracy with far too much money, sending their children to Oxford and pinching their accents to sound English. My family's like that. I suppose it's why I married you really, because you were rather odious.'

'We'll drink Burgundy from now on,' beginning to wonder uneasily what all this was leading to.

'Exactly. You often make these snide little remarks they go in for in Burgundy, like if it smells of the cork, it's a Bordeaux, and down there they all die of diabetes.'

'Why?' puzzled.

'Because they have to put in so much sugar, imbecile, you know how astringent that cheap Bordeaux is. And bourgeois policemen like Richard – you can't stand him and he sees it, and it isn't very clever to show it. Whereas a man like Henri you approve of because he got somewhere without any inherited positions, just by the force of his own two wrists – I don't blame you either.' She only stopped because her mouth was full. Colette never spoke with her mouth full. Incapable of it, just the way Robert de Saint-Loup was incapable of saying 'William' when talking about the Kaiser. Being well-brought-up he always said 'The Emperor William'. He stopped to fill up both glasses, pursuing the train of thought.

'Charlus,' he said.

'What?'

'You remember how nice Charlus is, getting cross with the French in wartime for being so crudely and so stupidly anti-German, and laughing tremendously at Monsieur de Norpois for being such a pompous old imbecile, and never reading the reports of criminal cases because he's so sorry for the condemned man, and one likes him so, and then the next minute one finds him in the bordel being chained up and beaten by the soldiers. Only how complex people are. I don't know you at all, really. I'm a bit shaken by the bombardment. Are there still frightful revelations to come?'

'There haven't been any yet,' said Colette tranquilly. 'Everything I've said has been quite superficial and obvious to anyone who takes the pains to look at you. Richard, for example, or Henri.'

'There was a lot of loud talk earlier on about my mistresses.'

'If this person, this hypothetical observer – not all that hypothetical just at present – were asking himself a question like that,' taking a little rest before helping herself to salad, '– have the last one before it gets cold – they'd start by looking at me, wouldn't they? Or he. They are, believe me.'

'Both your thought and your syntax – getting kind of tangled.'

'Sorry; give me a bit more of Mr Palmer's nice juice.'

'Mr Palmer's nice juice. He'll be most indignant.'

'They'd look, I think, for something you felt thoroughly at ease with, which isn't the case with me. Someone a little timid, perhaps rather reserved and uncertain of herself. And someone with a lot more warmth and spontaneity than me. Someone who shared your interests in literature and art, less narrow, unadventurous and boring than myself. And someone quite attractive, because you have high standards of presentability. I haven't thought of it often enough, but I'm very dull. You find me very dull.'

'Not just now.'

'Oh that's only because I'm getting drunk. And how often does that happen? You're too nice as a rule to tell me so, but secretly you do find me very dull. I am dull. Oh to be sure I do my duty. Unselfish in bed, and I look after my appearance and wear nice underclothes and so on. But it isn't at all interesting.'

'And where are we to find this paragon? It sounds a rare bird.'

'Oh I think that Vera would offer possibilities.'

'Vera!' Startled, Bernard knocked his glass over, caught it in mid-air, and looked astonished by the rapidity of his reflexes. Luckily, it had been empty.

'Yes, Vera. Were you surprised at my catching that, or at your catching the glass?'

'But good heavens,' gasping at the first argument he thought of, 'she's half paralysed.'

'She was,' blandly, 'but I notice she gets around.'

'But she's a friend of yours.'

'Certainly, and a good one.'

'She's not even attractive.'

'Don't play the imbecile, Bernard, she's magnificent. The slight difficulties of movement make her if anything more so.'

'You mean you find her attractive.'

'Intensely so.'

'Odd expression for a friend of yours.'

'You're defending yourself very feebly. You'll be suggesting we're Albertine and Andrée next. I'm not Les, you know. Nor, I'm very sure, is she.'

'You astound me.'

'Really? Just because I'm a judge and have some training as an observer?'

Bernard meditated on all this, while unwrapping the foil and pulling the cork, making rather a thing of smelling it, of the second bottle. The wine-waiter's act went on while he wiped the neck of the bottle out with a corner of his napkin, poured a bit out, held it up to get the light through it, swirled it around and smelt it.

'Now drink some,' said Colette a bit too curtly.

'You certainly got your own back.'

'No. That's not one of my characteristics. If I sleep with Henri it isn't out of any revenge feelings.'

'I only meant a heavy return of service. You turned the tables neatly upon me,' finally getting round to drinking some wine. 'Is it better than the first, or not quite as good?'

'Tastes to me exactly the same.'

'Very well; suppose we accept your hypothesis, which I don't grant by the way, and we were to assume all this to be true. Where do we go from there?'

'Ring them up and ask them round,' as though it were the most obvious thing on earth.

'Just like that? What about the slave of the phone? I mean I know he's not supposed to tap outgoing calls but . . .'

'Don't be idiotic, of course he listens to everything, but what's wrong with that? Henri is supposed to be detecting; he consults us or anyway we consult. Vera is a friend, she was here this morning, holding my hand. Tranquillize yourself, we weren't making love: the idea wouldn't have entered my head.'

'But it does now?'

'And then?' with an uproarious guffaw.

'You're drunk.'

'Slightly. Going to get slightly more so, by the look of it. I'm like the man in the Thurber story – I'm sitting in the catbird seat.'

'Tell me – what are you suggesting?'

'A party.'

'You're not serious,' said Bernard, much more shocked than he had thought he would be.

'Who's bourgeois now? Cheese?'

'*Du Roquefort d'abord, d'accord.*'

'And then you can go and get up a bottle of champagne,' she said gaily. 'Don't be so silly; they give this stuff to babies.'

'Will you ring?' asked Bernard politely, 'or shall I?'

'I'm nearest. What odds does it make? ... Hallo, Henri. You've had supper? Had a rest? Feel relaxed? Listen, we have ideas, plans, various proposals. We'd like you to come over. Would you like to come over? Oh yes, quite indispensable to bring Vera. Yes, positively so. Oh yes, I agree, in your private capacities. Oh, absolutely. Yes, of course Bernard's here with me. He's all for it. Yes yes, I quite agree.' Great carillon of laughter.

'You haven't any bugs fixed here in the living-room, have you, Monsieur Castang? No, of course I'm joking. Isn't it a good moment to joke? What do you want then? – that I should sit staring out of the window with the tears trickling down? I've had a horrible day. So has Bernard. So no doubt have you. So has Vera who played Sister of Mercy all morning. Before I face another day like that I'd like to loosen up completely. I also think this will serve several purposes. You will? Champion, champ.' She put the phone down.

'And talking of champ, whip down to the cellar.'

Bernard, with an air of digesting peacefully, was eating Roquefort and finishing the Bordeaux.

'Come on,' said Colette, 'we want to get all that rubbish away. Don't want the place smelling of hamburger.'

'What are you going to do?'

'Change. Put on a nice frock. Have a shower. Like I say, unwind. Tomorrow is a holiday. No need to go to the office. I have shelved, ha, my current affairs. So we weekend. Exactly as though we were going to the country with a couple of friends, and the town, and all concerning it – work, and formal manners, and the whole law-politics-commerce syndrome – is laid aside, and all those topics of conversation are taboo. Forget the electric light and the central heating, and just have the oil lamps and the firelight.'

'And play sardines.'

'And play sardines,' said Colette perfectly seriously.

And Rachel? Was she forgotten?

No, of course not. But nobody can go on speculating on a painful theme. By a tacit agreement neither of them mentioned Rachel.

\*

Where was Rachel? She was not happy. Neither, really, was she unhappy. She had made too many discoveries too fast to be able to do much thinking about whether she was unhappy or not. Just so, when in wartime one was suddenly whipped into the army, even those accustomed to all that was most idle and luxurious in a carefree existence, even someone who had led a Noël-Coward existence –

'Whose yacht is that?'

'The Duke of Westminster's, I expect. It generally is.'

– were not in the least worried or disconcerted at the new preoccupation with boots and keeping one's bedspace clean and finding their entire life held in the hollow of an illiterate Welsh corporal's stubby grubby hand. Just so could a noble lord, heir to an immensely wealthy estate in one of the most historic, picturesque and protected corners of England, when suddenly put in prison under conviction for a criminal offence, keep his balance and humour.

'Well, how do you find prison?'

'No worse than the Guards Depôt at Caterham, thank you.'

And the Guards Depôt had been just like going to school

123

again. Painful, to be sure, because one does not know the rules, and gets whacked for unconsciously disobeying an immense multitude of incomprehensible shibboleths. But a child as young as Rachel, who was not yet nine, is accustomed to severe rules in large quantities, even those laid down by persons quite as arbitrary as any fierce brick-faced noncommissioned officer. Children like rigid laws, and discuss them with as much solemnity and respect as any magistrate.

'*On a le droit . . .*'

'*On n'a pas le droit . . .*'

Young as she was it was not the first time. The school playground, the lavatories, the class, the mistress. Silence periods and rest periods, moments of immobility with arms folded and hands and feet still, when chattering and tics and grimaces were severely reproved.

'We do not mill aimlessly about.'

'We do not rush screaming through the passages.'

'We stand up when an adult enters the room. We say *"Bonjour Madame"*. We do not make a *schweinerei* with our play materials. We learn self-respect. We do not blow our nose on our sleeve. We do not have the right to jig about madly when we want to do pipi.'

Now that there were suddenly a million new rules, all perfectly incomprehensible, Rachel was not as disconcerted as she might have been had she gone to a 'free expression' school instead of a classical '*maternelle*' at four, and the 'big school' at six.

'Acceptable work,' read Rachel's first report. 'One might reproach Rachel with being a bit too head-in-cloud.' *Un peu tête-en-l'air*. And the odd blot in her exercise-book severely ringed in red ink and the remark '*étourdie*' with an exclamation-mark. Unconcentrated!

Rachel found these children singularly ill-brought-up.

In the car she had been very frightened. The young man was so violent. Not that she had been really frightened by the knife. He had opened it, and laid it on the ledge of the dashboard, and glared at her.

'You see that? That's to open the tripes of the animals. So you'll know that you keep quiet. If you don't keep quiet you know what will happen.' She didn't believe in the knife and its fearful threat. Indians on the television had such knives. They got struck down by arrows and bullets and fists and collapsed in a heap.

'Hollywood Indians,' said Papa. 'They die every day for ten francs a time.' She understood perfectly. They were actors. And the cowboys often spoke in those menacing tones, and despite the most appalling socks on the jaw they were never hurt. 'They are *cascadeurs*,' said Papa, 'professional fallers-down.' She knew how to do that too.

She had been much more frightened of the brutal way he drove the car, accelerating furiously, noisily, from the red lights, muttering threats at all who passed. A car, she knew, was much more dangerous than a knife or a gun. Mama had a gun in her handbag. Papa had a rifle in the country. Everyone in the country had guns, and these were plainly country people. But he drove much too fast.

They drove a very long way. Up hill and down, through innumerable villages. It was terribly hot in the car. She fell asleep. She didn't know whether she had walked, at the end, or whether she had been carried. There had been such a hot smell of hay and animals. Now there was a country smell, which was familiar, but somehow different. Wood smoke she recognized at once. Sour milk. A tarry smell of sun on creosoted wood which she knew and loved. Other smells not particularly countrified but still familiar, like the smell of Marie-Line at school who was negligent, and whose hair was not always washed and who didn't change her underclothes every day. The smell, highly disagreeable, of stale sweat and musty clothes, which was that of the dirty-laundry basket. And a close stuffy smell of chicken-feathers. But it was not dirty. The tiled floor was scrubbed, the enamelled stove was clean, the window-curtains were white. The people were poor, because as Mama said the poorer the people the fussier the lace window-curtains – and these were extremely fussy. She was in the hands of peasants. She was not particularly frightened of peasants. There was also a smell of potatoes, wine, and whitewash, exactly like the cellar in Aunt Elizabeth's country house.

It was the kitchen. They all sat at the table, a big table with an oilcloth cover. She got a chair by the stove. They looked at her with curiosity.

'So you got it?'

'Like you see, no?'

'No trouble?'

'Why would there be trouble? Easy as wink your eye. I always told you it would be easy.'

'But will it stay easy?'

'Ssshh.'

'You hungry, eh? You want bread-and-butter?'

She was hungry.

'Yes please, Monsieur.'

They were delighted. They all burst out laughing. What had she said that was funny?

'Yes please, Monsieur!' But the old woman got up and cut a big piece of bread, twice the size she would get at home. She didn't mind; she was hungry. She could eat all that. There was no butter. The old woman had a stale smell, but her apron looked clean. She smeared the bread with jam, sickly pineapple jam which Rachel did not like at all, but she did not think of making any complaint.

'Little pitchers,' said the old man warningly.

'Ach what?' said the old woman. 'She doesn't grasp. Nor will she. No risk.'

'Anyway,' said the young man, 'who's going to be dictated to? Had enough of being put down, right? Not having any more of that, right?' They all seemed very angry. But not, apparently, with her. They all broke off to stare at her, not unkindly. They seemed to approve. She ate her bread in small mouthfuls, and tried not to drop crumbs on the floor, which was freshly swept.

'Been properly brought up,' said the old man.

'What do you know about it?' said the old woman. 'What, brought up? They're allowed anything. But she'll learn.'

'She'll learn,' said the young one approvingly. 'We'll train her, what. Drill her a bit. Teach her what's what. How decent people behave.'

'She don't answer back, anyhow.'

'She better not. Soon see what she gets if she do. Back of my hand.' She could understand easily enough. It was French and not *patois*. They had a rough peasant accent, but it was recognizable. It was like the carpenter, in the country, who said 'Eh, Fifizou' when he saw her, and gave her a sweet. But he had a

126

soft voice. Why did they shout so? Were they angry with each other? The old woman had teeth missing, top and bottom, all the way round the sides. Two big snaggle stumps in front. Rachel was fascinated with these teeth. The old woman had a way of sucking at them.

'What are you staring at, eh? Don't you know it's rude, to stare at people? Where's your manners, eh?'

The old man was small and thin. He was an ordinary country-man, such as Rachel was quite familiar with, and was not afraid of, except when they killed pigs or birds, which they were always doing; they seemed to enjoy it. He had an old beret pulled on very tight right down over his forehead, making his ears stick out. Didn't it hurt? He had very tiny eyes, which glared at her, and looked very frightening, but she wasn't frightened. The eyes were somehow not vicious or cruel.

She didn't think the old woman was so very dreadful either, despite all the yelling. She seemed very worried. There was a perpetual anxious frown on her face. But when she sat at the table and started to clean a pile of green beans the frown cleared, and then the eyes seemed placid and quiet.

'Shall I help?' asked Rachel timidly.

The eyes swung round and the puzzled glare that made them look so angry came back for a moment. The old woman seemed to think she was being mocked.

'What you say?'

'I know how. I could help.' The glare went out and for a moment the eyes looked quite benignant; the pursed mouth relaxed its suspicious pucker.

'Well, that's good. Why not? Yes, you can help. You can look in the drawer. Get a little knife. Don't cut yourself.'

'May I bring my chair?'

'You may.' A pile of beans on a sheet of newspaper was pushed over. The old man sat immobile, watching her. The young one lit a cigarette, a yellow one with maize paper and very strong black tobacco. He had very blackened broken nails, and the skin seemed impregnated with dirty grease, as though he were a mechanic. He seemed very sullen; Rachel did not care for him at all. She did not understand how it was that she had thought him nice when they met by the roadside. In the car he had said nothing, except for the savage muttering at other drivers. Rachel had not been worried by that. Papa did it too occasionally when they went out to the country, and he was particularly tired after a hard week. He was *énervé*. He had that sort of impatience at home too, quite frequently, roaming nervously about the flat, what Mama called 'polar-bearing'. It was quite true; she had seen them at the zoo and on the television, walking continually about in a gruff nervous way, looking for something to criticize. It was at these times that he nattered about the food, or said he couldn't find any socks (they were there all the time in the drawer, under his nose: it was as though he just hadn't wanted to find them) or complained she hadn't brushed her hair properly, or made rather wounding remarks about Mama's clothes. He could be most irritatingly inconsistent, suddenly switching the television set off, punching the button far too hard as though he wanted to break it, just when there was a programme she wanted to see, muttering angrily and using one of his damaging, denigrating phrases which could be so hurtful.

'Sitting there on your passive bum, gazing aimlessly at that spineless trash.'

Mama got upset sometimes, and there were rows, when she was tired and what she called 'ragged'. She did not often look at the television, but sometimes she liked to sit and sew; a frock whose hem needed letting down, or her own broken shoulder-straps.

'I like sometimes just to sit and be female,' as she called it; a thing Rachel understood. Men had always to be doing things. Papa read, or wrote, or 'thought', sitting with a lot of papers twiddling his fountain-pen round and round in what really was an irritating fashion. Or shutting himself up in the spare room to paint – he painted landscapes in water colour which Rachel was not allowed to touch (anyway she liked her own box of *gouaches* much better; they were far brighter), making pencil drawings when they were in the country, with the margins full of neat little notes, and 'working them up' as he called it on a drawing board at home. Rachel admired them but he always laughed at her and said they were no good.

The young man, now, did nothing, but somehow this was much more ominous and troubling. He sat sprawled in an arm-

128

chair, and Rachel was slightly shocked at this, because the two older ones – could they be his father and mother? – sat on plain wooden chairs at the kitchen table and Rachel did not think this right. He was very much the king-of-the-castle, around here, it seemed: he sat slumped, with his long legs sprawled right out. He was quite handsome, Rachel thought, but there was something wrong with his looks. Vulgar, she rather thought: it was a word she did not really know the meaning of but which Mama used often for things she did not approve of, and Rachel understood why, though not quite how. It was hard to pinpoint. But he was uncouth, that certainly. He had thick brown hair which should have been nice, but it was matted and dull looking, and he had one of those checked caps on – in the house, too – like the greengrocer's boy had. And he had very long reddish 'sideboards', and his chin was badly shaved: it gave him a dirty look, and sort of scruffy. He bit his nails too, which was foul. (Jackie bit his nails, and his hands were horrible.) He fidgeted and sighed and shifted about. Why didn't he do something? The old woman sat placidly doing her beans. The old man hadn't anything to do, but he sat quite immobile and peaceful with his hands folded, seeming quite content.

Rachel sat with her head well down, top-and-tailing conscientiously at her pile of beans – it was a very big pile; she guessed there must be at least two kilos, if not more, and wondered why they needed so many. But she could not stop glancing up at the young man, because he fidgeted so dreadfully. And she was feeling fidgety herself. She hadn't gone to the lav since leaving school, and was beginning to want to very badly. She didn't want to irritate him, because he seemed so uncertain and this she felt as a danger, but she couldn't help it.

'What you staring at me for then? Just keep your eyes on your work. No call to go staring at me in that insolent way. Snotnose.' She felt dreadfully crushed and humiliated, because she hadn't really stared and certainly not in a rude fashion.

'Leave the child alone then,' said the old woman. 'You've got her and now you've got to know how to handle her.'

'I'll handle her,' muttered the young man fiercely. 'I'll break her in. She'll learn how to behave properly.'

'You better take it easy,' said the old woman. She had a funny way of talking, at once drawling and spitting, because of the lack of teeth. It was funny, with the drawn-out singsong peasant accent, but Rachel did not dare look up. 'She's working, and that's all right, and she didn't need telling, and that's all right, and she's only a little'un when all's said and done.'

Rachel felt a bit indignant at being called a little 'un, but did not dare say anything. Thank heavens, she was nearly at the end of her beans. It had been a big pile; she was getting very tired. And what about her homework? She hadn't seen her school bag since the young man had snatched it and flung it in the back of the car with the animals.

The young man seemed pleased, despite the reproof, which didn't worry him. He took his fingers out of his mouth to snigger.

'If you bite your nails like that when they're so dirty,' Mademoiselle Lassagne said to Jackie, 'you'll get worms.' Rachel had been terrified at this horrible notion. Jackie hadn't minded: he never did. Ough! She shuddered. But she certainly wasn't going to worry whether this nasty personage got worms. She rather hoped he did!

'The judge's daughter!' said the young man, sniggering again. 'So high and mighty, and look at it!' She felt angry. What was wrong with doing beans? She often did, at home. She wanted to say so but didn't dare.

'I'm against,' said the old man suddenly. 'I have been against all the time, and I still am.'

'Shut up, you.' Rachel was again shocked. Even if it wasn't his father, one should not talk like that to older people. The young man had said 'tu' too. Well, one said 'tu' to one's parents, but not in that tone of voice; one would get clipped over the ear. Though she didn't see who would clip this one over the ear; he was too big!

'I won't shut up,' said the old man, suddenly bawling very loudly. 'I've a right to my opinion, and I say it's a mistake, and could lead to big trouble.'

'Who's to know?' scoffed the young one. 'Who's going to tell – you? No! Who else? Carney? Marie-Thérèse? Don't be so bloody soppy.'

'And if someone saw?'

'Nobody saw. And nobody's going to see. We keep it indoors,

right? We don't ask for money, right? We don't look for trouble. We keep our mouths shut, and so do you.'

'I don't go boasting in the pub about how clever I am,' yelled the old man. 'But what I say is keep your nose out of trouble. And trouble there'll be. There'll be cops smelling about. I've said so all along.'

'You're that shitty you see cops under your bed in your piss-pot,' jeered the young man. 'Cops!' He spat, outrageously, on the clean floor. 'I know something about cops. You don't know nothing.'

'Proud now. Something to be proud of, having been picked up before. Sung small, then, you did. They could peg you then, just by smelling your breath. And lucky you were to get off with it as you did.'

The young one was all red, and absolutely flaming, like Jackie when he got into one of those awful tempers. Rachel felt frightened that they would come to blows. And if they did the old one would get the worst of it. He was so sort of scrawny. But the old woman intervened. She hadn't budged at all, just shovelled the beans into the pot and gone on sitting there, massive, with the huge pale face unwinking. She didn't raise her voice.

'Shut up the both of you. You, oldie, you talk about what you know. You never had no trouble with the cops because you're too bloody scared: you knuckle down and take your cap off to anybody, bowing down there like you was a serf. Like the boy says you're shitty. And you, Pierrot, you better pipe down too, your mouth's too big. What the old bugger says is right. You think you can handle everything because you flannelled them before. We can flannel them again, right, but we got to be smart and we got to keep it quiet. We're the bosses now, we got them where we want them, all right, but not to go showing off. One thing we can't do and that's let anybody see we got them by the knackers. It's enough we have, and it's enough we know it.'

Rachel found nothing odd about this. She hadn't grasped a word, except to know that somehow it involved herself, but she was impressed by the old woman. She was in a sort of way a judge. Like Mama. If there were quarrelling men in the court, Mama made them shut up. She had never been in the court, but she knew. Jackie knew all about it.

'Your mum's a judge. She sits up there on a special chair, and if they've been pegged for speeding she dishes out the fines. I know because Pop had a thing with a cretin who bumped him, and the insurance wanted to make it just knock-for-knock.' The all-knowing Jackie. 'He wasn't wearing that, and he shoved in a complaint for criminal negligence, and he went to court, and the judge told him he was right, and the other bugger lost his licence three months. That's what your mum does.'

'Well you're just wet so yah,' said Nathalie. 'Rachel's mum doesn't do that one bit and you're talking cock. She's the children's judge and I know because my father told me, and what she does is she'll have you, if you get caught pinching those pears which everyone knows come out of old Léon's orchard and he's fair hopping, and Mum said if I ate them it was as bad as pinching them and I'd be brought in front of Rachel's mum and then she'd have to pay damages because old Léon is always in and out of the court. And what's more, Jackie Sillières, you better watch out because Rachel's mum could send you to the Assistance Publique with the Arab children and that's what'll happen to you if you pinch any more pears.'

Jackie had been very noisy and aggressive but they all knew Nathalie was right. Rachel had kept quiet because she was unsure. The Assistance Publique sounded very threatening, and Arab children did get sent there, though she was not quite sure about it. It wasn't a prison. She had been there. She gave toys to the children, and wrote them letters, to Claudine who had hair that did up in thousands of tiny curls all over her head and was nice. It was an orphanage. Jackie would not go there. She wasn't quite sure where he would go. Perhaps to the Bon Pasteur, which was a very severe convent, where the teenage prostitutes went. She was a bit vague about what it was that teenage prostitutes did, but it was pretty wicked and the Bon Pasteur was rather like a prison. Come to think of it, it smelt rather like it did here.

But if Mama caught this young man? He had certainly done worse things than Jackie. Because he had stolen her, and that was worse than stealing pears. But the Bon Pasteur was inadequate. So was the Assistance Publique. And she didn't think he'd get sent to prison. She had heard Mama often enough saying that this was to be avoided. But this young man seemed too old for Mama anyway. Mama did children, and this was no child. He had whiskers. Perhaps he would go to prison. Adults went to prison. It was not Mama's affair. She herself had never been in the prison but she had seen it from outside, and very grim it was, worse than where the ogre lived who roasted little girls on the spit and ate them, though that was of course just a story. Mama said it was Victorian. She didn't quite know what that meant, except it was antique, and very primitive. You had to go to the lav on a bucket. She felt rather that this would be suitable for the young man, and recollected with a shudder that perhaps they went on a bucket here. He wouldn't mind. She would. And she'd soon find out because she couldn't hold out much longer.

'What you fidgeting for, eh?'

'Please, Madame . . .' She didn't want to say in front of that horrid young man. At school one didn't mind. Anywhere else she wouldn't mind. It was as Mama said a natural function and nothing to be ashamed of. The Queen of England had to sit on the lav too. What was hers like? Not a bucket. 'May I whisper?'

'No you mayn't. No hole-and-corner here.'

'Bad manners,' said the young man ominously.

'Wants to piss,' said the old boy, coming to her aid. She was grateful. She nodded at him. 'All right, little rabbit, that's O.K. I'll show you then.'

An evil sort of scullery. And one couldn't even lock the door.

'Used to have to go down the garden,' said the old man sniggering. 'Modern now.' If that was what they called modern . . . But she felt so much better when she had finished that courage remounted.

'Want to come with me, eh? Feed the beasts? All right, you can.'

'Don't let her outside,' screamed the old woman down the passage.

'Just the shed.' But he winked at her quite peaceably. 'Fussy, eh? Can't let you be seen. Do you no harm. There, that's rabbits. That's a guinea-pig. You seen that before? You can pick it up. That's right. Watch he don't piss down your front. Outside's the chickies and the ducks. There's baby ducks too.'

'Can I see them?'

'In the kitchen, maybe.'

'Hey oldie,' came a bawl down the passage, 'fetch me a beer.'

'Fetch it yourself, lazy sod,' bawled the oldie back with a surprising force of lung. 'I got to do the chickies out.'

'Tell the kid then.'

'Here, see that door. That's the cellar. Don't fall down the steps. There's crates on the floor. You know what a bottle-er-beer looks like? Fetch one. Better fetch two, 'cause Carney'll be back soon. When I've done the chickies I'll show you how to draw a jug-er-wine from the barrel. You got to learn. That's a kid's job. Make yourself useful.'

Rachel was not frightened of cellars, even strange dark ones. There were cobwebs and big spiders, but she was not frightened of them. She got the beer without trouble.

'That's right,' said the young man sourly. 'Don't shake it then. All right. Learn to obey, and then you won't get locked in the cellar. Because that's what we do, see, with kids which are troublesome or cheeky. And that's what you are, a deal too cheeky.'

'She ain't been cheeky yet,' said the old woman. 'Here kiddy, you come and help me fold these clothes, I got to iron, see? Can you iron?'

'Only dollies' clothes. I tried but I burned my arm. You can still see. There's a mark.'

'Got to learn, and that's the way. Burn once, you won't burn a second time. That's the way we teach'm. Pull it then, kiddy, pull it.'

'My name's Rachel.' She detested being called kiddy.

'Fancy name,' said the old woman with a snort. 'Christine'll be back soon. You can play with her. You can watch the television too. Nobody means you no harm. You just watch your step, you'll be all right. Teach you how to live is all. You don't know nothing. Need educating. Never seen the way real people live. Judges!' with immense contempt.

Rachel was stung.

'My mother works very hard. And I'm not frightened of work.'

' 'Ere, watch it. No cheek. Glad to hear it. You'll get plenty. As well as having a nice holiday.' The old woman's chuckle was sinister.

'How long do I have to stay?'

There was a guffaw through beer from the young man.

'Just as long as we thinks right, kiddo, and that's all you need to know.'

Rachel's heart sank. Nobody could possibly know where she was. Mama would try. Papa would look. Mama would tell policemen. Monsieur Castang, for example. He could come, and he could put this horrid young man and this horrid old woman in jail. But he wouldn't know where to come. She had no notion where she was. None of the roads were familiar. What she had seen of the village . . . she had seen nothing. In the car the young man had picked the knife off the dashboard, and told her to get down on the floor, and stay down, if she knew what was good for her.

The clothes folded, she was allowed to go back to her chair. She looked at the clock, which was comforting, because at home in the country they had one like it, in a wooden box with a glass front, and a brass dangler which clicked rapidly to and fro. It said ten to seven. She looked at the television set, which she had admired. It was very large, encased in veneer of extreme and obnoxious glossiness, which she found splendid, and had a brass trim and brass buttons, so that given a fur hat and red trousers it could have mounted guard outside Buckingham Palace and nobody would have noticed the difference.

'May I see?'

'Yes youngster, but you mayn't touch.' The old woman waddled across the floor and switched it on. The evening programmes were being announced by the usual vapid young woman who didn't know her lines. The sight flooded Rachel with joy and relief; this busty overdressed figure with the laboriously painted face and silly supercilious voice, ordinarily greeted with groans, was of a sudden infinitely dear and cherished like a doll one has had a very long time (which it much resembled). So in a far-flung country, surrounded by avaricious natives, the heart of the depressed tourist floods with sympathy at sight or sound of a fellow countryman. Rachel followed every affected gesture with warm love and tear-filled eyes and intense homesickness.

A loud noise of a car motor reversing with a roar made her look up.

'There's Carney,' said the old woman between thumps at the ironing board.

Rachel felt afraid. She had had time to get accustomed to this kitchen, and felt familiarity, almost affection towards it. The first shock of unhappiness had worn off. It was quiet here and somehow cosy, with the television going, the old woman ironing (a peaceable and reassuring set of movements) and the old man now again sitting quiet in his chair with a jug of wine and a glass. Even the dreadful young one had calmed his restless fidget, or the beer had calmed it for him. He was sitting apathetically gazing at the screen with slumped limbs. Even the noisy sucking way he smoked a cigarette had ceased to scrape upon her ears. At least he was no longer showing violence.

But now anxiety surged up and she tried to make herself smaller, crouching stiffly in her chair, dreading the moment when the door would open, as though when it did it would be to give passage to the executioner and his assistants. She felt the pains of foreboding and anticipation, so much keener a torment than any physical pain.

There were loud laughs and noisy voices. They were so noisy, all these people. The door was flung open with a great unnecessary bang. Except for the old man, who she had already realized carried little weight in this extraordinary household, all their movements were like that. The beans had been thrown in the pot like faggots of wood flung upon a stone hearth; the lid had gone on with a crash; even the water from the tap had gushed with violence. When the tap was turned off it gave loud shuddering jerks for no apparent reason, and a series of small explosions seemed to take place in the piping. (So too does the strapped body of a guillotined man continue to jerk and twitch after the head is severed: it is one of the most nightmarish features of this nightmarish scene.)

Yet it was a perfectly banal pair that entered, a man and woman of harmless and conventional aspect, and most banal of all pushing a young child in front of them, a little girl younger even than Rachel. The 'man' – for so Rachel continued to name him, even after discovering that he was the 'young man's' elder brother and that 'Carney' was a family form of Claude – was not a fearsome figure. Rachel saw at once that he was the type Papa described as 'rickety'; a thin thing with hollow cheeks, hollow chest, bent legs and round shoulders. Once extracted from his car, in which he was the terror of the highway (his lifelong dream was that he could, if not dispossessed and pillaged and trampled upon by the rich, have been a successful racing driver), he cut indeed a pathetic figure. He did not wear a working overall but a demoted Sunday suit, looking the more wretched because neither its exaggerated cut nor its cheap synthetic cloth had resisted six months' wear on best occasions. He would always have that draggled look of someone who has fallen in the pond and been pegged out to dry on the clothesline, still inside his garments. Perhaps because he was aware of this he carried himself jauntily, with the bobbish movements of a marvellously articulated and skilfully manipulated puppet. He was was always performing complicated movements; a perpetual cigarette jiggled in his bony fingers and flicked from one corner to another of his mobile mouth. As he came in he was juggling the car keys on his palm, tossing them up and catching them, flicking back his long dark hair, stroking his small moustache while his eyes jerked and snapped from side to side with an effect of a match being struck on each bony rasping eyesocket. Where his younger brother had the big slab-sided Flanders-mare build of the old woman, who even drowned in pale cool fat had still the solid muscles given by a hundred years of buckling down to the beetroot harvest under the skies of Artois, he had the loosely-jointed clothes-horse look of the old man, who in his sleeveless vest and bib-and-brace *salopette* had the scrawny neck of a plucked turkey and whose puckered blue jaw moved awkwardly and woodenly to and fro in an uncertain wobble the whole time, rather as though a wasp were continually buzzing about just at the back of his neck and he were trying to catch a glimpse of it, to know where to launch a smack from the desiccated forearm.

His wife was a very different sight. Quick, alert, pretty, well cared for. A tall, slim and shapely figure. A cascade of thick rich blonde hair with a natural wave, a well-turned pair of fine-boned and sun-tanned legs, a lusty look of life enjoyed, an upright healthy physique with a strongly-shaped head poised on a fine neck. Isn't she pretty, thought Rachel, with a touching belief that a pretty and healthy young woman will prove to be a kind and gentle young woman. It was indeed sad that the illu-

137

sion lasted so short a time. What had gone wrong? What unhappy handicap so marked and marred this pleasant, good-looking, still youthful female and turned her into a spitting viper? Even her name, Marie-Thérèse should have been that of a gentle, pretty, kind girl. An awkward poser it would be one day for a judge of instruction.

Had she been born with that voice, or had she acquired it after years of embittered suffering? It was the first thing, after the initial impression of health and vivacity, and the gift of physical good looks, to strike the onlooker.

What sharp, agonizing, penetrating pain had so struck and bitten into this strong young body? This perhaps unintelligent, but quick-learning, responsive young mind?

Dayspring mishandled.

Something that could be seen, still, in the face. A bright and sunny disposition checked and warped by misery. Turned violently in upon itself. Worse still; writhed and knotted into a wound that had festered, that had turned with adulthood into a well of poisonous hate.

That is a hard and bitter thing, which even an adult finds hard to grasp. Why is the world so full of malice? Why are we so evil?

To a child she was simply a harpy, in a simple literal sense, the classical Virgilian sense. *Nec saevior ulla pestis*: flesh-tearing carnivore, yet a woman. A young, pretty woman. *Tristius haud illis monstrum*: a sorrowful fact of existence.

Rachel was to learn that all her dread, of the thick floundering old woman, of the toothless old man – who could, still, bite like the netted weasel – of Pierrot, that suffused, stupid young bull – and there are paper bulls as well as paper tigers – and even of the jaunty Carney, manipulated like dough by his fearful consort, and dangerous because of this: all dread would be insignificant before that of seeing, hearing Marie-Thérèse. And, for an eight-year-old girl, being touched by her.

Melodrama. Yes. To be sure. A generation afraid of blowing its cool despises melodrama, and is the more frightened of it. But a police officer, and especially a P.J. officer, is not contemptuous of melodrama. He comes to know too, if he has any taste for reading, how oddly true to the facts of his existence are the nineteenth-century novelists. It is Stendhal and Balzac, Dickens and Dostoyevsky who give him the visions that to him are anchored in reality.

Thus Castang, who would come one day to see Marie-Thérèse as part of Victor Hugo's Thénardier family. A Punch-and-Judy show, a *grand guignol*. Certainly. But alive, real, present, dangerous. As Thénardier lands on the ground from his prison break, breathless, giddy, nearly dead with fear, he picks himself up and says 'Who shall we eat?'

Marie-Thérèse perhaps, by paradox, most resembled the most melodramatic of all nineteenth-century figures – Beethoven's Leonora.

The examining magistrate, an opera-lover, came eventually to this conclusion. It was not in the dossier sent to the Chambre de Mise en Accusation; it was not mentioned to advocates or written on any official piece of paper. But in his private notes it went down 'an evil Leonora – if such a thing is conceivable'.

The moment she came in at the door she broke out into a croaking shriek of laughter.

'The judge's child!' Rachel shrank away before the gloating face, paralysed.

*

An officer of Police Judiciaire does not make anything to boast about in the way of a living. Even with a few years of seniority he is at a modest clerkly level, and Castang lived in a street so apparently beyond his means that he had been suspected at times of taking bribes. It was really quite a small and humble flat on the second floor of a passably shabby nineteenth-century row but this street, besides being relatively close to the centre of the town, and a small pleasant bike-ride from the office, was much sought after; an address with considerable 'standing'. There were three reasons for this, all good. The street led nowhere in particular and was not much used by cars. It faced a disused canal whose water ambled at foot pace between grassy banks, with towing paths from the old horse-drawn barge days. It had an unusually wide pavement on which residents could park their cars in comfort between splendid big poplar trees of much age and beauty; these on the canal side. On the house side were planes. This was all very nice.

When Vera had had the accident which had left her legs

paralysed (not a road accident, not even a ski accident, but even more banal and boring a stupid fall while catapulting off the asymmetric bars used by girl gymnasts) they had been forced to conclude that she would be in a wheelchair for the rest of her life. No operation was possible. Nearly a year of physiotherapy, including a long and horrible stay in a re-education centre full of pathetic boys who had been in motorbike accidents, and a grandiose sea-water cure where her room-mate was an international ski girl with a ruptured Achilles tendon (amazingly patient on her crutches; the child was only eighteen, had nothing else to live for, and this had given Vera a new lease of fortitude), had made no improvement in her condition. Her top half was better looking, firmer muscled than it had ever been, but the sad wasted legs just would not obey. Castang had determined that if she was never going to go out much any more she was at least going to have a flat with a view, and a quiet street where she could at least sit on a balcony and draw trees, for Vera had some talent as a graphic artist, had been to the 'Beaux Arts' school as a teenager in Czechoslovakia, and even made a small amount of money as an illustrator, which was very good for her morale.

Professor Rabinowics, the doctor at the University Hospital who was her specialist and had become a friend, had pulled strings to find them this flat. He had been pessimistic about the future.

'Medicine has done all it can. But it has been known for these things to get better, not altogether spontaneously.'

'You mean I should go to Lourdes or something and pray for a miracle.'

'Well I'm far from despising that: it's a therapy like another, but it's not quite what I meant. I've no judgement to make about supernatural resources. The Madonna might cure you, and so come to that might a witch-doctor; I know one or two – alas, the Social Security Office won't repay them. What I wanted to say was that I may have exhausted my resources, but I'm not altogether convinced that you have exhausted yours.'

And in the end Rab had refused to give an opinion. Was it physical or metaphysical? Had Vera simply been her own witch-doctor? And – she was a baroque, jesuitical sort of Czech Catholic – had the Madonna lent a hand?

'More than likely,' said Rab. 'The X-rays are exceedingly difficult to interpret, but something happened to the lesion.' All that had happened perceptible to the human eye was that Vera had gone on stubbornly exercising her legs for nearly eighteen months. One day she stood up and didn't fall down. Some few days later (this had all been kept a dark secret) she had taken a wobbly step, and still hadn't fallen down.

Vera now walked, in a shuffly way; a bit odd. She couldn't keep it up for long. But she got around the flat, she hopped about a shop, she could get into (and out of, which was harder) a car. And the muscles of the legs were no longer wasted. As good as new, said Castang contemplating them with pride and satisfaction.

Neither the Madonna nor the witch-doctors had been efficacious in her attempts at having a baby, but this was a problem dating from before the fall.

She had wanted to give up the flat, which drained their resources. They never had anything in the bank.

'Not on your life,' said Castang, imposing a thoroughly male decision. It was a very small-bourgeois existence, with a canary and a little orange-tree.

Vera looked up as he came in, tired, sweaty and bearing marks of discouragement.

'That was a long day.'

'Very long, and singularly useless. I've nothing to show for it.'

'Do you want dinner now, or wait till you get it?'

'I'd like to wait a bit. Does it matter?'

'Not a bit; it's stew.'

'I must have a shower. A drink first to get up courage. I need to feel comfortable, but first I want to feel at home.'

'My poor boy.'

'You know, I'd like very much to bust this. I feel deeply involved. Implicated.' His hands sketched fold. '*Éntrlificoté*'.

'Yes. I can understand. I'm very fond of Colette; she's a good person. Since I feel bound with ties of affection as well as sympathy I don't feel able to make anything of it. I just sit numb, wondering how it must be for her. I can't arrive at seeing it from outside.'

'Better,' drinking half a glass of red wine and topping it up from the bottle. As cheap wine went, this was honest. It was almost honourable. He got it from the grower. One doesn't have to take bribes to be able to enjoy perks. 'Throw me the matches, would you? Richard asked this morning whether I'd perhaps let myself get over-friendly with Colette.'

'The ideas he gets.'

'Yes, well, it doesn't do to take him too literally. More a way of telling me his own mind was cantering around, wondering whether either of them would have a motive, say, for using the child as a weapon.'

'Meaning that she wasn't kidnapped at all?'

'I think she's been kidnapped all right. But Richard's a cautious bastard. He thinks about possible knowledge, eventual connivance, a conceivable obscure device or even plan.'

'That sounds plain silly to me.'

'If one just supposed, for example that Colette had a lover, would you know about it, do you think?'

'Good heavens, are you serious? You think we go about whispering teenage confidences into one another's ears? You can't be that naïve surely. Nor Richard, for goodness' sake. If he thinks Colette tells me about her private life he is an imbecile, and if he thinks I'd spy for him upon a friend – assuming she had given me any confidences about her personal problems – then he's infamous.'

'You wouldn't even tell me? – assuming I needed badly to know.'

'My poor wolf, I suppose I tell you pretty well everything I know or hear, since you're my husband, poor you, and I suppose if I came into possession of any knowledge involving a crime or a possible crime, or even just a felony, I'd tell the police. If it were a case of conscience, you know, the professional secret or the confessional secret, I suppose I'd be in a dilemma. It's never happened to me so I don't know. I imagine that it would worry me very much. I think, though, that if Colette had given me a personal confidence, feeling sure I would respect it, I'd hesitate a long while before blabbing, even to you. I'd want to feel strongly convinced that you had the right to know.'

'And that only the existence of a crime would give me that right, is that it?' finishing his glass and his cigarette.

'I suppose so. I haven't thought it out.'

'Do think it out – while I have a shower.'

'But, my darling, I don't have any such knowledge, believe me, so don't add to your anxieties I beg of you. Anyway, if Colette's lover is you,' laughing, 'presumably I'd be the last person she'd confide in. But surely I don't need to tell you that we're friends but that doesn't mean she confides. In any case she's a secret person who doesn't gush about her innermost. It would be very boring if she did. Does anybody? Adults don't, surely. They may be transparent persons, but they still have all sorts of secrets, or they wouldn't be adults.'

Castang, wearily, was undressing. He threw his dirty clothes on the bedroom floor, sighed, picked them up again and put them in the basket. He kept the bathroom door open to avoid a lot of stuffy condensation on the warm summer evening. He could hear Vera talking, but not what she said, because of the rush of water.

'Anyway,' Vera was saying, scooting her wheel-chair across into the kitchen, which was a lot quicker than walking, 'as Colette herself says, it's not what you do that counts, where the police are concerned – it's what it can be made to look like in a court.'

She put a flame under her vegetables and gave the stew a stir to be sure it wasn't sticking. He had forgotten – or been in too much of a hurry – to get any clean underclothes. Men! They left the bathroom door open, made a lot of noise and splashing, left loose water all over the bathroom floor – she did wish she could afford something better than beastly cheap plastic shower curtains – and then came rolling out all bare and hairy complaining that there were no clean underclothes. She went patiently into the bedroom to get them. A shirt button was off; she got a needle and thread. He was jumping about and yelling there because of turning on the cold water. The underclothes were old and worn thin, patched across the seat. The shirt collar needed turning. She could thank God it hadn't been her hands that got paralysed. She made virtually all her own clothes, and mended all his. Hm. One could always find excuses to be grateful for not having children.

He appeared with a wet towel; also a thing worn thin and needing replacing. Warmth and moisture made the hair on the stringy forearms fluff up; his legs were still plastered. The big stitched scar on his back, running from the bottom of his ribs

143

up to the shoulderblade, was white and crinkly: he had been ripped by a shell splinter and sewn up casually. Every time she looked at it she couldn't help thinking she would have made a better job with a needle and thread than that. Still, field hospitals in Indochina . . . not exactly proliferating in creature comforts.

Face hollowed by fatigue; muscles sunken, queer nose a bit flattened by boxing. The hair when wet could be seen getting a bit thin on top. Too young to be looking that middle-aged.

Vera thought that if he were Colette's lover Colette had made a good choice.

He was in no hurry to dress: he sat there contented waiting for the warm evening air to dry his skin thoroughly. The chair, which was rattan and had a washable cushion, would take no harm. He took a second drink, a thing he rarely did. She bit off her thread and tossed him the shirt.

'Photograph,' she giggled. 'Unbuttoned policeman.'

He laughed.

'Yes, one's there all day, neat and functional, the severity you know, and the official importance. Now, Mrs Whoosis, I want you to think carefully. Police Judiciaire, just answer the questions. I suppose some take it home with them. Bullying their wives, having the children brought up with military exactitude. Law and order in the home. Go and get your hair cut. Show me your school exercise books, and if your marks fall below the acceptable level I'll deprive you of pleasures; no going out, no television, watch it or I'll take the belt to you. There are some like that, too weak to be able to take the uniform off; they have to be wearing it even in bed. And there are some one knows of, who go bloody near the limit of what is officially permissible, and even beyond it, at work. Abattoir types. Always talk in a yell, always got their hands loose to make some boy's ears ring – nastily expert in giving a slap without its leaving a mark. They're not bad, most of them, just coarsened, just naturally bastardly, but I think a lot go home and are perfectly reasonable and quiet with their family. Nearly all get pretty calloused. So do doctors, or dentists, or whatever. Make up your mind not to get calloused and it's one long grind.'

'And poor.'

'And poor. Come home and your wife goes on about turning

144

a shirt collar, and you start thinking of all the nice contributions you could be getting for turning a blind eye. Half the time you're turning a blind eye anyhow, and it eats in to think you could be getting paid, and pretty well paid, for doing nothing. You don't need to connive at any crime; only the very stupid ones do that – you know, taking a kickback from the sale of drugs in a café. All you need to do is take the borderline stuff, the old-fashioned misdemeanours. Well, Mister Chose, you do realize that it's a technical infraction, it's in the code, but since it's not really a moral issue nowadays in these changing times I'm prepared to be indulgent, and now what about our widows and orphans. A good P.J. cop doesn't have to take any bribes at all. He leaves that to the municipal small fry, tapping the business men in exchange for not making a fuss over illegal parking on the pavement. In the P.J. you don't need anything crude like money changing hands. I do you a favour, you do me a favour. See that the children get good marks at school, see that my wife gets her hairdressing free and her clothes at sale prices. See that I get a good buy on a watch or a car or a suit. All you need do is respect your own standing at your own level. Once you're a commissaire it becomes a bit more sophisticated. Make sure I have a surefire stock-exchange tip. I'd like to join the golf club, but I find the dues kind of high. I like to go to starred restaurants, and don't give me this crap about the tables all being reserved.'

'And you had to go and marry a Czech communist.'

'Come off it, communists take far more bribes than we do.'

'An artist, then.'

'That's better. If I started playing the golf-club game it'd just make you sick.'

'So petty. I'd rather be poor.'

'I'd like to be rich for a change.'

'Make up to Colette, quietly. A judge of instruction can do a cop a lot of good, on the quiet. See that he's well thought of by his superiors. That the Proc thinks him a good fellow, in line for a few rewards. That he'll get transferred to a good district in Paris.'

'Most of the Paris cops I know have requests in to be transferred to the provinces. Too far to go, to get home when off duty.'

'Those are the stupid ones. The good ones have unobtrusive flats in historical buildings where the rents are pegged.'

'I know one who has a flat in the Rue Bonaparte. Building is classified – there's no lift. And not much space. But there's a garden behind the house . . . and I know another, on the courtyard, a hôtel particulier in the Rue de Sèvres. Both work in the sixth arrondissement. Five minutes' gentle stroll to work in the morning, stopping for coffee and a couple of fresh croissants. They don't need anything old-fashioned like a car to get to work, and they don't climb in no metro neither. The rent's peppercorn, with antique furniture thrown in. They've never taken a bribe in their lives.'

'And yet you're clever enough. It's your wife who is stupid.'

'All she has to do is accommodate. Like if her husband is friendly with a magistrate, see that the magistrate's husband is kept happy.'

'Yes. It all goes nice and smooth. And then the stupid magistrate's stupid child gets itself kidnapped. So you being a pal, they ring you up quick to make sure that a press blanket is put on, and all the scandal stays inside the family.'

'That's right. But I've got to be very careful that that bastard Richard doesn't get into the act, because he wants to make quite sure the Proc won't get cross with him.'

'Children are very embarrassing.'

'One does far better not to have any.'

'Poor Colette, she's under considerable strain,' said Vera reflectively. 'She is very tense under that relaxed exterior. Eaten up by all sorts of anxieties. Worries about how the child sees her, and how the child judges her. My mummy is a magistrate. That's bad. My mummy is a bit of a whore, really. That's not very good either. She's far too fixated on the child's opinion of her.'

'You think she'd better have another one? By me maybe?'

Vera looked at him wryly.

'That's a bit like saying I ought to stir my stumps, isn't it? If I can't manage with you, I'd better jog Bernard into collecting his responsibilities. Vera thinks herself an artist, silly bitch. Restless dissatisfied woman; give her a baby, do her a world of good. And Henri will know perfectly well, and it gives him a good efficient lever. Make Castang a commissaire, we'll find someone who is decidedly superfluous to requirement. Uh – prompt me.'

'Lasserre. He's a lazy bugger; Richard does all his work. Adjunct commissaire is a good job to have; the screw is reasonable and the responsibility minimal. Post Monsieur Lasserre to Pézénas and give me his job.'

'Can I get the dinner on the table? Put your shirt on, do; I'm not having men with hairy armpits at the dinner table, even if you aren't even an adjunct commissaire. Really, it is the child who is the great stumbling-block.'

'You're telling me. Bernard becomes thoroughly unbalanced. Colette can't be relied upon. What does she do? – fly into a panic and phone me. I'm involved right from the start. If anything goes wrong Richard blames me. If I get it sorted out Richard takes all the credit. Because either way the Proc is breathing down his neck. I'm in the middle getting screwed. And the worst is, first I'm intensely worried about what happens to Rachel. She's my mistress's adored child. Second, as a police operation, she's turning out singularly difficult and ungrateful. Where is the child? What has happened to her? Nobody has the faintest idea.'

'Nobody?' said Vera, ladling stew. 'Not even the faintest?' Because these tirades were not unknown after wearisome days, full of a lot of futile stumbling about, and when newly married she used to have horrid visions of a husband sacked for incompetence, or transferred to some barbarous hamlet in the extreme backwoods of the Massif Central. She no longer took them quite so seriously.

'Throughout the entire day I discovered one grain of fact – literally the size of a pea. Which isn't linked to anything, may be sheer coincidence, and even if connected, and that remains pure speculation, isn't helpful, because what is the rabbit population of France? There's no evidence that any kidnapping ever took place. Balances us between two uneasy notions. That a dangerous maniac somehow gained possession of the child, which would mean giving what we know to the press and appealing for information. Not a happy thought, and we labour under the tremendous handicap of twenty-four hours lost. Or that there never was any kidnapping, that either Bernard or Colette, you can take your choice, has been playing an immense comedy, in a quite unbalanced and indeed dangerously irrational fashion. Richard has been toying with this notion, how seriously I don't know. Nor what – if anything – he might have to go on. Are there any more beans?'

'Didn't he give you any instructions?'

'He just went enigmatic. Told me to continue probing the background. What do we know, after all, about them? Precious little. What do you know, even?'

'Poor Colette. She is an awful fool in ways. She's a good judge, I should think; I've never seen her at work.'

'She bears that reputation,' said Castang.

'I only know her outside, and then she can say things of startling silliness. Whether she does them or not . . . What are you going to do?'

'Go over there after supper, in the rôle of family friend. They haven't realized it yet, but the police can put a searchlight on one's private life which is unpleasantly bright, upon occasion.'

'Think if it were us,' said Vera, softly.

'I am,' he said, 'but the point's got to be cleared up. Startling silliness, you said. Like for instance?'

'Are you examining me?'

'Yes,' briefly. 'Look, of course it's never very nice to be in an investigation of a serious crime against the person. You have to go trampling in on people's privacy. All sorts of little details that aren't necessarily damaging but that they'd rather keep to themselves or that they wouldn't mind telling a doctor inside his professional secrecy, but having it typed out and read back to them makes them wriggle. A magistrate, or a policeman, has his own professional secrecy too of course. But these dossiers are seen by a lot of people, the smallest of details might come to acquire importance – it might be something the president of a tribunal decided to bring out in open court, that you'd been sleeping with your sister or something. We get pretty depersonalized about this, even brutalized. But it still comes as a shock when it happens to oneself, or to one's friends.'

'Yes,' said Vera unhappily.

'You don't really understand, do you?'

'Not altogether.'

'This – Colette's a magistrate, she knows all this. So like a good magistrate – or a good policeman – she keeps it all compartmentalized. Her professional mentality doesn't leak into her private life. If she's examining the parents of some child that set the place on fire she doesn't stop to ask herself 'Suppose this were me'. You do that because you're an artist, but justice – or police work – doesn't get done that way. I might be under-estimating her, I don't know. But I don't think she's grasped the fact yet that this time it's her under the lamp, and that if Richard wants he can reach a long way into her privacy. Inclu-ding that of her friends.'

'You're saying – if I've understood – that if the hypothesis is correct, and you're her lover, it would come out.'

'Yes.'

'And if Bernard was my lover, that too.'

'Correct, Madame. For all I know Richard's got someone watching this house.'

Vera took a cigarette, a thing she did two or three times a week. 'Colette has never told me anything like that,' she said slowly. 'When I said she was capable of silliness I meant quite banal things. She has a weakness for astrology, and fortune-telling, and magic – she has a childish side. And foolish notions. There's no harm in telling you.'

'Whether there is or not – you better bloody tell me.'

'Oh well, the other day, we were talking about holidays, and she brought up that old gag about having separate holidays. You know the theory. Saturnalia when the law does not run. One is happily married and one has a good husband, but when one goes on holiday one puts the wedding-ring in the handbag and one goes looking for adventure, and the husband goes off on his side, and this is simply lovely, and very adult and mature and an enriching experience and all that, and nobody tells and nobody asks – oh, you know.'

'A vulgar, silly, and dangerous fantasy.'

'That's what I told Colette,' said Vera dryly.

'Does she do things like that?'

'I don't suppose she does more than toy with them. If she did them she probably wouldn't tell me. Or it might be her way of setting aside the hidebound bourgeois traditionalist upbringing she's so ashamed of.'

'Stupid cow,' muttered Castang angrily.

'She's vulnerable. Needs constant reassurance. Tense under

149

that air of relaxation. Look how she drives that car. Far too fast.'

'But well.'

'Sure,' said Vera. 'Familiar syndrome. When women are good drivers they are very good, equal to any man. Same with magistrates.'

'But she's perfectly aware she's good, and accepted as good. It's ridiculous; she doesn't need to go proving it to herself the whole while.'

'She always wonders whether she's taken seriously. Always over-sensitive to a suggestion of humiliation. She feels that at present. I got a long tirade this morning. All about she knew it was absurd but she couldn't rid herself of a feeling that this had all been arranged to discredit her.'

'Now that is interesting.'

'It's idiotic. I told her so.'

'Bernard's more the one really to have secret feelings of in-adequacy or notions of being humiliated. Being sensitive about commerce, or anxious lest people find out about yoghurt and start sniggering.'

'But it's perfectly honest, to sell yoghurt.'

'Of course it is. We're accustomed to being despised by the neighbours for being in the police. It's thought of as a dirty job. Yoghurt sounds to me like a paradise of healthy clean living.' And he couldn't resist laughing at himself. It was true, ridiculous as it sounded. Several of their neighbours felt that having a cop in the building lowered their standing. Even when they themselves worked in insurance companies, and as Vera remarked there's nothing lower than that.

'What are you laughing at?' she asked, relieved.

'Oh, just that this afternoon I was interviewing Bernard's boss. Partner, by courtesy. Now there's a fellow who's quite singleminded about his yoghurt. Thinks of nothing else. Humourless. Rather admires Bernard for being sensitive and all that. Poor old Bernard, who is sensitive all right, about not taking yoghurt seriously enough. And has some resentfulness at his being sensitive about Colette being a judge, while he's just a dirty little sales manager.'

'Something the way I'm sensitive about you being a P.J. cop and a good one? Whereas I'm a draggy little Czech peasant with broken legs. A bloody hindrance, and that can't even give you a baby.'

He looked at her across the table, face emptied of expression.

'Sure. Like I'm sensitive about being a dirty little muckraking cop, sniffing at old clothes through a magnifying glass and getting very humiliated about my wife being an artist.'

'So we both try not to pity ourselves. Looking it in the eye, you rather fancy Colette. I'm unsurprised. She's exceedingly attractive.'

'Maybe – when I'm very tired; like now. Discouraged. At that moment she might make my head swim a bit.'

'Not an open-air object like the rustic wife smelling of sweat and cherry-orchards. What perfume does she use?'

'How should I know?' he laughed. 'Chamade probably.'

'What does it mean?'

'Medieval term for surrender,' grinning at her.

There was a small awkward silence.

'I wouldn't altogether feel surprise or grievance,' said Vera, 'if you were her lover.'

'As Richard thinks I am. What would you feel?'

'I'd think it my duty to keep my mouth shut. What is unsaid is better left unsaid. Even if what is thought cannot be unthought.'

'A policeman finds the same. One starts turning up things that had been better left unturned.'

'Everyone – however placid and serene their life – needs a lot of courage to keep it running. Without grief and pain. Without thinking a lot of things better left unthought.'

'Colette is wondering whether this hasn't all been arranged to discredit her. Richard's little theory begins to gain ground – that Bernard is capable of cooking up a drama to sabotage her.'

'Why do people take lovers?' abruptly. The sudden naïveté – Vera's speciality. The only way to take it was seriously.

'They haven't enough illusions?'

'A sign of fundamental feebleness? Piffling? Except for the very young.'

'Yes – at eighteen, cocufying some pompous old bore is the ideal.'

'After that, surely, a sign of stultification. Prolonged im-

151

maturity, like Louis Quinze. Hm,' said Vera reflectively, 'I'm stultified all right.'

The telephone rang. Castang picked it up languidly. A small frown formed straight away between the eyes. As the voice went on, now and then suddenly too high and too loud, forcing him to make a face and hold the receiver away from his ear, Vera watched. She was too far away to pick up the spare earpiece and listen in, and it was too much trouble to satisfy her curiosity, even though she recognized Colette's voice, or intonations rather: the voice itself was shrill and edgy. A drama? She watched Castang's face changing from irritation to boredom, then to a sort of good humour, and gradually back to a kind of interest, going a bit further than just curiosity.

'She's pie-eyed,' putting the phone down. 'Come to our party.'

'Party's well on the way to judge by her voice.'

'Mm. In a mood to do silly things all right; risky things too. And Bernard's in no condition to stop her. She wants me to bring you.'

'You're going to the party?'

'I was going anyway, as I told you: detecting to do. I was putting it off. Waiting another half-hour won't make me any more thrilled. But what about you?'

'I'm more than game,' said Vera enigmatically. 'Help me change my frock.'

*

They got into the car together. Castang had put on a seersucker shirt, and after some thought a linen jacket, to conceal the fact that he was wearing a gun. Taking one's gun to a party, thought Vera: hm . . . She was wearing an ankle-length cotton frock. Loose enough for her too to wear a gun. But it would take a lot of time and effort to get at it. Unless somebody strips me. Perhaps I should take my bow and arrow. Will you show me how to put my fingers on the string? Emma, came Mr Knightley's voice, you are behaving foolishly.

Castang drove, always very serious and deliberate at the wheel of a car, and looking both ways the whole time. This extreme caution struck her. She remarked on it, jovially.

'I've my wife with me,' said Castang in a toneless grunt. It didn't sound as though he were warming up to enjoy himself.

Colette carried a gun in her bag. She had told Vera a rambling tale of bringing it out the other day for the first time to point at a night-time lover boy. As long as this doesn't become a habit . . .

The street was deserted, the Résidence Dampierre wrapped in discreet bourgeois tranquillity. Whether or not the inhabitants had peace of mind, nothing must be allowed to show. Broad deep generous curtains of full-length velvet drawn across their windows. The windows themselves firmly shut, even on a June night. The night air noxious, pernicious, most unhealthy. The sounds, and smells, and dusts and din of traffic must be most painstakingly excluded. And to be sure, anything going on within must be kept in. Not just an eye-patch, thought Vera, but a nicely cut, pretty velvet mask. Mask! – a whole veil. Our velvet hand adjusts our veil. The countenance must not be seen to be distorted by pain or fear. The screams must be stifled.

A line of verse came from somewhere into her mind. What had brought that there? Velvet, perhaps. 'Peace of mind becomes me . . . – yes, of course – As soft white velvet hands become a man . . .' Oddly touching scrap of verse. The silent scream of Albertine Sarrazin at the barred window of Amiens prison. She'd had no velvet curtain there.

'. . . As on half-healed wound a dressing – a dressing of diamond.' She said it well, thought Vera. The softness of gauze and the hardness of the hardest grit: abrasiveness of diamond dust. No mere grindstone could cause such exquisite pain to the film of new, tender pink skin. And yet precious, that pain . . . precious as diamonds . . .

What had kept Albertine going? Not her pride in herself, in her writing. Simple. Simple love, pride in her man, love for the man who had not had soft velvet hands.

Soft and delicate this interior. Not velvet but beautiful lined linen curtains of a soft straw-colour. Vera had never been able to afford any curtains at all in her own living-room, and had to be content with venetian blinds, and really rather wished that Henri would pick up a few bribes from time to time. And shantung lampshades of that same straw colour, with lines like straw in the weave. And pale beautiful straw-coloured champagne. Oy! Krug 1966. No less.

And even soft straw-coloured music. Bernard's immensely

expensive high-fidelity record-player, and one of Colette's delightful collection of 'nostalgia' records. She had something for every mood. Noël Coward's song about the room with a view. Hoagy Carmichael – Lauren Bacall's song from *To Have and Have Not* – ha. The vintage of 1942: hadn't that also been a good champagne year? And 'My Defences are Down'. The hell they are. All we need now is Richard Tauber to sing 'You are my Heart's Delight'. Colette had that too. As well as Tauber singing Mozart; better and more bitter. And playing at present she had Nelson Eddy and Jeanette MacDonald giving her wildly laughable version of 'Indian Love Call'. Delicious!

'Why'n't you take off your jacket?' asked Colette in her soft, party-slurred voice.

'Because I'm wearing a gun underneath,' crisp.

'And he can't take his trousers off for the same reason.' Bernard being funny. This piece of undergraduate wit went down badly.

'Go sniff some glue or something.'

'Oh come, Henri darling, don't be so acid.'

'The people are nice and the drinks are good, but the kind of party where the women get shrill and somebody ends up yelling "Let's all sleep with one another's husbands" is just crappy.'

'Henri,' said Colette, 'that was rather a wounding thing to say.'

'Where did this elaborate fantasy start? Don't think I'm against; I thought it funny. Just that if we end up believing it true we can hardly be surprised if everybody else does too. There's no rumour so tenacious as the one you start yourself.'

'What on earth are you making such a fuss about?' asked Colette languidly. 'Who has to go running to disprove rumours that don't even exist? You're being a self-important prig.'

'I'm a cop,' said Castang, 'with enough experience to know there's another cop outside.'

'You mean the slave of the phone down in the basement? – that he really is listening to all our conversations?'

'I don't know whether he is or not,' tranquilly. 'It would be perfectly possible. I doubt it, because you're a magistrate, and other magistrates might not take kindly to the idea of eavesdropping: it might happen to them some day. And because you're a magistrate you're entitled to a good deal of protection, and by the same token you'd be unusually vulnerable in the case of anybody cooking up a rumour about you. As for me, I'm unimportant; nobody much cares who I sleep with. But it would be enough to have a suggestion made, say that your husband was friendly with my wife, for a lot of people to conclude that I was conspiring with you to cover it up.'

'But this is preposterous – you don't mean to say Richard imagines that . . .'

'Why not? You did.'

Colette looked at him with a sort of weary disbelief.

'My dear boy; I don't know whether the imaginative Monsieur Richard is trying to protect his department from any eventual criticism, or is setting you up as a scapegoat in the event of Monsieur Besson taking a dim view, but I don't know what you're using for brains. I am, despite my youth and innocence, aware of the dangers of a magistrate having things in his or her life – even private life – that he or she would prefer to conceal. And I'm aware that cops very easily get frightened lest even their wives' friendships should compromise their career. I suppose I shouldn't be surprised that an old wife like Richard has the mentality of the John Birch Society. I had thought better of you. I had imagined Vera's husband capable of understanding that a time sometimes comes when one just doesn't give a damn; when one wishes to give way to feelings that were originally those of a spontaneous and generous character. When one feels so hemmed about and encompassed by malice that one wishes to break out.'

She was taking deep breaths in order not to yell.

'I don't have much experience as a magistrate, or of life, but quite enough to know that the whole of society is based upon thinking ill of others, and that the chief pleasure of the human animal in all walks of life is back-biting.' She was working herself up now into a fine rage: what Bernard – who was wise enough to keep his mouth shut – called 'lashing her tail'.

'So that as one small section of educated persons we try to have a belief in civilization. Which is what? Perhaps a tiny effort now and again to raise ourselves above the level of plant biologists and fortune tellers, to believe that we aren't just animals concerned with nothing but fear, aggression and the satisfaction of the belly.'

Castang was just thinking that a university education served this much purpose at least, that emotional problems always got placed at the level of intellectual argument, when she came abruptly down to personalities.

'You're such an imbecile that you can't even see why I wanted to get drunk. It wasn't just for crude oblivion, you know. And I suppose I can't blame Richard if he has so little understanding as really to believe that Bernard or myself would use Rachel as a weapon against the other, whatever dirty tricks we may be capable of.'

'Good,' said Castang, 'I suppose you're right and I am a horrible prig. In all justice though, don't believe I'm bothered by evil notions Richard gets into his head. I came here to tease him a bit, it's true. You alarmed me because I thought you were getting a bit too reckless. The press is like a champagne bottle: if you want to get the cork off without noise it's as well not to shake it too roughly. You don't want to go to bed with me in the least; you've a vague notion of humiliating yourself and punishing Bernard for getting you in the shit, and punishing yourself for wanting to give him pain, and we're handy bananas.'

'Bananas?' asked Bernard, puzzled.

'Back in Cayenne – the Islands of Salvation, well named – the executioner used to test the guillotine on a banana stalk. Right thickness, right resistance.'

'Henri,' said Bernard softly, grinning, 'tell me one thing honestly. Did you believe – but it was there a moment you believed – that I was sleeping with your wife?'

'Oh if you want me to be quite honest . . . I'm a policeman; do you really believe I'll ever be that honest?'

'Wouldn't do you any harm to try,' said Colette.

'All right then if I'm going to be absolutely honest – for an instant. A very fleeting instant.' All three were laughing at Vera's outraged face. 'I would be readier, on the whole, to believe myself Colette's lover.'

'The wish being father to the thought,' said Vera tartly.

'Because we're really more reckless. Artists never are really. They pretend to be; big bohemian act of utter responsibility to an irresponsible ideal.'

'Huh?'

'All that asserting of their independence, pretending the rules don't apply to them. But unless they're very stupid there's generally a cold cunning little mind working away there, well able to judge what they will and what they won't get away with.'

Colette burst out laughing.

'So much for you and your kitchen-maids,' she told Bernard.

'Crime,' Castang told her meaningly, 'is only committed by the bourgeois.'

'You're calling yourself a bourgeois now?' Vera asked, interested.

'All policemen are bourgeois – conditioned by the rules of a bourgeois society, the principal characteristic of which is, as Colette pointed out, the willingness, readiness and insistence upon thinking ill of other people.'

'Did you come here thinking I'd go to bed with you?' asked Colette curiously.

'There was a moment when you felt quite ready to,' he told her.

'That's not an answer to my question,' said the magistrate.

'No Madame la Juge. Put it that I was aware that the moment existed.'

'Touché,' said Bernard.

'You conjugating that in the masculine or the feminine?' she wanted to know.

'I'll get you off the hook,' said Castang. 'I came here really to do a bit of work. As your partner Jérome puts it succinctly, no knickers-down allowed in my factory.'

'Now who's touché?' remarked Colette.

'I came to the conclusion I hadn't done a proper day's work.'

The whole atmosphere changed. It was like a refrigerator which has had what technicians blandly call the 'intelligence' to find itself constipated with masses of ice, and switches itself on to defrost. At a certain moment it decides that it is sufficiently purged, and starts freezing again.

'I want to put a certain number of questions.' Even the record-player in the corner, coming to the end of its meal of discs, fell silent.

'Your country house . . .'

'It's not really a house,' said Bernard automatically, 'it's just a shack still really. We own a certain amount of terrain, that's

157

all. Why don't you come out and see this weekend? – when we have Rachel back.'

'I may be out there even quicker.'

'But this is very odd. Are you thinking it has anything to do with . . .?'

'I don't know. It's been an odd day. Richard as you know has been mucking about – I suppose that's the right word – at the Palais all day. Looking at dossiers. Wondering why.'

'It is the right word,' muttered Colette. 'Shit-shovelling.'

'I spent the day hereabouts, tactically, huh, working out how. Going up and down the hill. Somewhere on that hill . . . she left the school. She set out for home. Carrying her bag. There's no doubt about it. The alleyway from the village – doesn't matter which, because they both meet at that Rampe.'

'It's odd; I've hardly ever been that way – I suppose because we don't do much in the village.'

'I shop there occasionally,' said Colette, 'and take the short cut home. But I've never noticed it particularly. One doesn't somehow, living up here.'

'Exactly. It's part of the village. Whereas you're townspeople, living out here by accident.'

'It's a sort of playground for the children.'

'And where – this preoccupied me – would she have been momentarily out of sight and away from the attention of the other children, the people who live there, all the potential witnesses to anything outside the ordinary pattern? There's precious little. There are just two places which form culs-de-sac, which might be fertile ground for the criminal attempt we now feel sure has taken place. I went over these very carefully, because I have the absolute conviction that she passed by there. Nothing else makes any sense. There's not a shred of a suggestion that she deviated from a familiar path. I'm not going to bore you by a round-by-round commentary. I brought a boy with me who had a camera, and he took pictures, a great many in close detail. There's nothing in them of any interest. Confused traces of feet and tyre tracks, too blurred to mean anything on that dry ground. The usual litter – well, that's police work; photos of old cigarette stubs and chewing-gum wrappers: one just does it to be thorough, just because somewhere, some time, one might find a link.

'In one of these blank corners we found a very promising suspect; dotty old boy with delusions and grievances about justice, quite unbalanced, lives there in ambush: for a moment there we thought we had it taped, whipped along to your colleague, Colette, got a search-warrant, and came up with a handful of dust – nothing, a dud – well, one's accustomed to that.

'The other place seemed as likely; children play forts there, and Indians, and probably father-and-mother: sort of overflow to a building site. But less promising too because overlooked by a nosy old biddy, and I'm witness she doesn't miss much. Technically less possibility. Good, I'm beginning to sound like Richard but it started giving some outline of the person, or brain if there's more than one, we have to deal with. Someone cunning, sly, and who'd thought out a clever trap. I don't mean intelligent in an intellectual sense: more in a military way: someone who knew how not to be conspicuous, how not to attract attention. I'm sure too it was planned, thought out by someone who took a good look at the terrain and knew instinctively where best to place his ambush. A countryman, I'd bet, because it's not an urban landscape, it hasn't the characteristics of an urban ambush, and also because there's a piece of physical evidence; it's not connected in any way, but neither is it connected to anything else, around here.'

'And this is?' inquired the judge coldly.

'I said a handful of dust; should have said rabbit-shit. A rabbit was wandering about there. I make three conclusions. People have rabbits anywhere, also there, but nobody lets them loose, because as it was put to me flatly there're too many cars and too many boys. Now that's, you'll agree, a good bait for an eight-year-old girl. Ambles about and hops. Cuddly – no urban, I mean flat-bred, child resists that. Because it's the most satisfying sort of toy. An urban mentality could perfectly well think of that, it seems to me, but where would he get a rabbit, how would he handle it, where would he keep it? It's the weak part, which stinks of contrivance and fiction, in *The Hound of the Baskervilles*. Fellow had to invent a whole enormous melodrama of pathless bogs and abandoned moorlands and unworked mines and whatnot, because of where to keep the bloody hound, which is a hell of an awkward thing. He's a sort of undersized harmless-looking butterfly chaser, and how does he organize this savage beast, painting its muzzle with phosphorus and all – it's just idiotic, unless of course you happen to fall under the spell of that Sherlock crap, which needs, to be at all convincing, the assumption that all policemen from start to finish are totally cretinous as well as craven. The Scotland Yard Inspector, when he sees the hound, gives a yell of terror and falls flat on his face, though a moment before he was making with the big pistol. That's typical faking. In real life of course the slowest and most rustic village cop would have, one, cleared the whole job up in three days and two, told that great bull-shitter Holmes to fuck off out of that and stop his fancy posturing. Sorry Mister, the law-enforcement around here is me. Now, sorry for the parenthesis, the country cop here is me, and the hound's a rabbit, and that's a thing a countryman thinks of and uses because he can handle it effortlessly, it's unforced, it's natural; sorry, I'm getting heated. Richard doesn't see it, because he's full of fancy Freudian notions about Bernard having cooked this up as a fancy way of punishing Colette's clever little adulteries. Which is, if you'll forgive the expression, a load of rabbit-shit.'

'Prolix,' said the judge, 'and you could have spared us the fiction bit, but a cogent argument.'

'Somebody whom nobody'd notice, in what is after all a kind of no-man's land but has a village atmosphere still. Somebody who could park an old car there with a bit of hay and some rabbits in the back. Somebody who could talk to a child without arousing automatic fear and distrust. Young, old, male, female, dotty, undotty, a howling psychopath or just a dimwit peasant with a grievance, which is all old Léon, the suspect I mentioned, is really. I haven't a clue, but I'm interested in your neighbours in the country.'

Bernard looked at him blankly. I can see, the look said, why you're barking up this particular tree, but there's nothing in it: I've climbed it.

'Well,' polite, 'of course it's true that you've never been out there. I mean to say, yes, there's a tiny one-horse dorp, which overlooks the valley, and of course all the peasant homes are built carefully facing away from the view, and then there's a bum road which makes a big loop and rejoins the main road about five kilometres further, and up there it's even prettier. The view's getting spoiled of course because people are building. We have a big field, and a few trees, and a big brambly hedge which shelters us from the road. It's all very humble – just a prefab wooden chalet. But we've managed to get a well sunk, and a septic tank, and electricity, and we'd like to build, but keeping small and very simple: fieldstone, and a terrace for looking at the sunset.' Castang nodded.

'And as for the neighbours there aren't any, because one side is a sort of broken ravine and the other side is a dentist from the town and we've no troubles there because we agree to disregard the other and we both put up a belt of trees to form a hedge.'

'And the people you bought the land from – no grievances? No dispute about the boundaries?'

'No – all marked clearly in the cadastral survey.'

'And Colette's never had any legal dealings with the villagers or even in the district? – drunk boys beating up the local dance hall or whatever? Or even just local rancour?'

'No,' she said. 'Villagers – you know . . . As long as one doesn't pretend to ostentation or airs of superiority.'

'And above all not mix in local politics,' added Bernard.

'Just a question of tact really. Be polite to everybody, the more so when they're a bit sour, buy a bit from the local shop, let them cut the hay on the field.'

'Mm,' said Castang.

The telephone rang.

\*

Rachel had watched the television with Christine, who sat quiet and said nothing, and didn't show much curiosity. But Christine was much smaller than her, and a year or more younger. She still had all her milk teeth. Or 'all' thought Rachel, is a manner of speaking as Papa says. Her mouth smelt, and Rachel tried not to get too near her. The teeth were all discoloured, with sort of blue patches. She knew about that, because Papa went on at her about eating sweets, and had terrifying tales about English children, who all had false teeth. It was more disgusting than terrifying: like here. She went to Monsieur Combes too, who was not at all terrifying, though Mama pretended he was, calling him the 'Anticlerical' and making jokes about pulling Jesuits'

161

teeth out which Rachel failed to understand, because Monsieur Combes was the gentlest soul alive, spoke in a soft whisper like Mère Marie-Dominique (but she rather hated her, because of a slimy way of talking about 'the dear child') and above all was always honest.

'This won't hurt at all' – it didn't.

'This might hurt a little – tell me if it does and I'll stop' – and he did.

'This will hurt a lot but only for a second.' He didn't tell lies.

Time passed not unpleasantly. The young man, and the atrocious greasy Carney, and the old man too sat watching the television, drinking beer, and jug-er-wine, sucking their teeth (Monsieur Combes would be anticlerical with them all right; all rotten, noted Rachel scandalized) and saying nothing. And the hideous young woman sat smoking like a chimney, looking at the television, looking at her a lot. Rachel tried not to look, not to see, and not to think.

The old woman put big black frying-pans on the stove. The food smelt good, though it looked queer, whenever she dared give a round-the-corner glance. When it was ready the old woman gave a sort of grunt, and they just all 'drew up' as they were around the table. It wasn't cleared or anything: the beer glasses and the jug-er-wine and the ashtrays (stolen she knew from cafés because they had 'Cinzano' written on them) stayed as they were. Greasy steel cutlery was handed out; soup bowls were slapped in front of everyone. Nobody paid any heed; they just went on looking at the telly. The soup was *bouillon gras* with white beans and bits of carrot. It looked horrid but tasted good: she was hungry. It was the kind of farmer's soup Papa always said he loved. Everyone tore off great hunks of bread, and they all soaked that in the soup till it was like porridge, and then sucked that up: bouh.

There was a lot to eat. There were pancakes, very big thick ones, with bits of bacon in and onions, and big pieces of parsley. They smelt simply delicious but were very clawky. She couldn't finish hers, and was frightened, because at home she had to finish her plate no matter what. But she was – unexpectedly – supported by Marie-Thérèse. She didn't finish hers either.

'Those things would choke an elephant,' she said in her hoarse growl. And Christine didn't get any, and left half her soup, and was not punished. The men ate all theirs, and a big panful of sauté potatoes too. Rachel loved sauté potatoes, and didn't get any, and didn't dare ask.

Then there were beans, the beans she had helped with, and in which she felt a sort of proprietary pride, so that she ate them gladly though she had hardly any appetite left, and was glad she did because they were delicious; one had to be fair, much nicer than green beans at home, cooked just right, still all crisp and crunchy and with a marvellous flavour, and she knew this was because they were out of the garden, and it was like that special restaurant where she had once been taken where Papa and Mama went once a year just to eat asparagus because it too had just been picked.

Then there was cheese which she didn't get offered and was glad of it, because she didn't like cheese, and couldn't eat any more anyway. She hoped there would be fruit, because in the country there generally was, and was disappointed because there wasn't any, not even cherries.

'All right,' said the old woman when they were finished. 'Go play with Christine.' She was relieved because she had wondered whether she shouldn't volunteer to help with the washing up. In the country she always did it with Papa, because there was no machine for the dishes there. Papa washed, very meticulous and exact, everything in its proper place, and she dried. She couldn't wash because the water was too hot for her hands. Mama 'cleared'. Papa said that women had no notion how to wash up properly, and Mama said in that case why didn't he cook too, and sometimes they got heated and exchanged insults, but it never lasted long.

'Don't ever let the sun go down on your anger,' as Mama put it.

Christine was not much fun to play with. She was passive, as Mademoiselle Lassagne said about fat Véronique. And there were innumerable things which weren't allowed. She wasn't allowed out, but Christine wasn't either. It was unhealthy. Children needed fresh air. That was perhaps why she was so puddingy and had rotten teeth. And she didn't know how to skip or how to play with a ball. They played *marelle* where you mark squares with chalk and hop from one foot and nudge a stone from one square to another, but Christine was no good. Too small anyway. And she kept showing off.

'You haven't got animals in your home.' 'You haven't a garden.'

'You haven't even dogs.'

Well, one wouldn't want dogs like that. There were three, and they were shut in a sort of wire enclosure, which was very dirty, and they'd done caca all over the place, and they smelt simply horrible, and they spat when you went at all close. She got a bit of beastly saliva on the back of her hand and rubbed it as though it burnt: bouh. And that stupid Christine seemed not even to notice how they smelt. She was snoof. Papa's word for someone who can't smell; like deaf. But she was too little: she didn't understand. At the same time she was quite clean. She had a checked overall as apron. Rachel wished she had an apron. She'd left hers at school, because it wasn't the day for changing it. Her skirt was stained, and her top grubby, and Mama would be cross, and Rachel understood that because she wasn't happy about it. She wished she were at home, and could have a shower and get a clean frock. No shower here. Not even a bathroom. No wonder everything smelt so.

Marie-Thérèse suddenly appeared. Rachel winced because she thought she would get a slap. But it was Christine that got the slap. For no apparent reason. She didn't seem to mind. Used to it, perhaps. She didn't even cry. Snivelled a bit, but Rachel knew perfectly that one can always produce a snivel; it doesn't mean necessarily one is hurt or anything. She snivelled herself, even though Mama said cuttingly that snivellers were to be despised. But she wouldn't snivel here: she'd rather die.

'All right. Bed.' And they went. Just like that. They didn't have to wash. Their hair wasn't done. Christine had hers cut short in a mop, but it was dull and dirty. Rachel's was long, and had been loose all day. It had gone straggly. She would have liked to brush it. She couldn't plait it by herself, or put it up. There wasn't a brush. There wasn't even a comb.

They went to the attic. The attic was nice, with rough boards, and a good smell of hay. Christine had a wooden bed. She had only a folding canvas camp bed on a metal frame, but she didn't mind that: it was much the same as she had when they were in the shack. But there were nasty features. The blanket smelt musty. The sheet was clean, though. And that beastly little Christine had a pot to pee in, filthy little beast. She wasn't going to pee in any pot! The lav was repugnant, but she'd rather go down two flights of wooden ladder and stairs, and go out near those horrible dogs which barked and threw themselves against the wire grille and spat through it: anything rather than pee in a pot which one kept in one's bedroom all night; that was the pink limit, as Granny said. Granny was Mama's mother, and had a country house with a marvellous smell outside Toulouse, and when they were there Rachel got a bedroom with wonderful faded flowers printed on cotton, which Granny called 'chintz' – funny word which made her laugh.

She wasn't frightened of a strange bed. She had slept in many odd hotels, and in the country she had camped with Papa, on a bed made of freshly cut spruce branches. Under the sky even. There was a *chouette* – a barn owl, which was frightening; Dracula might come. But Papa had his rifle, and a tomahawk.

Nobody came to *border* the two little girls. Mama came – not always but regularly – to 'tuck one in': this was a female ritual, which men did not understand: Papa did not know how. She didn't care. Nobody would want to be *bordée* by Marie-Thérèse: thanks, one would rather have Dracula. Come to think of it Marie-Thérèse much resembled Dracula. She at least had white teeth, but such biting teeth.

The worst of all was that the little pig made such a fuss about the window. It was only a skylight, but it would open, and Rachel wanted to open it. And that idiotic baby-pig Christine yapped and cowered and complained and said she'd call Ma. It was dangerous, she said. Dangerous! As though Dracula would come. There wasn't any Dracula. Rachel knew that perfectly well. One was very frightened of him, but he didn't exist, which was silly but there it was. There were plenty of things which didn't exist, but which one accepted. To set against Dracula there was the guardian angel, and the *Sainte Vierge*, the *Bonne Mère* who looked after small children. She had never seen them, and plenty of people said they didn't exist, but they kept off Dracula.

'Yah,' said Rachel silently. 'Beastly baby.'

She began to cry, rackingly, but stifling it under that musty blanket. Christine might not be asleep, and she wasn't going to cry in front of that rotten-toothed snot. Anything rather than alert that horrible Marie-Thérèse.

She wished Jackie was here. He'd open the window. She wondered for a long time whether she dared. Finally she crept out and opened it. Bouh, it was stiff. But she managed it noiselessly.

Deathly tired, aching, crying again a bit, Rachel fell asleep, with despite everything a sense of triumph. She couldn't get away, but at least she'd got the window open.

The cock woke her up, crowing, in the morning.

She dressed as quickly as she could. The house seemed still but she couldn't tell; somebody might come creeping. The old woman puffed and grunted, and the stairs creaked under her weight, but she had noticed that the young woman could move catlike when she wanted, perfectly noiseless. Very like a cat, too, that baleful, unwinking green gaze.

Only she couldn't stay still like a cat: she fidgeted and picked at her fingernails.

Rachel was worried about her clothes. Her undies were not too bad, and would do another day at a pinch. And it was a pinch. But she had tried her best not to get them grimy. Mama would certainly have made her change her pants but Mama, desolatingly, was not here. Mama would be very worried. And Papa would be upset, and when he got upset he was liable to get very cross with her. How to make them understand that it wasn't her fault? And that it was even very unfair. She hadn't done anything that was forbidden. She had followed the usual path: well, not perhaps quite the usual path but she hadn't been in the mood for playing with Jackie. He was so noisy sometimes. And she and Véronique had had a tiff. Not really a quarrel; they'd 'had words' and Véronique had *boudé*, gone off without speaking to her.

Perhaps she was being punished for being nasty to Véronique. She had been stolen. People did steal little girls sometimes, and did horrible things to them. Such people were not in their right mind. That was one of the reasons why one had to come straight home, and leave a note if one went out to play again after having one's *goûter*. And the principal reason why one must not talk to strange men or even women, nor let them talk to one.

Well, she hadn't. It wasn't for that she was being punished.

She hadn't done anything, truly. She had only looked at the rabbit. Had it been wrong, to pick up the rabbit? It was from that moment only that things had gone wrong. But the young man hadn't been cross at her picking it up. On the contrary, he had seemed pleased. Surely it wasn't that which had made him so cross and touchy. Later, she knew very well, he was cross and nervous because he had stolen her, and was afraid of being seen and noticed. Did he know that Mama was a judge, and could send all the police in the town after him? Rachel was sure she had, too, but they hadn't found her. She was well hidden. She didn't know how far they had come, but it was a long way.

The pants had to do. What she would do tonight she didn't know. Perhaps Papa, or the police, would have come by then. But they would need to be strong.

She had had to sleep in her vest and knickers; a dirty thing to do, but she had no pyjamas, and no nighty. Prisoners, and she knew she was a prisoner, got given special clothes when they went to prison. Rough scratchy prison clothes, because they were being punished. Would she get given prison clothes? She hoped so. She wouldn't mind their being scratchy so long as they were clean. This house was so dirty. Not really dirty that there was dust everywhere and a filthy mess and everything slummy and untidy. But it did smell so.

Christine slept in her knickers, under her nighty. A dirty thing to do. One more reason for despising the little horror.

Her socks were very dirty. They would just have to do.

Rachel crept downstairs very softly. In the kitchen the clock with the loud tick and the vulgar bonging chime said twenty to six. Early. There was no sound in the house. She put on her shoes carefully, not to make a clatter. She wanted badly to do pipi; she tried not to think about this. That place was so horrid and stinky. And it would make a noise. She would put it off as long as she could hold out.

She studied the door which led to outside. There was a big lock, and the key in it. There were big bolts as well.

Suddenly a wild flutter of hope rose in Rachel. The door led to the street. Not far away, she knew, was a village. How far? She didn't know. But even if it were far, a kilometre, she could perhaps run. If they were all still sleeping. A kilometre was no further than the distance to school. She could run. It was downhill too. By six there would be people, a baker open. In the country people were early. But would the baker be perhaps friends with these dreadful people? In the country they were all in clans. Papa had always said that one must never get involved with the village people because they were all cousins or cousins-in-law. And they stuck together, to their wife's cousins as to their own. *Maqués ensemble* was Papa's phrase. But surely there'd be someone who would think it not right to keep little girls prisoner. Somebody would agree to phone the gendarmerie. Perhaps the gendarmes would be still in bed, but they'd get up for a surety when they were told that a little girl was held prisoner, and had escaped. Come quick before the dreadful people find out, and chase me.

Rachel took a chair, very softly, climbed up, and tugged at the top bolt. It was oiled; it came quite easily. So did the bottom bolt. That left the lock. She wrestled with it. It was very stiff. The big key gave plenty of grip, but she was not strong; it didn't turn easily. She got up on the chair to get more leverage.

It turned: it was coming.

Behind her a harsh voice cackled with laughter.

She turned in a great hurry, terrified that it was the cat, the dreaded dreadful Marie-Thérèse. It wasn't, thank God. It was the old woman. Rachel had been so concentrated on wrestling with the horrible great key she hadn't heard anyone. And all dressed too, in her skirt and her apron, and the woolly bedroom slippers she wore all the time. She was angry; her hand went up: Rachel cowered. But she did not get the smack she expected. The old woman laughed again, hoarsely.

'Thought you'd run away, ey? Thought you'd open the door without noise. But I was watching. It wouldn't work even when I wasn't. There's a bell on it, outside, see. Can't open it without the bell rings.'

'But there wasn't; last night I mean.' Again the cackle.

'Puts it on at night, we do. Can't nobody open the door without I hear.' And suddenly angry, 'Cheeky little bitch.'

The hand swung up again, but Rachel was a quick learner. The hand flew up, but it didn't always fly down. It was a menace, no more. She had seen the hand fly up to cuff Christine too, for whining. Christine was a great whiner. Papa, who was peppery, would have cuffed Christine a few times. Even Mademoiselle

Lassagne, who never cuffed anyone, would have become impatient.

'Now Christine, stop pitying yourself. That's the way to earn a slap.'

Because Mademoiselle Lassagne virtually never gave anyone a slap, this was the ultimate menace. Even Jackie dreaded a slap from that thin hand with its sparkly diamond ring. ('Mademoiselle has a boy friend!') These great meaty hands flew up far more often, and somehow the menace wore off. Devalued, as Papa said laughing.

'You watch it, and no cheekiness, or you get the back of my hand.'

They weren't 'out of their mind'. Or Rachel didn't think so. The young man, twitching and muttering. Maybe he was out of his mind. And ghoulish Dracula-Marie-Thérèse. She could well be out of her mind. Still she hadn't hit Rachel yet. Christine had got slapped. Four times; Rachel had counted. For not having poured milk for the cats (the animals, here, seemed to have a much better life than the children). For wailing when the television got switched to the other channel. For having dirty underclothes (but they still hadn't been changed, and Rachel had really found that difficult to understand. 'You just go on wearing them, dirty pup, or I'll rub your nose in them.' Rachel had cowered, under her blanket). And for talking, late at night. Marie-Thérèse had 'come creeping'.

'You keep your mouth shut now, hear me. You get a clip round the ear-ole now.' And she'd got it, though mostly on the hair, and Rachel had been ashamed for her. To yell so hard for relatively little, though it would hurt, that bony knuckly hand.

She got breakfast. This was nice. A big bowl of milky coffee, and she only got coffee at home on Sundays. It wasn't as nice coffee, having a strong taste of caramel and chicory and not really very much taste of coffee, but was, recognizably, coffee, and not just baby cocoa.

Carney appeared, unshaven and horrible, sullenly sourly saying nothing but unlocking the door.

'Hey. The bolts are drawn.'

'Yes. The little'un thought it'd make a getaway.'

And two thick satisfied cackles of laughter. But not really cruel. More just brutal.

'Is brutality worse than cruelty?' Mama asked Vera one day. Nice and pretty Vera, who taught her how to dance and do gymnastics, and whom she was allowed to call 'Vera' and not 'Madame Castang'. Vera who had bad legs and limped, but who had such finely-shaped and terribly strong pretty hands; short and somehow stubby but somehow too beautifully shaped. Vera who had made her such a lovely drawing of horses playing and prancing, which she had pinned up in her room. Her eyes filled with tears.

'Stop snivelling, little'un.'

'No,' said Vera, 'surely brutality can never be as bad as cruelty. Brutality is just stupidity. I ought to know. Once I had a cruel schoolmistress. She made us suffer in a quiet voice.'

Oh Vera. Even with her limping legs, Vera was very tough. And Vera was a gymnast and knew judo too. 'Next time Jackie is horrid to you, you catch him so, and drop your shoulder and swing your hip so – oh you, you've too much tummy.'

'Do it again,' laughing to find herself on the floor.

'So! You try that – that'll astonish Jackie's weak nerves!'

All dirty as he was with black bristles all over, Carney went out, and she heard a car start noisily, and he was back a few minutes later with wonderful big country bread smelling good, *miches*, big round blackened loaves. The old woman cut them in thick slices in the old-fashioned peasant way, the first time Rachel had ever seen it, clutching them up to her huge solid apron-bosom, and making a sign of the cross over them with the fist holding the knife, and cutting them into the apron. It did not astonish Rachel. Mama did the same thing, in a different way. Sometimes laughing a little, but always serious, 'because I come of a bourgeois family', Mama always made a cross over bread, with her finger, the way Papa with his thumb made a cross on her forehead when he said good night. Rachel was never allowed to waste or throw away bread. 'But why?' 'Because it is our daily bread,' said Mama, quite fiercely, 'and we ask God daily for our bread, and we are grateful, because you know very well how many children have to do without. And because it is the greatest of all symbols; Christ chose the bread to be him, and it is our promise and our hope.' Which Rachel understood perfectly well. And whether they were brutal, or cruel, or both, it was somehow less bad.

And it was nice bread too. And she could dip it in her coffee, which at home was forbidden.

Infinitely to her relief, Carney took away Marie-Thérèse 'to work'. And infinitely to her own surprise and anger with herself, they took away Christine. She cried, and was ashamed. Christine was such a drip, and a dirty little thing into the bargain. But Rachel had looked forward to playing with her. And was jealous too, because Christine was bumped into an overall, and had her face scrubbed (but her hair wasn't properly brushed, and she didn't do her teeth) because she had to go to school, and at that minute Rachel wished she were going to school with almost as much passion as she normally wished to be going home after an ordinary, quiet, rather boring day's school.

The young man wasn't there either. It was midmorning before she plucked up the courage to ask the old man where he was.

'He's at work.'

'But at night?' puzzled.

'Sure. They're on shift. He's on nights this week. He'll be back,' with that toothless sly giggle smelling brassy of old wine and nasty old corks and the horrible coppery taste of the thick heavy little pot Mama used for making sauce hollandaise on fish days, which always had to be so particularly scrubbed and burnished.

But the morning was quiet. The old ones pottered about. Only once was Rachel harshly treated, really imprisoned, when the butcher's van suddenly parked and tooted just outside the door, and the old one suddenly took her by the collar and pushed her in the 'larder' and locked the door on her. Rachel decided not to kick, at the door, and not to scream, because the hand which went up would, she knew, this time come down, hard.

'You make a noise, and I'll . . .' She was quiet, and she was let out inside a quarter of an hour.

She was not allowed out. She would have liked to go out and do some gardening. At home in the country she could do gardening. She had a garden, with snowdrops and crocuses in spring, and different things in summer (this year she had orange and yellow and red nasturtiums, and taller, elegant, feathery blue flax flowers, of a very lovely blue which Papa said was her eyes). And for the autumn, at the back of her border, there were orange and yellow chrysanths, but a totally different orange-and-yellow from the nasturtiums, much deeper, much more autumny, and also tall rain-smelling Michaelmas daisies. It was dreadfully much work because there were so many weeds, and there were slugs and other nasty beasts, and sometimes she rather hated the garden and was bored with it, but here she would have gladly gardened, but it was not allowed, and she had to peel potatoes, which was not nice, and courgettes which had a rough unattractive skin, and aubergines which were lovely, so dark and blue-violet and beautiful, but beastly difficult and slippery and tiring.

The old woman would have helped her, she thought, because rough as she was she wasn't really beastly, but just at that minute the young man appeared. He was beastly. She had to fetch beer again, and minister to him, and put away his boots, and peel the vegetables alone, and she didn't cut herself but it nicked into her finger at the side and the thumb on the ball and made them sore, but she had to do it.

'No lazing,' he said. 'Get on with it, and if it's not properly done you get the stick across your arse, understand?' She didn't think she would be beaten, not really beaten on the behind with a stick. But she wasn't going to risk finding out. Being beaten would be fearful enough, but being beaten by that horrid, atrocious, ghastly young man would be the most horrible thing she could imagine. Even being beaten by Marie-Thérèse would not be worse. Still, she wasn't beaten, but only because she worked terribly hard. After dinner, thank God, she was allowed to lie down on the bed and sleep. The young man went to bed as well. Thank God. She didn't sleep properly, because when she woke up it was the same time as yesterday, when she had been stolen. The young man was not there with his hot greedy not-right-in-the-head eyes, but she had been prisoner a whole day and a whole night. And Papa had not come, nor had the gendarmes, and she was helpless, and the kitchen floor had to be swept and washed, and a sort of dreadful routine had set in, and soon the filthy Carney would be back again, and the dreadful woman with him, and that horrid Christine whom she no longer looked forward to playing with though she had been longing to all day, and her undies were filthy now, and so was her frock with no apron, and what was she going to do?

172

The day passed quietly enough, and even quickly, because there was lots to do. The house was much bigger than it looked. At the back there was a warren of rooms in one of which the old ones slept, in the middle of a strange heap of tools and flowerpots, and upstairs a kind of 'flat' where Carney lived: these rooms smelt of Marie-Thérèse, a sort of shrill scent in which the only element Rachel could distinguish was the smell of carnations, and she loathed carnations. She didn't know why, but they were nearly her most unfavourite flower. She was afraid to go into these rooms. There was a hairbrush with a lot of hair caught in its bristles, which made her shudder. She had to sweep these rooms and dust them, which was like Cinderella and not really disagreeable at all, or need not have been were it not for the hairbrush. The old woman floundered about, and abused her shrilly a few times, but she had learned not to be too alarmed at this, and that the yelling was not totally stranger to a sort of rough kindness. And everyone else was away. Even the old man had set out early with a scythe, to cut the tall grass and make hay of it. And when he came back she brought him a juger-wine, which she had learned how to draw properly, from the barrel in the cellar, and afterwards she went with him while he did the animals, in the strange conglomeration of sheds and shacks at the back, cunningly built with the weirdest odds and ends: a true 'bidonville'. Already she had learned not to mind the hot jungly animaly smell. It was only the enclosure where the dogs were kept that frightened her: nasty beasts, leaping and slavering and throwing themselves against the wire and barking hysterically every time she was seen by them. But it was not really because of the dogs that she had so terrible a fright.

They were going to look at the baby ducks when her eye was caught by another enclosure of wire, wedged between the dogs and the house of the rabbits, with a wall built of old boards, and a lean-to sort of roof of fir-poles supporting old tiles, which was empty. The pig had been kept there, Christine had told her, but the pig had been killed for bacon, with a very sharp knife and a great pot of boiling water ... Rachel had not wanted to listen to that bit, but she had listened. The old man had cleared it out since last night, and there was a bundle of fresh hay there.

'Are you going to get another pig?' Rachel asked.

The old man grinned his toothless grin.

'That's for you,' he said.

Rachel shrank away, frozen, feeling herself go quite white and bloodless.

She had heard of people fainting, but had never understood how it was done, and now she realized, because she felt her legs would refuse to hold her up. They were witches. Now she knew why Marie-Thérèse was like Dracula. They were going to keep her like the pig, and make her fat and then one morning they would come with the very sharp knife and the great pot of boiling water... She had wondered and wondered why they had stolen her. She knew now. It was to eat her. Like cannibals but there were no cannibals here. There were witches, though. Jackie had told her that people used to believe this about Jews, and this was why some people still didn't like Jews. It didn't sound very likely, in fact a typical Jackie fantasy, but Papa when asked said it was true, that at one time the peasants used to believe this. She could see now; the witches were cunning, and when a little girl vanished they blamed it on the Jews. The horrible old man cackled at her terror.

'Joke,' he said with his piggy little eyes all shiny. Rachel knew it wasn't a joke. She crept into the kitchen and sat on her chair, not daring to move at all. The old woman said nothing. Perhaps despite everything the old woman would save her. But Marie-Thérèse was stronger, as well as being a witch. When Marie-Thérèse came back ...

But when she came back (Rachel had prayed against all hope that the car would break down, that something, anything would happen; and when she heard as she had known she would the noise of the motor outside she thought she would faint, again; she prayed she would, so that she would be unconscious and not know, when the terrible fierce hands reached out to take hold of her ...) nothing happened. The witch just looked at her with dull bored eyes, and only said irritably, 'Go play with Christine. I'm tired; I don't want to look at yer.' Only too thankful, Rachel crept out. But she could not play; she felt so dulled and tired, and her legs would not carry her. She sat down in the angle of the wall and the floor, outside in the passage, and Christine nothing loath sat down alongside, smelling as usual of pipi but Rachel was too numb to object. As long as nobody came out.

But nobody came out. The old woman was making the supper, and the old man was tired now, and the young one, who had been busy all afternoon in the side cellar which was like a junk-yard full of rusty iron and bits of old motors, seemed tired too; he had got his own beer, and had been sitting for nearly an hour, dully staring and smoking and biting his nails, and seemed un-interested in her.

She didn't want to know, and at the same time she did want dreadfully to know. She wanted to listen. She knew that listen-ing at doors was bad manners and she didn't care. What man-ners had these people? She wanted to know because there was a corner of her mind that still refused to believe in the knife and the witches, and she had to know, and in there they were talking about her: she knew that because Papa too said 'go out and play' when he was going to talk about her. And Christine wouldn't give her away because she wanted to listen too. Rachel hated that but somehow accepted it.

It was easy to listen because they shouted. They always did shout. Every conversation was like an argument. But they were arguing too. They mumbled, and when they all shouted together it was difficult to disentangle. But she could get the drift. And the drift was at least partly reassuring. They were frightened. They wanted to get rid of her. But it was not at all reassuring as it developed, because they were frightened, and they might kill her: that much she knew from Mama.

'Why do people kill people?'

'Nearly always because they are frightened.'

'But why are they frightened?'

'Sometimes because they are ill and suffer pain, or imagine they do. And sometimes for no reason. Why are you fright-ened? No reason at all, generally. It happens to us, and then we have to try and reason our way out of it.'

'I'm sicka the sight ofa.'

'Easy for you. You're away all day. What did you wanta for, then?'

'We got what we wanted. Made them shit. They're frightened all right.'

'You can't just bringa back.'

'Too true. Place'll be crawling with cops. Just take her away 'n' leta loose some place.'

'She'll tell.'

'What can she tell? We've been over all that. I told ya I'll tell ya again, they'll never catch on. Not in a million years.'

'Dopy just to leta go now we gota. Screwem a bit first.'

'How?'

'Telephone.'

'You think that's clever? Be listening. I know how they work. Ya voice give ya away.'

'I'm not going to leta go just like that. Where's the satisfaction? I want to hearem squeak. What else was it good for? You're not going to phone anyway, you're such a fool, you'd give it away.'

'Fool is it? Who gota? Who thought how to geta? Not you. And you keep your mouth shut, where I am, see, the whores keep still and let the men talk.'

'You hearing that, Carney? You going to stand for that?'

'You shut up. Carney can shut up too or I'll beltem. I never married no prostitute.'

The voice of the witch would have gone through all the walls in the house.

'You shut up and you hear me, Pierrot stupid cretin, what are you but a pig peasant? Where I come from the girls keep quiet for their men and not for no yobbo out the cowshed with the shit sticking the straw in's hair, you just try me, monkey, and you'll find I don't need no Carney to help handle you, when the cops got you you sung real small.'

'Shut up the both of you,' the old woman's voice. 'You, Pierrot, don't use that talk about your brother's woman, and you, girl, mind that evil mouth of yours and let the man speak.'

'I was always against.'

'You're against anything might threaten your belly, 's all you think of. Think y'selves all smart for gettinga, any kid with half a bollock could do as much, but how to handle it then takes brains and who got brains? Me.'

'And me.'

'Y' got a few dots 'n' you too scared to use'm. S'now I'll tell you, 'n' belt up 'n' listen. Phone you say. Right, I'm all for it, make them shit and hear them at it, I ask nothing better. Tellem we gota, now come'n'finda. Or what's left ofa.' And the witch broke into a squawk of laughter so horrible that Rachel could not bear to hear any further. She crawled away along the passage and up the stairs, the harsh voice pursuing.

'Not from no phone box because that they can trace. Y'got to have an automatic phone because that they can't and we know that where I come from which isn't the sticks, and you just leave this to me. You can listen if you like, get a kick out of it.'

Rachel heard no more. She dragged herself up to the attic, lay down on her bed, and thought she was going to cry, but somehow she was too numb for that. She fell asleep. She hadn't paid any attention to Christine. The little slop would run and tell, no doubt. She just didn't care. Nobody could help her now. The witch was too strong.

\*

When the phone rang they were none of them alert for it: even Bernard's fibres had been loosened to the extent that he only rolled himself along the sofa towards the stupid thing. Jérome, probably, fussing about tomorrow's 'board meeting' as he called the weekly sit-in with the accountant and the sales head.

'Delavigne,' he said in a voice which was not slurred – he had not had all that much to drink, just enough to be comfortable.

'That you, Delavigne?' said a woman's voice, sharp and suspicious.

'In person,' said Bernard boredly. Sounded like a long-distance operator. Probably be Martial – ridiculous name for a salesman – from Barcelona: they were making inroads on the holiday-camp circuit, and he would be fussing again about supplies.

'You lost anything, Delavigne?' said the sharp grating woman's voice, instead of the expected, 'Hold the line please.'

Bernard sat up abruptly. Colette was already snatching the spare earpiece. Castang's hand came down gently on hers, and held it between their two ears.

'Who is calling please?' said Bernard in a neutral voice.

'Ha!' Screech of laughter, jangling the mike. 'Like to know that, I bet. This is confidential. Friend, say, who wishes you well.'

'What is it then? Get on with it, whatever it is.' Good, thought Castang. You're not stupid, whatever else. That's the way; irritate her, make her clack.

'You'd love to know, ey? Just love it.'

'You've got a wrong number,' said Bernard, and hung up.

'Bloody good,' said Castang, delighted.

'But ... why did you cut off? It's news – news of whatever kind, we must hear it.' Colette, innocently bewildered.

'Have no fear,' said Castang. 'She'll ring back. Hasn't sung her song. Don't worry. This is it. Let it ring three or four times, Bern, get her stretched.' When the phone rang again they all four sat as though paralysed, glaring at it greedily, as though it were a chilled bottle of Roederer, beautifully sweating with condensation, appeared by magic down in the obscure rockface chamber, in the deep places of the salt mine. The sweat was standing on Bernard's forehead.

'Patience,' said Castang gently, bringing his voice up over the jarring ring of the phone. 'For-ti-tude.'

'You being funny, Delavigne? I'm the one who's laughing.'

'Let me in on the joke. What is all this?'

'You'd like to find what you lost, wouldn't you?'

'What do I have to do – offer a reward?'

'You think everything's for sale, don't you, because you never had any dealings with honest people, ever. You got a lot to learn. You need to start getting a bit grateful and learn to be less proud-stomached. How did your first day go? You know what I reckon? – that in a few more days you won't be sounding so cocky.'

'You rang up just for a nice chat, is that it?' Bernard was keeping his voice even but his free hand was making nervous circling gestures, asking for something. Colette and Castang stared at him puzzled. It was Vera who looked in her handbag, hitched herself off the edge of her chair, and gave him a paper hanky. Bernard gave her a grateful look and mopped at his face and neck. The voice was coming faster as it gained in confidence.

'A nice chat, a nice chat,' mimicking his voice sarcastically, 'yes, that's what it is for me because this time it's us that's on top, we can take things easy, we don't have to come and go when you blow the whistle. I got news for your wife too, if she is your wife. She's the judge, huh, sits there without a worry in the world giving orders. Saying,' mock pinched accent, 'Oh, pleeceman, take these ruffians away and lock them up. But this time I'm giving the orders and you're there sweating.'

Bernard's hand with the hanky in it stopped abruptly and he gave a startled glance at the telephone; a thing to make one laugh, ordinarily.

'If you have a proposition, make it.' His fist with the balled-up hanky made a jagged jab at his glass: Castang picked it up and put it carefully in his hand. He tucked the receiver into his neck while he swallowed and fumbled for a cigarette he couldn't find: he was sitting on the packet.

'Oh, a proposition?' The voice was secure now: it had him reined in. 'You mean like some sort of contract where you give us something and we give you what you want, is that it? Let me tell you, I wouldn't make any agreement with you, not over as much as a pound of tomatoes. I wouldn't trust you not to break it, because I know your lot, nothing but a pack of twisters.'

'Since you've just rung up to call me names,' said Bernard calmly, 'consider it done and go on back to bed.'

'Not so fast, big shot, just remember we're on top now and we tell you what can be done and what can't be done. You want her back, don't you?'

'Naturally.'

'Nat-u-rally,' mimicking. 'All cold, like you couldn't care one way or another, trying to beat the price down.'

Bernard took the phone away from his ear, put it down on his lap, closed his eyes and breathed very slowly, deep in, deep out, wiped his face again, and picked the thing up afresh.

'What use is this? Suggest something concrete, straightforwardly, and I'll give you a straightforward answer. As far as I have understood you're not looking for money. Apparently you feel some sense of grievance against me – or is it against my wife?'

A chuckle came over the line, rich and juicy.

'Sure. You'd like me to tell you. And my name and address while I'm at it.'

'I don't care what you tell me. Stay as anonymous as you please. Just tell me what you want in exchange for bringing the child back.'

'Don't want anything. There you are. That surprised you, ey? With you, it's always nothing for nothing and not much for sixpence. Looking to make deals, trying to get bargains. And we're not bargaining. We got you where we want you. We got your kid, and maybe we let it go and maybe we don't, and maybe we just drop it on a roadside on its bare arse like any stinking vagabond tinker because that's all you are. And maybe we do that tomorrow or some other day or whenever we think we got time to spare. And take that to wipe your arse on because you won't get better.'

'If you want nothing from me,' Bernard was trying to keep his voice down, and not to get shrill, 'I can't see what use it was to ring me up.'

'I wanted to make you shit, you bastard. And no mistake about it, I have, and I will, and I'm laughing.' And with an abrupt clank the phone rang off.

Colette let herself slide on to her knees on the floor and buried her face on her elbows in the seat of the chair. Bernard went on wiping his face automatically, his jaw muscles twitching, staring straight in front of him. Vera had turned herself sideways and was studying a picture on the wall with intense concentration, horribly ashamed at being a helpless bystander to suffering.

Castang looked at the three of them and for a moment did nothing at all. Then he leaned over and picked the phone up.

He clicked the receiver, waited a second, and then said, 'Johnny? You got it all? ... no, I think bring it up. Just reverse it to your mark, snip it off and come up with it; we'll get a better result up here. Yes, just rethread and set it on automatic record: I want you here too; your opinion's going to be vital.' He put the phone down, considered for a second, leaned over, smacked Colette lightly on the bottom, and said, 'Oops-a-daisy, girl: half-time. Our turn to play with the wind. I've never had the chance to do that to a judge before. Organize your face; the police will be here in a moment. Efface the traces of the orgy; this is your lover speaking. God's teeth, Vera, stop letting your imagination run riot. Bernard, tell me I'm not mistaken, and that the fancy high-fidelity set has a tape-recorder incorporated.'

'What was it again? – bare-arsed stinking vagabond tinker?'

'You'll hear it again. In fact you'll hear it so many times that anaesthesia will have set in, worn off and been replaced by common or garden nausea. Open the door, would you, that's Johnny. Hallo, Johnny, didn't I tell you this would pay off sooner or later? Can you make this machine go? – blimey it's got more switches and little red lights than the cockpit of a jet. Well, snip a bit off this and splice it up or something. Come on Bernard, show us how to switch this damn thing on.' There was a soft heavy amplifier hum, a loud scratching noise, and a voice suddenly boomed out 'Delavigne', sounding like Adolf Hitler in the Nuremburg stadium. 'Jesus, turn it down. No, stop it. Get a good balance first, the woofers and the tweeters and all the rest. Pity we've a double distortion, first from the crappy phone mike and then from the lousy black box amplifier. Try your best, Johnny.' The loudspeakers in the corner of the room boomed and whispered and spoke: 'Delavigne, Delavigne, Delavigne. That you Delavigne, that you, that you, that you, that you.'

'Godssake, Johnny.'

'Won't do better than that.'

'Ladies and gentlemen take your seats, *Gone with the Wind* is about to begin. Just an easy conversational volume, Johnny, no need to take the neighbours into our confidence. Look, the two of you. We've crossed over. The wind is now blowing down our side of the pitch. We've been knocked about a bit, but we're very lucky. Unless I'm much mistaken there's jam enough in this to catch any number of wasps with. Concentrate all you can. Have you heard the voice before? Can you place it in any context? Does it carry any association? Never mind any associations of words for the present, just concentrate on the voice; sorry, I'm repeating myself.'

'You seem excited,' said Colette sourly.

'You bet your ass, Shah, as Lauren Bacall said to the Peacock Throne when told she was a good dancer.'

'Damn it, he's happy,' said Bernard sarcastically.

'The voice; just listen to the voice.'

The recording was played through.

'No,' said Colette.

'Zero, I'm afraid,' said Bernard.

'What sort of accent would you call that, Johnny?'

'Overlaid,' said the technician stolidly. 'Predominance parigot.'

'Parigot hell, that's peasant. Jump to the bit in the middle where she got excited. Now give me a *rallentando*. Stop. Now get that. *Cassé* and *causé*. That's peasant. *Ca-ah-ssé. Cau-u-sé.*'

'What I meant by overlaid. Underneath I think it's parigot.'

'I'm not sure but that it isn't the other way round. Peasant who went up to Ivy and acquired the rhythms. We'll get a language expert. This is going to be easy.'

'I thought a recording wasn't evidence of anything.'

'Can't one have the call traced?' The two sentences were spoken together.

'Mixing it up,' said Castang, 'both remarks are bullshit. Tracing a call is a thing only done in detective stories. Could be anything, La Rochelle, Valenciennes, for all we know. And a recording isn't evidence, but what it leads to is.'

'Easy,' said Johnny. 'Can't count the relays this end, but the way it comes through, the quality of the tone. There's not all that much amplification added – in fact it's relatively faint. If you want a quick guess the way I originally heard it I'd say inside the department – not much over fifty kilometres either way. Need a phone engineer for an informed guess. Playing it off my box will give us the original power, and at least a notion of the relay used.'

'Get Richard on to that first thing. Now the words. The words are full of clues like a stuffed tomato.'

'Aren't you reading too much into this?' asked Colette in a voice made dispassionate.

'I'm not talking about the tone,' said Castang. 'Like your tone, and with knowledge of the facts we would say you were trying not to set your hopes too high. We're looking at the choice of words; expressions.'

They played it again twice.

'Now,' said Castang, 'it's a party game. Whose little notebook has the most annotations?'

He had had a couple of glasses of red plonk at home. And one glass of champagne. Just enough to set the motor going.

Vera had found something to look at and feel satisfaction. Almost happiness. The man had been utterly miserable with helpless frustration. A whole day, and nothing but double handfuls of air to show for all his work. And a bit of rabbit-shit, which he'd been too discouraged even to laugh about. He'd been brought so low that he'd even dallied with the notion of something totally reckless and irresponsible like bedding poor Colette (who'd have loved that, and been childishly comforted at somebody else being as deep in the shit as she was herself, poor wretch). But now he could move again, and show everyone he was a cop after all.

'There's a whole heap,' he was saying with pleasure, 'of interesting characteristics, which we ought to be able to straighten out into guidelines. You've all three got good analytical minds.

'The voice: you say you don't recognize it, but since she knows you it's a fair bet you know her. You may never have heard her speak much. A woman who has lived some time or been brought up in Paris, but is probably of peasant origin, and we can say – linking this to the rabbits – lives in all likelihood in a country district, isolated perhaps but in this region, judging by the accent. Does that mean anything to either of you? Some disgruntled ex-employee, Bernard? Recall that Jérome is proud of knowing everyone who works for him, and at a pinch we can get him to listen to this recording. A witness of some kind, Colette, in a case you instructed or judged? Think.

'Second point: pure malice. No ransom involved. This hasn't been done cold-bloodedly for money, but in hot blood and poisoned with hatred and unbalanced envy. Makes it all miles easier. There's a tremendous grievance against one or other of you or both. In fact one could go as far as to say that the grievance is against you as a family rather than as individuals. They attack you through your family. Isn't it a good bet to suggest that the grievance they imagine is something they – because there's obviously a clan – felt is an attack upon their family? Now – we ought to be able to do something with all that.'

'My mind's a perfect blank,' said Bernard puzzled. 'I've never sacked anyone. It's a thing I'm so bad at that Jérome always does it. I'm generally regarded as a soft touch for the hard-luck tales.'

'They seem confident of being safe from discovery,' said Colette, who had pulled herself together and was ready to discuss things calmly. 'I don't quite see, Henri, if it's as easy as you seem to suppose, how they would not realize that it would point to them. I mean a peasant may be ignorant and uneducated by our standards of looking at things, but they're notoriously cunning. It's almost impossible, as any judge knows, to bring a successful charge against a peasant. You know – sly. Wriggling out of things. The witnesses are all perjured.'

'Sure. But I'm hoping that sheer rancour, and everything in that voice stank of sheer rancour, will be blinding them somewhat.'

'Lord God,' said Bernard. 'Sheer rancour. You can't surely just accept that as a sufficient motive for the cold-blooded kidnapping of a helpless small child.'

Castang made an irritable gesture.

'I see that, and there's probably some ulterior motive we don't know about, some morsel of self-interest: they are probably going to try to turn this to their advantage somehow, even without money. As Richard suggested, the dropping of a charge or the liberation of a prisoner. Rachel must be a hostage for something or someone. But I'd like to say that this must be a great relief to you. You can be sure henceforward of one very important thing, that Rachel is not only alive and uninjured but safe and even relatively well-cared-for. She's a valuable hostage and they'll look after her.'

'That woman sounded so cruel,' said Colette bleakly.

'Brutal maybe. But I think the threats are mostly just big mouth.'

'I don't think I agree with you, Bernard,' said Vera suddenly. 'I think it might, yes, be sheer rancour. You're neither of you peasants. Henri is a little Parisian stump-in-the-gutter. But I'm a peasant, I was born in a shack with an earth floor, and got my first shoes when I was ten. I know of dreadful things done out of sheer rancour. I remember a man's legs being cut with a scythe, so badly that he never walked again – the tendons were severed – on account of a cat that he'd killed several years before.'

'There's generally money involved,' said Castang with his police experience.

'An ancient lawsuit,' said Colette, looking at Vera lovingly, 'or a disputed heritage. A girl jilted or a boy betrayed.'

'You none of you know me,' said Vera. 'I'm a very rancorous unforgiving person.'

They all stared at her aghast. Vera! The gentlest of souls.

'But then it's dottiness,' said Bernard, troubled. 'If it's blind unreasoning rancour on such slight grounds then such people are out of their minds. They may do the most dreadful things to Rachel.'

184

'Not legal dottiness,' said Colette.

'Not dotty from a peasant point of view,' said Vera. 'To us it would be all quite rational and comprehensible. And I don't think you need worry. They – we – wouldn't avenge ourselves upon a child. Animals – yes. Poison all the chickens. Even hamstring a horse. It would be like putting weedkiller on the neighbours' dahlias. But the innocence of a child would be respected.'

'I hope you're right,' said Bernard, looking at her with the uncomprehending eyes of a hamstrung horse.

'We're sitting here getting morbid,' said Castang. 'A while back I was accused, with some justice, of excessive priggery. This isn't doing us any good. What we need is a change of scenery. Let's go out and have a few drinks.'

'Huh?' said Bernard drearily.

'We can't go out, surely,' from Colette.

'Why not? She won't ring again. Her idea is that we should stew now in our juice and suffer grinding torments. Why play it her way? We leave Johnny here to finish the bottle' – Johnny had been, as was his habit, sitting silent and immobile, waiting to be spoken to. He grinned at this – 'and bugger off to a bordel. I'm in the mood for doing something illegal.'

'It's all right, Madame,' said Johnny to Colette, comfortingly. 'You don't do any good now. She'll know that from now on the police will be listening. If she rings again it'll be an effort to cover her tracks. I'll stall her with some talk. The recorder in the basement is on automatic. If you care to go out as Monsieur Castang suggests I'll be here. You've got a wonderful high-fidelity – if you'd allow me I'd play myself some music,' humbly.

'Of course I'll "allow you",' said Colette, touched.

'Settled,' said Castang. 'Let's go to some dirty scruffy nightclub and look at the striptease, and drink home-made champagne, and be obscene. That's where we'll get ideas. Here we've gone stale.'

'Madame la Juge in a dirty cabaret,' Colette, tickled.

'Nobody will recognize you. We'll take Bernard's car. Nobody will recognize me either, with all these bourgeois women out on a dirty-minded slumming trip.'

'The idea,' said Bernard, 'is good.'

'Nearly as good as sleeping with one another's wives,' said Vera with an irony so gentle that it scarcely touched the others.

'Let's go and have a pee,' said Colette to her. 'Nightclub lavs . . .'

'Know any good addresses?' asked Bernard.

'I know a really filthy dump full of Spaniards,' said Castang happily, 'where the pubic hair gets shoved practically in your face.'

'Lead me to it,' said Bernard, delighted.

'Don't forget it's to stimulate your memory,' with one of those gross laughs that men exchange while the women are safely in the bathroom.

*

There was no light at all except a flickering candle here and there. Candles were the general theme; a naked girl on the tiny dancefloor was doing suggestive things with a lighted candle, covering herself with grease.

'Like a dirty picture painted by Georges de la Tour,' said Bernard, interested.

The champagne was so nasty that Castang poured his surreptitiously in the bucket. The girls were delighted, as only really virtuous women are when dipped agreeably into an atmosphere of vice. The stools at the completely unlit bar were full of boneless whores slumped dully on the bar top waiting for business to perk up. They would not be too dreadfully disappointed, thought Castang, even in the pitch dark, because the clientèle is either German politicians popped over to see what money can be made out of our shaky aircraft industry, or English Members of Parliament studying European notions of democratic rule. Plus of course Spaniards, being happily filthy-minded because of censorship. Pass the butter, as Brando said to Schneider.

'Dammit,' said Bernard, ' – can anybody read the label on this bottle? – my mind's still a blank.'

'Never mind about the label,' prompted Castang gently. 'Just find something you have done, maybe deep in the past, as Vera said, which might have split family solidarity in a peasant community.'

As usual in nightclubs the sexes had split up. The men sat there with their legs stretched out in a lordly manner, 'looking the whores over' (except that it was too dark to see), while the girls were giggling together in a corner at private female and feminine jokes. The stripper writhed and illuminated her pubic hair with candle-light, and gave a loud yell in an effort to wake up all the stunned parliamentarians with constituencies in Somerset. Who had been looking forward all day, poor dears, to luscious French food, and French whore-by-nights to follow. What they got was steak and chips, and a very wearied stripper from Jugoslavia: the package trip to Lloret would have been cheaper. Luckily they were euphoric from a plethora of champagne made in large stainless-steel vats in the Rhineland.

'How long have you had that country cottage?' asked Castang suddenly. 'Do you always spend your holidays there?'

'I spend mine there – I hate the seaside in summer. Colette mostly goes for an extra month to Arcachon, sitting in a black bikini under a parasol getting all bronzed and sexy and yelling at the child. "Rachel darling",' in a high soprano that made two whores look round, "don't go near the dirty water, darling." '

'What's wrong with Arcachon?' asked Castang, interested.

'My belly hangs out over my bikini,' said Bernard gloomily.

'So does everybody else's.'

'Yes, but instead of bronzing I just go red, and scratch all night, because there's nothing to eat but polluted shellfish tasting of diesel oil.'

'So you'd rather a mountain holiday? Where d'you go?'

'Just to the country, but when we were poor and didn't have the shack we used to go to my parents' house, but Colette of course didn't care for that much. Once we borrowed a cottage belonging to my Aunt Joséphine.'

'Tante Joséphine,' Colette struck in as her ear caught the word, 'I was just thinking about her. Do you remember the row?'

'Oh good God, you mean when I gave the boy a smack. That was utterly trivial though.'

'Tell me about Tante Joséphine,' said Castang persuasively. 'Nothing's too trivial.'

'Oh it was silly,' said Colette laughing. 'Bernard's Tante Joséphine is a terrible old biddy who reads the financial pages and rings up her stockbroker every five minutes. She's a compulsive gambler only she plays the Bourse instead of the casino because the odds are better.'

'She has a cottage over in the valley of the Aube, heaven

knows why except there's a vineyard goes with it and she thinks it posh to be a landowner,' said Bernard laughing, 'and if you've got carrots you're a backwoodsman, but if you've vines, even when they're no good at all, you're gentlefolk. She's a horror.'

'And she lent you her cottage?'

'Oh it was one year, ages ago, Colette was still a student, and I wasn't making anything, and it was all the holiday we had. Rachel was tiny, still getting pushed about in a pram. There was a squabble with the farmer across the valley who claimed it was his right to pick the fruit-trees, which was all lies of course: that's all – as trivial as it sounds.'

'Go into more detail. What boy? What smack?'

'Oh well; it was just cheek. I mean we couldn't care less about the fruit: there was loads, but he was taking advantage of us. You know – Joséphine watches every penny, and would have driven a bargain, and after all I felt I had to watch her interest, and he was bare-faced; sent the boy to strip a tree, so I went down to shoo him out of that and the boy – he was about fifteen – was rather insolent and I gave him a clip around the ear: this is really too absurd.'

'Maybe,' said Castang.

'And did the farmer across the valley,' asked Vera softly, 'keep rabbits?'

'As I recall a whole zoo. I never noticed rabbits in particular but it's possible. He wasn't a real farmer; one of those peasants who do a little bit of everything – bit of wine, a few chickens, a pig – the fruit-trees, I suppose, made an attractive perk. Joséphine said afterwards he was always trying to diddle her over them and he must have thought us green ducks after that tough old turkey.'

'That's quite clear,' said Castang. 'Where is this place?'

'Bellac-sur-Aube – up at the top of the valley that goes down to Lotte. Goodish step from hereabouts – what, it must be over a hundred kilometres: it's the next department.'

'Not that far. Up to Lotte is within our region, inside our competence. Is there a tribunal in Lotte?'

'Canton tribunal,' said Colette, 'Correctionelle would come to us and assize of course,'

'You're not seriously thinking . . . ?' said Bernard.

'Don't know whether I am or not. Good grief, look at this one; is it a man or a woman?'

It occupied their curiosity for nearly ten minutes, slinking about in a tight sequined frock and pretending to beat up a very obviously female young thing in pathetic rags which tore off, as Vera remarked, rather too easily and who, as Colette remarked, was rather old for a schoolgirl. Her habiliments were removed with much prancing and whipcracking amid a variety of conventionally Lesbian offers, after which the sequined frock got skinned off, displaying odiously frilly undies, which gave the game away to Castang: he was after all, a detective. A smart tussle ensued with the by now naked nubile one, as a climax to which the frilly undies and the blonde wig shot off in a heap to disclose a rather poorly-equipped male, who was greeted with jeers as well as cheers, and some catcalling from the Spaniards, who plainly had no very high opinion of his slightly limp attributes.

'What on earth are we doing here?' asked Colette crossly.

'Quite right,' said Castang. 'I've been thinking of a verification we could make.'

'What of?' asked Vera, which provoked a laugh. Despite protestation, Bernard was judged incompetent to drive further and it was Castang who wheeled the Citroën out of the parking-lot.

'Where are we going? A better bordel?'

'The best of bordels,' he promised, 'and which I can drive to blind, drunk, or asleep.' Nobody was surprised when this turned out to be the courtyard of the Cité Administrative, where the regional service of the P.J. has its offices. Vera stayed in the car: the P.J. offices were even less treat than a bordel.

The P.J.'s night shift was still, this early in the evening, for it was only midnight, occupied in catching up on its paperwork. Adjunct Commissaire Lasserre, the commander of this lethargic platoon, was himself a lethargic person, inclined to be fat and greasy-haired. They had some difficulty with him, because he didn't like Castang, and Castang didn't like him.

'You're up late.'

'We got a bit of an alert.'

'Yes, so Johnny tells me. Doesn't sound very helpful.'

'There may be a bit of a lead somewhere in Richard's papers.'

'Come now, Castang, I can't allow you to frig about with Richard's desk unless he authorizes it.'

'What do you want me to do, phone him at this hour? – he'll be delighted.'

'What is it you want, anyhow?'

'He has a list that was made today of all the cases judged by Madame Delavigne in the last couple of years.'

'Are you crackers? – that's a confidential document belonging to the Palais, and it's restricted. Not for just everyone's eyes. Commissaire or over.'

'That being so I'll ring the Proc and ask for a ruling, since Madame Delavigne would like to refresh her memory.'

Colette was not insensitive to this appeal for support.

'Really, Monsieur Lasserre, I think you could stretch the point, since you're aware, of course, what has been happening.'

'That's all very well, Madame, but you realize that I am only responsible to Monsieur Richard without a direct intervention from the Parquet.'

'In my capacity as judge, however . . .'

'With all respect, Madame, the judge in charge of the dossier hasn't left me instructions covering the eventuality, and while of course I'd be delighted to do anything I possibly could as a person my official responsibility is involved.'

'Yes, Monsieur Lasserre, of course. Would you like me to give you an official service note absolving you from all responsibility, which I take entirely upon myself? It could be added to the dossier. You see, that way nobody could accuse Monsieur Castang of overstepping the regulations.'

'I hardly see, Madame, what justifies me in going rummaging among Monsieur Richard's private papers in his desk when after all he will be here tomorrow morning and at that moment I feel sure that you'd have only to ask him unofficially . . .'

'Yes, Monsieur Lassere, but in the meantime there is a bewildered and unhappy child somewhere in the night. With your permission I will ring Monsieur Besson and ask for his authorization for access to my own files.'

'Come, Madame, please don't let's allow this to slip on to an emotional level – I know they're your files, and there's no necessity for us to disturb Monsieur Besson: I'm simply obliged to point out that this extract from the Palais archive is an official document belonging to this office for which in Monsieur Richard's absence I am answerable, but in the circumstances I am happy to bend a regulation and allow you to see it. Monsieur Castang on the other hand –'

'Please put an end to this,' said Colette in her magistrate's tone. 'You know perfectly well that Monsieur Besson gave full powers to Monsieur Castang to conduct this investigation, and that in consequence he is clearly entitled to access to any relevant documents concerning it, no matter what their origin, and since you remark I am not the judge charged with the dossier I think it best that you should get that confirmed by Monsieur Besson personally.'

'I beg your pardon, Madame, but the moment you see in me an agent in any way prejudiced I retire. You must believe that I am only carrying out the orders of my superiors, and you know that Commissaire Richard is extremely punctilious about departmental discipline, and since I am directly answerable to him for everything during the hours of night-time . . .'

'Monsieur Lasserre, your scruples do you credit and count upon me, I shall not fail to establish your credit, in as far as the warm recommendations of a magistrate can carry weight with your superiors, the very next occasion I find myself in Monsieur Besson's office.'

'*Je vous en prie, Madame.*'

The two of them went together into Richard's office.

'Now the bastard's certain you're my mistress. Or I'm your lover, if we're to follow departmental procedure.'

'Hush.'

'That's all right, now he's gone off in a huff. Here it is on his desk in full view, as that bastard knew perfectly well: not locked up in the drawer or anything. Blimey, what a lot there are. I'd no idea there was so much juvenile crime. Still, in nearly a thousand square kilometres.'

'It's just names and addresses. Here,' ripping out the paper-clip, 'you take this half.' There was a silence.

'I hope Bernard's not seducing my wife in the Cité Administrative courtyard.'

'He's more likely to be asleep. Heavens, what a lot there are.'

'How big a place is Bellac? It would be a postal address?'

'Yes, just about.'

It was Castang who found it, which was fair.

'What was the name of the farmer over the valley from Tante Joséphine?'

'I've no idea,' said Colette. 'I never had anything to do with them. I remember that Bernard came back and said there was warfare over the fruit-trees. The orchard was down at the bottom of the valley, the far side of the vine slopes. Almost out of sight of the house. You know how Bernard is – a man takes a certain relish in defending the property. I suppose they thought we wouldn't notice a few miserable baskets of cherries. I'm sure I never did. We used to picnic down there, with Rachel in a basket. I do recall vaguely there was a scruffy boy. When Bernard said he'd given him a slap I thought nothing of it.'

'So the name Pierre Gaboriau means nothing to you?'

'No – wait now. Wasn't it dangerous driving?'

'Quite right, Madame la Juge. An unintentional homicide.'

'It's over a year ago,' murmured Colette. 'Are you thinking . . . ?'

'I'm thinking it's a cross-reference,' said Castang calmly. 'That's until we link it up.'

'Gaboriau. I remember it now quite well. Rather nasty boy, sullen, with all sorts of grievances. Not a speck of remorse of course, that's always what's so discouraging. It's everybody's fault but theirs. Terribly commonplace, alas. The boy was still under eighteen and officially a juvenile. They went to a Saturday night ball and got drunk and crashed on the way back and the other boy was killed, and this one got scarcely a scratch; the ways of God are inscrutable.'

'But surely the insurance refused to pay, then?' said the policeman.

'There was a complex argument and the ramifications now escape me. But briefly, there was a clever defence, to the effect that the other boy knew perfectly that the first was a juvenile, had no licence and no insurance, and was drunk and incompetent to drive anyway. There was no way out on the civil side: the responsibility was divided. It went to appeal but was flung out. On the criminal side, which was where I judged it, it is always difficult to know how much to assign to the parents. He was about six months in jail pending, and I think I decided that that was quite enough. Banned from driving for ten years and some supervisory measures but I forget what: out there in the country it doesn't go for much anyway, with the shortage of personnel there is, absolutely chronic in these scattered outlying districts. It worried me at the time: I can't recall much more than that offhand.'

'Let's jump before Lasserre catches us having a kiss-up.'

'Really Henri, you are impossible sometimes.'

Bernard, shaken into wakefulness and jogged, was unhelpful. 'Monsieur Mouton, or something like that. I don't remember any Gaboriau. You're barking up the wrong tree. I always said, it was something utterly trivial. Can't possibly be this.'

From the dark at the back of the car, where she had been knitting, or telling her beads, or heaven-knew-what – one never did quite know what Vera was up to – a placid voice said, 'Was there a Madame Mouton?'

'Not Mouton, but something like that. Heavens yes, frightful old cow, came storming out yelling when the boy ran home crying after I'd slapped him. We had a right battle there in the orchard,' recalled Bernard with relish. 'Said the boy had bad ears, mastoid and I don't know what, and I'd slapped him and this would be a drama, etcetera. I told the old bitch that was just too bad, and they should have thought of that before sending their brat climbing up robbing other people's cherry-trees. Defeat of angry stout party. End of story. Flea in ear. General withdrawal breathing fire and threats of chopping down cherry-tree. Disregarded same. Retired with honours of war. You're just not telling me this is serious.'

'Had Madame Mouton been married before?' asked Vera implacably.

'No idea.'

'I think we check.' Castang, unrelenting.

'How in God's name?' sleepily.

'Palace of Justice archives.'

'How the hell do you do that this hour of night?'

'We get the concierge out of bed,' said Castang ruthlessly.

This was optimistic. Nobody had ever tried to get into the Palais de Justice at night before: nobody had ever wanted to. There were enough massive bolts and bars and heavy wrought-iron trellis work to contain King Kong: in fact one would not be surprised to find a live dinosaur plodding pathetically about those gloomy corridors, sadly searching for something to eat. But what do they protect, these bars? To be sure, the Degradation of a Public Monument is an article in the penal code. Perhaps, somewhere, is an uneasy realization that a few people are scattered about somewhere who really care about justice, and who might be tempted to start their reforms by knocking the whole frightful pile down.

Some detective work was needed to find out where the concierge lodged, and much further physical effort to get him out of the arms of Morpheus, and much tact to soothe his savage breast. When at last a Newgate-like series of bolts had been undone, with a steady undercurrent of grumbling, Colette made haste to neutralize any latent anti-feminist feeling with a large tip. Castang didn't have to work in the place: she did. Like all public buildings in France the Palais de Justice is ruled entirely by the concierge. They get very arbitrary and incline strongly to megalomania. Even the Proc listened humbly with downcast eyes when – as frequently happened – he got buttonholed and made to listen to a tirade about cigarette-ends on the barristers' robing-room floor.

'And if there's ashtrays provided they gets stole. Advocates! I know a few what should be in jail,' darkly. Monsieur Besson was tempted to say that he did, too.

'I'm afraid we're going to find an awful mess,' said Colette apologetically. They did. Her secretary ('a nice, bright young girl') and herself had had many a brilliant idea for simplifying and modernizing the magisterial filing systems, all frustrated by her greffier, a gentleman of the old school, given to scathing remarks about bright young men from business-administration schools, 'whatever those are', and with a dislike of metal office furniture ('where's my tin-opener?'). Aphorisms abounded. 'Wood is noble.' 'Dust is honourable', and of course the classic, 'I can lay my hand on anything blindfolded.' What was so infuriating was that he could. He'd had to, this day, with the instructing judge and the Proc and the P.J. (a disgrace, that) calling for the most unlikely things. He'd gone off late in a notable huff, leaving everything nicely arranged on the floor, the way he knew how it should all go back.

It took Colette, as a consequence, nearly half an hour to find Gaboriau, Pierre. She had spent this time on her knees on the floor.

'Very good, and suitable for magistrates,' said Castang, sitting all male and lordly at her desk in her chair. She looked at her grimy hands with distaste and went off to wash them, cross and edgy, and just too tired to give vent to it. Poor Henri – washing with Sunlight soap and wondering why one ever bothered with anything else, since this was so much nicer – she hoped he was right; almost as much for his sake as for her own.

When she toiled back into the office Castang was sitting smoking and thought-collecting with so blank a face that she knew he had been disappointed and told herself calmly that she wasn't going to cry or anything: there wasn't a tear left in her.

'I'm sorry, Henri,' she managed to say..

'Sorry, my dear girl? What for? Everything is done. Except the hardest part. Which is going to be knocking up a judge at this hour.'

'Oh Henri, don't torture me.'

'Torturing you now; I could rape you in the middle of your own files if it wasn't for that pig of a concierge. Be rather piquant.' She did realize dimly that this was only an expression of tension relieved; a very great tension, perhaps indeed a breaking-strain.

'Tell me what you have found,' she said softly.

He held up a file and patted it.

'Madame Mouton, whose name I may say is Moustier, because as Vera acutely suggested she's been married before, is formerly Gaboriau. It's all in the file. Every damn thing is in the file. Very thorough, our legal system. It's all there. Every scrap of it. A complete case. All we need now is to go and get Rachel.'

'Then why is the hard part to come?' uncomprehending and unable to believe this.

'Because I can't move without a warrant, and we want to move fast.'

'But surely that can be managed.' Signing a warrant was something Colette did every day: they got handed out like theatre tickets.

'Not quite so easy, I'm afraid. You saw the way Lasserre was. I agree; he's a lazy fat greasy bugger. He's also my hierarchical superior. Even if I get a warrant, it would be putting myself hopelessly in the wrong to try and bypass him by getting Richard out of bed. Whether it's arrest or even just search it's in a country district and only gendarmerie can execute it. We'll have to wait till morning.'

'I can't. I won't.' Threatening hysteria. 'If you are really serious – Henri, are you certain?'

'Yes.'

'Then, oh I don't care – let's go and see Monsieur Besson. No – it's old Jeremiah. God help me, he doesn't like me much. Whether I appeal to him as a woman or as a colleague, I can't see him . . . no, I won't give up. I'll come with you; I'll cover you. I'll take the entire responsibility. You're not just cuddling me? You are sure?'

'Sure as that the earth goes round the sun – no, I'm not in the least sure of that. Never mind: I'm sure. I won't waste time: I'll give my argument to the judge.'

The concierge was glowering at being kept so long. His glance would have accused them of making love on the floor of Colette's office, but luckily such enormities had not entered his head.

'I'm so sorry, Monsieur Mangin. But it really was important. I can't tell you how important. Something absolutely vital to me or I'd never have disturbed you.'

Monsieur Mangin looked at her with sympathy. He knows, Colette thought wildly. Better not ask how. Concierges always know everything.

'That's all right, Madame Delavigne. Happy to be of service to you.' For the rest of her life Colette would never know whether this was just an assumed air of importance, or whether he really had known.

Bernard and Vera were both asleep in the car. Or asleep . . . well . . . the way one might sleep on a platform in Crewe station at three in the morning, sitting on a suitcase.

'My God. At this hour.'

It was another thing she would never know. Was it just because it was the police at two in the morning? Was it because she was a young woman as well as a colleague? The judge did not come down in any orange-striped pyjamas. No; he was dressed, down to his tie, and brought such a chill with him into the dark little study that it was no warm June night with the big clattering bugs wheeling round the lime-trees outside. Office hours in November in Goose Bay, Labrador.

But he showed no impatience, no irritability. In a way one would have preferred that. That dry business-like tone; that way of looking at the two of them as though they were just two more unshaved and sweaty ruffians clattering in with the handcuffs still on.

'Spare me the details, please. I feel sure, Monsieur Castang, that you would like to give a multiplicity of details to palliate the impression of haste and confusion. But no details, please.'

Colette's mouth was full of her tongue: she could feel it right down into her throat muscles. She kept her lips shut.

'Yes sir,' said Castang respectfully. 'Monsieur Delavigne, while defending the interest of a relation who has a country property in this village, was forced into a hostile attitude some years ago, and was sufficiently irritated to slap a teenage boy caught flagrantly stealing fruit. We have identified the same boy as one who while still a minor was brought before Madame here on a homicide-by-imprudence following a dangerous-driving charge. It escaped everyone. A dissimilarity in names; a woman twice married. The juxtaposition is casual and trivial, but the psychiatrist's report on this boy is cogent. And cumulative. I don't want to say it is conclusive until you have read it, sir.'

The judge read it, took off his glasses, and said, 'At two in the morning, one is naturally eager to take things as conclusive.'

'The one item of physical evidence left upon the putative scene of the kidnapping was a scatter of rabbit-droppings. It points strongly to a pattern of this nature.'

'It pointed, with equal force, to the decidedly unbalanced man on whose terrain this hypothetical rabbit had been exercising itself,' said the judge levelly, holding the earpieces of his glasses by the fingertips, dancing them gently up and down. 'You went then in a high state of enthusiastic excitement to Monsieur Richard and convinced him that a search-warrant should be forthcoming. If I'm not mistaken, Castang . . .'

'No sir,' cursing that old Léon from the bottom of his heart.

'He has placed a verbal complaint before the Parquet for wrongful search and seizure. He promises a written complaint. He was sent to me – he gave me an exceedingly tiresome quarter of an hour. He talked a great deal about the abuse of powers. That was this evening. Now, a few hours later, you come to me with another tale of unbalanced peasants nurturing grievances. Two tales: two too many, Monsieur Castang.'

'With respect, Monsieur le Juge, Commissaire Richard agreed that it was indispensable to eliminate that old man from the inquiry. I don't think it quite fair to blame the P.J. for his being a monomaniac with a grievance against the courts of justice.'

'And what proves to me, Monsieur Castang, that this is not another instance of uneducated persons with an imaginary grievance?'

'With respect, sir, the existence of one old man who is notoriously a trouble-maker in legal circles – one could call him a professional lover of litigation – cannot excuse me from pursuing another line of inquiry because of the similarity. Could that similarity not be superficial?'

'And could it not be said, Monsieur Castang, that seeing you at this hour, in Madame Delavigne's company – and, be it said only in the privacy of this room, smelling of alcohol – it would be a natural conclusion to imagine you emotionally involved in this affair, to a degree that I would prefer to think does not concern me?'

'Sir,' said Castang slowly, 'even if you think it unforgivable I have to say one thing. I think that Monsieur Richard knows me sufficiently well not to take such a suggestion seriously.'

The judge did not show, by as much as a twitch in his expression, that he had heard this. He tapped his glasses slowly on the dossier Castang had brought.

'This file, Madame Delavigne – which belongs I think in your archive – you have taken this from the Palais? Just now? As a result of this idea you had late at night?'

'That is correct, Monsieur le Juge.'

There was a short silence.

'Castang, I am going to ask you to be good enough to wait for a moment in my hall. I wish to speak to Madame Delavigne in private.' Castang got up wordlessly and left.

'Madame Delavigne . . . Colette, my child, I must speak to

you bluntly. You are a magistrate. Are you thoroughly aware of what you are doing and what you may be risking?'

'Yes,' said Colette flatly. 'Have you another question, Monsieur le Juge? I will answer it with scrupulous truth. Knowing what it may mean.'

'*En connaissance de cause,*' repeated the judge reflectively. He raised his eyes suddenly. 'Are you prepared to give me a word of honour? Even though that term has become meaningless?'

'I give you my word of honour as a woman and as a magistrate, and believe me I know that my career and my life are in balance. I am no man's mistress.' He looked at her for some time, nodded, put his glasses on, went back to a second reading of the dossier.

'When you judged this boy – with considerable leniency as it appears to me – you were utterly unaware of his identity as a youth your husband had punished on another occasion with a slap?'

'Totally. I do not rely upon the discrepancy in names. I had no idea of these people's name. Even the slap was reported to me later at a remove, and I did not attach importance to it, then or at any time.'

'Was any complaint made to authority, as a result of the slap?'

'I have absolute trust in my husband when he tells me not, and that even if there had been, it would have been thrown out. Flagrant provocation. There was never doubt, as he tells me, as to the ownership of the fruit-trees.'

'It is alarmingly tenuous,' said the judge slowly. 'I can of course see that there is a cumulative effect . . . I am an old man, Colette. You are a young woman at the threshold of your career. I have made judicial mistakes. Some of them have had grave consequences. I believe – I can do no more than believe, but as to my belief you have my word of honour as I have yours – I believe as God sees and will judge me that I have never instructed a case, and forwarded the papers to the Chamber of Accusation containing my intimate conviction that a crime had been committed, without the certainty that I held that criminal. Forgive me – you are a young girl. Have you measured your responsibility, my child?'

'Yes,' whispered Colette. 'Not here. This is my child. I am only its mother.'

'Quite so. The more responsibility for me. Suppose I said to you – we have had a variety of scandals lately. Where, conceivably, a judge of instruction might be thought to have acted impetuously, – giving way, shall I say, to the pressures of publicity. Maybe – even without feeling the absolute certainty that the police investigation had been properly carried out.'

Colette said nothing to that, having nothing to say.

'You come to me with a heart-rending situation. The police come with a line of facile patter.' He had got up and was walking jerkily up and down, stopping to twitch the curtains straight with an automatic gesture. 'I should tell you to drink a tisane and go to bed. And send that young man home to compose a report for his superiors. I'm not suggesting that the elements collected here are worthless. They can be verified. But you have shown me nothing that explains, for example, this telephone call you have received.'

She felt that all her energy had dribbled away. She did not know what to answer. In other circumstances she would be saying these things herself. She had said them, frequently.

'Monsieur le Juge . . .' she said feebly.

'Yes?'

'Do what you can for me.'

He walked to the door, opened it, called 'Castang, come in, would you,' and went to sit down at his desk.

'Castang, this telephone call – there was no specific menace?'

'To abandon the child somewhere. What alarms one the most and convinces me that we should not lose time is the mixture of violent impulse in these people with the realization of possible consequences. I'm afraid . . .' He hesitated: he hadn't wished to say this in front of Colette. 'They were able to make a careful, calculated plan to possess themselves of the child. Now that they've got her they don't know what to do with her. No long-term thought. They've achieved their main point, presumably, of acquiring a sadistic satisfaction at giving pain and anxiety. They say they'll let her go. It must surely occur to them that she knows enough to identify them; to recognize them at least. They feel safe from discovery. But will they – by daylight – still feel safe?'

The judge glanced sideways at Colette. She was sitting dully staring in front of her, too tired even to move her eyes. She gave no sign of having heard. His fingertips fidgeted as though he wished to drum them on the desk. He reached for his pocket, produced a silver fountain pen, uncapped it, opened the drawer of his desk.

'I'll give you a warrant for arrest,' abruptly. 'Search won't help you at this hour of the night. You realize what that means?' Castang nodded. 'You . . .' blunt. 'I had no very great difficulty this afternoon. An old man who is a public nuisance in more ways than one. But this . . . You know what it smells of, Castang? An operation arbitrarily decided and enforced in the middle of the night, an inquiry where the press has been stifled, an affair which any advocate would draw as a private war between individuals, where a magistrate was using police force to a private end? It smells of the Gestapo, Castang. Have you thought of that? You know what it will mean to you? Have you seen yourself in a court, an officer of Police Judiciaire openly accused of abusing your powers out of private interest and corrupt friendship? You'd destroy her too, you know that? The entire public would conclude you were her lover. And your wife . . . Before I give you this warrant – thought of all that? Resolute? Very well.' The magistrate made the quick automatic gesture with which one signs one's name on the piece of paper which is a cheque or a hire-purchase agreement. He held it out.

'There is your warrant. The rest concerns you. I'll telephone Lasserre – make your own arrangements with the local gendarmerie. Before you put it in your pocket . . .' he glanced at his watch. 'Two thirty. In less than six hours Commissaire Richard will be back at his desk and you will have the opportunity to place the responsibility where it belongs. No? Good.' He got up. He stared at Colette, who got up too automatically and smoothed her skirt. He smiled suddenly, and turned back to Castang with a completely unexpected sprightliness.

'You've read *The Three Musketeers*?'

'Yes,' flabbergasted.

'Recall the passage in which Richelieu says, "Young man, I promise you that if I can say again what I have just said, I will say it." '

Castang sketched a sort of bow and went out. The judge took Colette by the shoulders, gently.

'I've done what you asked. What I could,' he said gently.

Bernard was not asleep this time. He was walking up and down the pavement beside his car, with the mechanical jerkiness of a sentry outside the palace.

'Drop me back at the P.J. office,' said Castang tonelessly. 'I've got to get a car.'

'And us?' asked Bernard aghast. 'What are we to do?'

'Nothing at all, I'm afraid. Tisane and bed, as the judge has sensibly suggested.'

'You come back with me,' said Vera. 'My turn for hospitality.'

'And it's one telephone number I don't have to look up in the book,' said Castang.

'I'd like some coffee, I think,' said Colette in a perfectly relaxed tone. 'And some bacon and eggs, or onion soup or something.'

'I'll peel onions,' said Vera. 'I'd rather enjoy the activity.'

\*

'You got him to give you that?' said Lasserre with a kind of admiration.

'Oh he didn't lose the opportunity of telling me I'd get bust like a burnt match.'

'Well, mate. 'S your funeral.'

'You don't sound as happy as you might.'

'Look, cock,' said Lasserre unforced, 'I don't give a damn whether you're sleeping with her or not. Because if you do that, all I can say is you've earned her.'

'I'll remember you in my will,' said Castang, not nastily.

'You're not mad at me?'

'Not a bit. I'd have done the same.'

'I wish you joy. No, hell, I wish you success. Really. Straight up.'

'Thanks,' said Castang, starting the motor.

'Jesus, it's heavy. Be a storm in the hills. Well, we could do with the rain.'

'A good hailstorm. I'll stand out in it, in the middle of the field. Bloody scarecrow.'

'You said it.' The car drove off out of the courtyard.

'Richard will guillotine you, mate,' said Monsieur Lassere out loud. 'And I suppose you'll imagine that it will make me dead happy. Which isn't necessarily so.' He looked up at the dark clouded sky, and wished it would break. He could do with a shower.

Castang drove. From here it was about a hundred kilometres. Be lucky to do it in under two hours. Thunder out there in the hills, that was a certainty. Knock the dust off the car. He shifted into top gear.

Three robbers sat in a cave.

One of them said to the other 'Tell me a story, Antonio.' And so the story began.

' "Three robbers sat in a cave . . ." '

Third gear. Second gear. Fourth gear.

\*

'You gave it away,' said the young man furiously. 'Thought yourself smart.'

'Shut up,' said the young woman fiercely. 'Know all, know nothing.'

'I don't think there's any sense, in keeping her,' said the old woman.

'Never did,' said the old man.

'Shut up, you. We're free to do as we please.'

'They could be listening. They do that. Tap the lines, like.'

'Shut up.'

'Nothing to do with it. They can't find us, there's nothing whatever to give us away. No need for you to start getting scared.'

'They could recognize your voice.'

'Who could? Who's heard my voice? Who knows me?'

'Not that we're thinking of. What good is she to us, now?'

'Get rid of her.'

'What could she say?'

'Describe us. Give names. That's what.'

'Describe us! Give names! You think a kid that age is able to? What you got, inside that head of yours?'

'She's asleep. Take her, put her in the car, drive her out a good way. Dump her on the road. She'll come to no harm.'

'Get a bit wet, maybe.'

'She'll wander about. She hasn't got a clue.'

'Clue enough to say "Marie-Thérèse"! I told you you shouldn't mention any names.'

'Look, don't be so goddamned wet. How many are there in France?'

'I told you, I always told you, she'd blab.'

'Shut up. What d'you want then? You think we should knock her on the head or something? You know what that'd be? Murder, that's what.'

'I'm not having any of that talk. That's not for us. We're not like that. She's just a kid. I'm not having her injured.'

'Nobody says injured. Blindfold her like, turn her around a few times.'

'And do it now.'

'Going to be a storm.'

'So she gets wet. Do we never get wet? Don't be such a bloody drip. Now it's dark. You want to do it by daylight?'

'Suppose she sees the car number?'

'Oh yeh and suppose she sees the colour of your eyes. You can turn the lights out, can't you? What could she ever tell? I ask you, what could she ever tell? Doesn't amount to a row of beans.'

'Enough to put us in jail, maybe. They'd say it was kidnapping.'

'Nix, unless you ask for money, isn't any kidnapping. We just took her for a ride.'

'Well, I say it's kidnapping.' It was Carney. 'I think it is even when you don't ask for money. And I say it's bloody risky. Who knows what she can tell?'

'You out of your bleeding mind or something?'

'I don't see what you're all on about. Look at all those Vietnamese kids. Napalm and stuff. Doesn't have to hurt. Back of the neck, like a rabbit, like. Then you know you're safe. I mean you're certain.'

'I'm not having any of that talk.'

'Look, just shut up. Or I knock you on the back of the neck.'

'You and who else?'

'Shut up. Stuff it. Too much talk.'

'Too much beer talking.'

'We're agreed, right?'
'We're agreed, right.'

*

It was one of the scattered, straggling villages, strung out along a main road, commonplace all over France. Hilaire Belloc, in *The Path to Rome*, says they are a sign of Roman civilization. Villages huddled together in a heap of protection are a sign of barbarism. There is truth in this. But there are different sorts of barbarism. Village like any other, thought Castang, sliding down the main street, which was the only street: shuttered café, deserted petrol-pump; usual village *mairie* half school and half fire-station: not a soul awake. Houses sealed, shutters blind, chickens all locked up behind high walls: fox trots down the centre of the street, one hundred per cent frustrated. Right down the other end of the village, a house with a sort of little barrack built on behind it. A milky illuminated sign saying 'Gendarmerie'. Castang parked his car. Nobody was astir. The duty officer was 'kipping' on a camp bed. He rang the night bell. A light went on. A sort of uncombed orang-outang in boots opened the door.

The folklore of the country gendarme, or of any 'village cop', as rustic but shrewd, all boots and heavy breathing, licking the stub of his pencil in a laborious transference of semi-literacy into administrative jargon, is one of the clichés dear to clued-puzzle detective stories, but has no more than a few superficial shreds of truth. The gendarmerie is one of the most disciplined bodies in France. So it should be: it is a military body organized in a military hierarchy. It is also extremely sophisticated, for as a relatively small body, thinly spread over a large and amazingly varied terrain, it is hard worked and has learned to apply a great deal of ingenuity to combating the chronic shortage of men and material, for a parsimonious government keeps it extremely short of money. It sees, daily, a cross-section of the follies and futilities of mankind that would stagger any urban police force. But what, perhaps, gives it an exceptional quality more than all else is the power it possesses and uses so sparingly. The gendarme is pretty well everything his municipal colleague is, as well as handyman in the fire and ambulance services, public works and rural engineering, but he is also an officer of judicial police. Out in the wilds, where the twentieth century sometimes

205

knocks its nose upon the seventeenth, commissaires and magistrates and Procs are far off and seldom seen. The extremely elaborate separation of powers, with subtle distinctions between legislative and executive, which prevails in the city, and ensures that no Gestapos arise upon the territory of the republic, is in the country fused. A country gendarme is in title an 'officer of police judiciaire' and compared to him Castang is very small fry.

It wasn't an orang-outang at all: this was no more than a trick of the light behind the glass door. Crumpled slacks and sweaty shirt-sleeves – the thunder kept muttering in the hills and the atmosphere was close and oppressive – did not prevent him from looking trim and alert. He gave a massive yawn, but it was nearly four in the morning.

'Come on in.' Lightning flickered over the hills, looking pale and ineffectual. 'I wish it'd make up its bleeding mind.' The two men stood on the doorstep together, looking up at the unseen charged clouds. A few scattered drops of warm heavy rain sploshed on the dusty leaves.

'When it does come,' gloomily, 'probably be hail and rip all the vines to bits. Or create a flash flood. Probably be out bleeding-bridge-building, before morning.' The gloom had no self-pity in it. He didn't sound as though it would be a treat, but he wasn't complaining.

'Where's the patrol?'

'Out looking after some Dutch tourists,' without even a grin, 'who brought their own grub with them and got food-poisoning as a consequence.' He flipped the switch on the shortwave transmitter and said, 'All right, Sam, pick up thy musket, lad, how goes it?'

'Ya, boy, I hear you,' came the voice horribly distorted by thunder and static. 'Going down the valley, the three of them in the back. Ten minutes from the clinic: no real worry, not in coma, just galloping dysentery. Deliver them, right, and then back to pick up all their camping stuff or some bugger'll pinch it. Thirty, no say forty minutes.'

'O.K. Logged. Out. Right, sir, what's on your mind?'

'I'll give you a quick breakdown,' said Castang, 'so you can see whether we have to call the brigadier, because I've a notion we'll need him.'

'Ho,' said the gendarme. He listened in silent patience, and said 'Ho' again at the end.

'Yes, I better call the brig. You want some coffee? Nes, I should say. I leave you alone a moment.'

When the brigadier appeared it was in pyjamas, with the rumpled schoolboyish look of a man just woken up, the placid manner of a man used to it, and a considerable five o'clock shadow. He sat down at the desk, spooned Nes into a teacup, said 'See that the water's boiling', and looked at Castang with mild expectancy.

'I gather you want me to execute a warrant,' putting his reading glasses on. 'Yes ... Well ... We can't go doing that in the middle of the night, can we now? Right, well, it's only two hours to sunrise. Let's see what we know. We don't keep files on every rabbit in the neighbourhood, you know. Gilbert, look in that cabinet there, the "Things Judged" one, and find me Gaboriau.'

'I dare say,' said Castang 'that what isn't in the file might be as interesting as what is.' The brigadier looked at him impassively.

'Don't get me wrong; there's no offence meant. But you're none too sure of yourself, are you? All right, all right; a nod's as good as a wink. You have a warrant signed by the judge of instruction. There's no name on it but you've got these people in mind. And it's sort of collective, huh?'

'There's a whole clan of these people – as far as I know. I'm hoping you'll know more.'

'Easy does it. Mine's a large district. Bellac is ten kilometres up the road. Orders are orders. You've a warrant for me, I'll execute it. But we better not have any excesses of zeal because I'd be answerable for them. You come out here hotfoot in the middle of the night and wake me up – no no, I'm not criticizing. But there's no name on this warrant. That's fair enough; you know about this young man, and you tell me about an old couple, and there's a young woman been on the telephone, and taking it all round we'd like to know a bit more, you and me both, that's reasonable, isn't it? So we look at this dossier first. Gaboriau – yes, now I remember him, cheeky young sod. Still, not a very helpful observation, that. Now let's see who signed this original report on that road accident. Sauvage. Well now,

Gilbert, seems to me you might get Sauvage out of bed. Not getting impatient, are you?' said the brigadier.

'No. I'm not going to go about telling you how to do your job.'

'Then we're happy. I was wondering, or let's say the thought crosed my mind like, that you might be a bit hipped at what seems an absence of zeal, like, which a judge might think was as bad as too much. But I don't mind telling you,' mildly, 'I like to look before I leap.'

'I don't mind telling you,' said Castang, slipping without trouble into this habit of deliberation, 'that it's all right by me. I suppose I seem about as welcome as the dysentery charging in like this, twitching and biting my nails, but I've been on the go since this time yesterday.'

'Man,' said the brigadier, 'don't you think it. A kidnap case – yes I know; we had it on our telex last night. And a judge behind it. And a P.J. officer with a warrant. You're going to get everything we can give you. Including, I hope, a bit of thought. Talking of dysentery, where's the patrol, Gilbert?'

'Be back any minute.'

'Then you might make us some real coffee. And be ready to nip out, like, for when Arthur gets his first batch of bread out of the oven. Now this is Sauvage. Jesus, man, where d'you get those pyjamas? This is Monsieur Castang from the P.J. and he wants to know something about the family Moustier in Bellac.'

'They got a grievance,' said Monsieur Sauvage sitting down and scratching with a hand like the blade of a Caterpillar back hoe. 'I don't know what it's about, but whatever it is they got a grievance.' The resemblance was increased by his pyjamas, which were 'Caterpillar' yellow.

'I've only got one question really,' said Castang. 'In this clan – is there by any chance a young or youngish woman who speaks with something of a parigot accent?'

'I'm not quite sure how that goes. There's a lot of screaming fishwives around there.'

'Got a tape-recorder around here?' asked Castang.

*

Time passed easily, out here in the country. The car patrol rolled in, encumbered with much camping material and an amazing number of opened tins, most of which seemed to contain apple sauce, and some sordid remnants of cooked chicken to be sent to the lab for analysis. This took everyone's appetite away, until Officer Triboulet finally arrived with fresh bread, and invited Castang to breakfast. Officer Triboulet got into trouble for having left the milk out. The thunder had turned it sour. But the storm had passed over without breaking, which everyone agreed was just as well, since the grapes were at a vulnerable stage. They always are, thought Castang, but kept his mouth shut. Breakfast finished, with a good deal of jam dropped on the table, the *maréchaussée* departed for a wash and reappeared unrecognizable, not just with gleaming shaves but in freshly pressed khaki gabardines.

'We won't take the jeep,' said the brigadier. 'The van's more discreet, like, in case we have some arresting to do.'

Castang had had time to ring Vera.

'I was asleep.' Her voice came thick and clogged. 'Sorry, darling – I didn't drink much, but it was still too much. They've gone home, at last. End of the tether. And you?'

Yes. The last twenty-four hours were now earning compound interest.

'Going up against this place now. Virtually certain. But . . . no, skip it. Just keep hoping for the best. Stay in bed. I've no idea when I'll be back, but if you want me, or if you hear from Richard before I get the chance to phone in, ring the gendarmerie here.'

He didn't phone Commissaire Lasserre. He had nothing to say.

'Can I borrow your razor?' he asked the brigadier.

Rachel was within grasp. A quarter of an hour's drive. It didn't somehow sound as a trumpet call. He was very tired, and he didn't feel there were any reserves left.

Oh well. Even in that ghastly shit-hole of Dien Bien Phu, Bigeard had kept his paratroops shaved. They hadn't had any reserves, either. Why did he feel so depressed? Rachel was within grasp.

Sauvage drove. Up the valley, around a big bare hump of limestone, and suddenly a beautiful, gentle, irrigated vista. And the high hills as backdrop.

'Up at the top,' said Sauvage briefly, changing gear: the tyres scrabbled on the stony track.

The Volkswagen minibus slammed to a stop noisily, and several dogs began a hysterical barking. A big slab-faced, slab-sided oldish woman peered out with a mask of black blank hostile suspicion. The brigadier jumped out like a boy of twenty and sketched a dazzling salute.

'*Bonjour Madame,*' bearing in at that door like a woodpecker.

'What's this then? What you want? Hey, you go easy there. Private property.' The brigadier took his képi off politely, laid it on the kitchen table, and said, 'This gentleman is an officer of the police judicaire from the city.' The old woman showed no sign of being impressed at all.

'What's that then? Looks like an insurance salesman.'

'No need to be impolite,' said the brigadier crisply. 'Now then. Monsieur Castang here is the bearer of authorization signed by the judge of instruction to search these premises. So I'd be obliged, Madame, if you would ask everybody present in this house to gather here in this room. All right? Right, Sauvage, just take a look out the back, would you?'

'Hey hey. Not so free, there, you. What is this?'

'Here is the authority to search, Madame. I must ask you not to cause obstruction.'

'You can't go pulling women out of bed. Here, you, where d'you think you're going?'

'Just seeing where the door leads to,' said Monsieur Sauvage comfortably.

'Nobody's pulling women out of bed. Just call them, would you?'

'My son Pierrot's day off: he needs his sleep.'

'Yes, sure. We have our beauty sleep broken too. And you've a daughter, I believe.'

'No I haven't, Mr Clever. You're barking up some wrong tree.'

'That will be quite simple for you to demonstrate then,' said the brigadier. 'Step-daughter or daughter-in-law or whatever she is, we'd be glad of the opportunity of seeing her.'

'Well,' said a ferocious voice. 'You see her. And so what?'

Handsome, thought Castang with spontaneous admiration. That may not be quite altogether the word, in view of handsome-is-as-handsome-does, but pretty is altogether too faded a word. A woman like wood charcoal. Just blow on her, quite

210

gently, and the sullen red will glow bright, and the concentration of heat will astonish you.

A mass of blonde hair round a keen, aquiline, slightly gipsy face fair snapping with vitality. Some body, too. She was wearing nothing but a short salmon-pink nylon nightdress and faded baby-blue mules with pompons on them. Splendid legs were naked to mid-thigh. Splendid breasts were pushed out aggressively, the ferocious nipples dark as the barrel of a gun showing up brutally through the semi-transparent material.

'What the hell are you? What the hell you want? What d'you think you're doing here? Now or any other time?'

'Here,' said the old woman, not very shocked or embarrassed, but just sufficiently both to have her style cramped, 'you better put something on.'

Castang had heard from the first syllable that this was his quarry. Despite himself, he was impressed.

'Ach what?' said the vision. 'Show them my arse, they wouldn't dare hiccup. What d'you mean by this here, hey? Out of here, this is private property. Lady here in her nightdress, you buzz off, understood, and make it quick.'

The brigadier had put on an utterly wooden face. His voice stalked stiffly over regulation phrases.

'Being present in virtue of a warrant duly signed by a judge of the requisite tribunal I'm under no obligation to withdraw and you'd better go and put some clothes on.'

'Want to get an eyeful, do you, dirty-minded prat that you are. Well you won't get it.'

The brigadier called forth all Castang's admiration at that moment. He didn't budge at all.

'My dear, you could show me your beautiful curls all the way up to your navel and it would just be dandelion salad to me: I'm a married man. And Now Go Dress,' in a ferocious bark that stopped the dogs in the yard, rendered insane by Officer Sauvage stumping about at the back door. He came in to see what all the row was about, and stood transfixed at the pink nylon bottom. The young woman didn't budge any more than the brigadier did.

'I'll put my clothes on in my good time and on my orders, not yours, hick.' Her eyes came round to Castang. 'Who're you? A bailiff?'

He leaned his bottom peacefully against the table.

'My name is Castang. I'm an officer of judicial police. We've met. Which is to say I had the pleasure of listening to you on the telephone last night.'

The fine eyes under their finely-arched eyebrows snapped at him. She whisked round abruptly to the door.

'Get out of my way, you,' she said to Sauvage. He did, politely.

The whole body arched indomitably at them. For a moment he really thought she was going to hitch up the nightdress and say 'Kiss it'. He could see the buttocks clench. She hesitated, and then whisked out. Slamming the door. The brigadier said nothing. Castang admired this disciplined silence.

'Careful,' he muttered. 'Create a short circuit.'

'Ask the men – and the women too –' woodenly, 'to get dressed.'

The old woman stood her ground.

'They'll get dressed when they want. When it's time to go to work. I stay here. Keep my eye on you. No knowing what you might not try to pinch.'

'All right,' said the brigadier. 'All the jokes are now over. Up the stairs, Sauvage: too much obstruction. You too, Castang; you know what you're looking for. You'd better keep quiet, Madame. Politeness is one thing, respect is another. And law is something else. You choose to play it the hard way.'

'Robbers,' screamed the old woman. Sauvage was mounting the stairs placidly, in an armour of indifference Castang – with a fine view of his backside – regarded with respect.

His technique, too, left nothing to be desired. Without once losing a polite stolidity he routed through the whole house, as unimpressed by the young woman's fervent access of modesty – 'You can't come in here: I'm dressing' – as he had been by the opposite. Getting spat on; getting her nightdress flung in his face; it all bothered him about as much as a fly.

From the attic to the cellar, and they paid particular attention to both, there was no sign whatever of Rachel. In the one there was a little girl, who screamed with quite unfeigned fear, and in the other there was exactly what you might expect. Nothing anywhere showed the slightest sign of any departure from the normal. Castang avoided looking at Sauvage, but saw enough of him to realize that Sauvage was taking pains not to catch his eye. No reproach. But brother, where do we go from here?

They finally got the whole band assembled in the kitchen, muttering and mouthing threats. They were going to go down straight away to the town to lay a complaint. They would get lawyers, they would tell the press, there was justice in this country, they would soon show that the poor were not to be trodden upon, and exploited, and abused, and fucked about by a pack of stinking fuzz that was nothing but a Gestapo under the thumb of the rich and paid – and bribed – to abuse the poor. Castang put on the same impassive front as his allies, who were showing a remarkable solidarity. His courage, though, was not high. It was always, notoriously, difficult to prove anything in the face of a clan of peasants. Even if everybody knew they were guilty as hell. God knew what breath of suspicious mistrust had alerted them. They *were* guilty as hell. He knew it. But what did he have? A slightly drunken, disjointed, inconclusive, trivial tale of a rustic squabble involving Bernard. The completely irrelevant fact that this sullen young ruffian had been judged once – a year ago – for drunken driving and manslaughter by Colette. And a tape-recording of a phone call, which was not evidence of anything: no court would touch it with a ten-foot pole. No court would want anything to do with a circumstantial suspicion case against a peasant family. Various unpleasant, inconclusive and thoroughly depressing landmarks in the history of criminal trials were at the forefront of his mind. Gaston Dominici ... Marie Besnard ... that nest of maddened hornets in Bruay-en-Artois ... For a three-ha'penny P.J. cop, even backed up by his commissaire, even backed up by the whole family of judges of instruction, to be sure of the So-and-So's' guilt was not enough. Not nearly enough ...

The brigadier, appearing completely unfazed, was addressing the assembled populace.

'According to information received you fall, the lot of you, under a grave imputation of a very serious crime. The instructing judge delivers me in consequence this warrant for inquiry, search and examination, and if necessary arrest. You lot better be very careful. You better forget all that nonsense pretty quick about running to complain to the canton tribunal and all the rest of it, because that stuff could have a nasty backfire. You lot

213

can go to work: yes yes, stop fussing. You others can go about your normal business. I leave you free for the moment, with the warning that you are all bound to hold yourselves at the disposition of justice at any moment and without notice. And you better be very careful.'

'Bullshit,' said the old woman.

'You can't hold what's in the past against me. That's already judged. Victimization, that is,' said the young man.

'You've kept me late for work,' said the other young man. 'I lose by that and I bleeding well sue for compensation.'

'I'll have you filthy fuckers,' said the young woman. 'Oh yes, I know how to go about that. I come from Paris, I know a trick or two for you lot. Bursting into my bedroom when I got no clothes on; I'll sue you lot for rape. And abuse of power. And wrongful arrest. Illegal force and constraint. Oh yes – and I'll go to the office of *France-Dimanche* too. We'll knock you lot off your perch. I know a few what's going to lose their jobs.'

'You better stop quacking – or else you really will be late for work,' said the brigadier unmoved.

In a dignified and menacing manner, the forces of the law withdrew to previously prepared positions.

'Not very clever,' was all the brigadier said on the way back. Sauvage said nothing at all.

'Well?' said the brigadier back in his office, alone with Castang.

'Got a black eye there.'

'Yes,' in an elaborately not-blaming-you tone.

'You could hear for yourself. That screaming cow's the one who made the phone call. There's no mistake.'

'No.'

'The child has to be found.'

'Yes.'

'And even if we do find the child . . .'

'Yes. And how. And when. And where.'

'I haven't wanted to think about it.'

'I can understand that,' said the brigadier shortly. 'I've got plenty of work. And I'll have to make a report on this to the lieutenant. You see? I don't know what you're aiming to do, right now.'

214

'I'm going to go and give that some serious thought,' said Castang.

'You heading back to town?' not without a certain sympathy, because that fellow there was buggered, if ever he saw a fellow buggered, and the ground under his shoes was getting kind of hot. Whereas he himself was covered completely, from start to finish. And it wasn't a lot of chat from that trouble-brewing shit-stirring crowd of peasants that would worry him. He felt quite sorry for Castang. Still, for an experienced man, he'd sort of stuck his neck out rather far.

There was a new gendarme on the desk, one he hadn't seen.

'I'm going down the village,' said Castang.

'O.K.,' indifferently.

'What's the pub like?'

'Nothing much. Their white wine's honest. Reasonably.' Both were words one could stretch.

It was the old man from Hanoi who came into his mind. At that little old café back in the village there . . . where the white wine was honest, even if nothing else was. The old man who had laughed at him, who'd seen too many dead children, too many good soldiers thrown away in futile operations, too many bright young officers left to fertilize fields. Who had remarked that even a senior civil servant would never have a secure retirement just on his lousy pension. What did taking a few bribes matter one way or another? The district still got peaceably and even surprisingly efficiently administered.

He, Castang, didn't have any children. He ought to be grateful for that, instead of letting it chew at him. Hell, he'd got so chewed at, between Vera and Colette – a tiresome bitch, that – he'd got all nibbled away on one side and had lost his balance.

Well, he had his law degree anyway. And a certain amount of experience. There would be a job somewhere. They wouldn't starve to death or anything. They might even do a sight better than they were doing right now, because this was a thankless job if ever he saw one. Bernard and Colette had loyalty, and would do what they could, and that could be quite a lot. Richard had loyalty too, and would give him the fairest deal possible. It wasn't disgrace. Everyone would give him a good recommendation.

The kind of good recommendation you give a fellow when you want to see his back limping off-stage fast.

Whoever let him down, gently or not, with or without a lot of lip-service. Vera would not. It might have been said – it had been said – that he'd made an imprudent marriage and it hadn't done him any good. But he had, by God, a woman who would stick with him no matter how sodomized he got.

Was there anything he could do? Ring the office? Ring Colette and Bernard? Ring Vera?

What could he say to any of them? What interest would it have to anyone? Unless he got Rachel back he wasn't worth a licked postmarked ha'penny stamp to man or beast. He ordered another glass of white wine, drearily. Sitting here in this dimwit dump getting sozzled. Go home to bed, fool. Get some sleep. That at least will knit up a few of the ravelled sleeves of care.

He didn't even notice the phone ringing. Ten veal cutlets to-day, butcher, six entrecôtes. Oh, and a bit of calves' liver if you've got any. Day like this, we could easily do twenty chance lunches with the tourists.

'Your name Castang? Phone for you.' He lurched over.

'Gendarmerie here. The city's on the phone for you. Your commissaire. I told him you'd ring back.'

'Thanks.' It had caught up with him sooner than he'd expected. But why try to put it off? He might as well have driven back straight away, taken his castor-oil and gone to sit patiently on the pot till the effect appeared.

Hell, he might as well ring and get it over. And ring from here: what good would discretion do him now?

'Hallo. Give me the boss. Of course it's me; who the hell did you think it was?' Even his voice had apparently gone unrecognizable.

Or had the word got around so fast on the grapevine that Castang had slipped on a banana-skin and bust his stupid arse?

'Castang here.'

'Where the hell are you then?' Richard's voice, cool and drawling, clear as though in the same room. Sounding utterly unworried. Fair enough. He didn't have any worries. He hadn't gone and got himself amorously mixed up with any pretty young women who happened to be magistrates.

'Village pub.'

'I see,' said Richard much too brightly. Sounding if possible amused. Castang the Entertainer. We've had the performing seals; now bring the clowns on. 'Good. Now listen carefully.' Oh yes. He knew it all by heart. But he'd listen real carefully.

'You pissed or something?'

'No. My voice might be funny. I've been up all night.'

'Serve you right.' Oh all right, don't rub it in.

'But foaming,' said Richard frivolously. 'Red-eyed. Dotty. Sinking your teeth in the wallpaper.'

'Look, spare me the wit.'

'I'll spare you the wit, buster. Running round the countryside without telling me. With a negligent roll of those big muscular shoulders, put on to impress lover girl. All done by little me. Me bigchief Hollywood Indian, me solve crime without any bleeding commissaires. Me act big hero. Me get bullet in belly last reel, but me make heroic deathbed, tell girl me love her truly with last gasp. Is that what you're up to?'

'All right,' yelled Castang. 'Skip that, and I'll spare you my withdrawal symptoms.'

'Christ, boy, how much trouble can you make me! Proc's been taking my skin off.'

'Tell him I shit on him, pending the moment I tell him myself. If he's hiding behind the administrative channels I'm not.'

'Look, are you drunk?'

'Not yet.'

'Well, shut up, will you?'

'Yes sir. Yes sir.'

'I've had a series of complicated telephone calls.'

'Who'd have thought it?'

'Fabre's rung me. Raynal rang Fabre. Gendarmerie headquarters rang Raynal. Some bright eager lad – like you – out in the sticks has shown zeal.'

'Yes, I know, I was there.'

'Look, keep your mouth shut. The child is found.'

'What?'

'The child, Rachel Delavigne, is found.'

'Hold the line.'

He just didn't care any more. As long as she hadn't seen it coming. As long as they hadn't made her suffer. A chop in the

217

back of the neck, the way they did the rabbits, which at least was no worse than a guillotine. The body might twitch. So did a rabbit's. But the mouth wouldn't talk, any more than the rabbit's would.

'Give me another glass of that stuff.' And drank it. And went back.

'Sorry, but you do realize. Something of a shock.'

'You're not paid to be in shock.' Joke. 'So's she in shock.'

'That's one way of putting it.'

'Look, Castang, straighten yourself out, even if you have been up all night. I said the child's in shock, and mildly hysterical.'

'You mean she's alive?' said Castang stupidly.

'Are you? Get your goddam arse over there. Vicq: it's about thirty kilometres from you, over the line. And take a tube full of Alka Seltzer. And stop mucking about. I send you because you're nearest. And get yourself woken up, because this child's parents are in a flaming uproar, and I've got to handle them. All right, boy? Move.'

He did his best. Fastened his safety-belt, and drove carefully under a hundred kilometres an hour, and everything.

*

Rachel was alive. Very much alive. The storm had broken where she'd been. She'd been absolutely drenched. There'd been hail, too. She hadn't sheltered under a tree because she knew that was a dangerous thing to do. She'd gone on walking. A farmer who'd been trying to keep the hail off his vines, and who'd got up early to know the worst, had found her in his field. Lying under the vines, like a dead bird. His wife had undressed her and wrapped her in a blanket and given her hot milk. And called the doctor.

'Well, there's a considerable degree of shock. What d'you think – dark, thunder, lightning, rain, hail, and some enormous fear behind. If she could speak at all she'd be gibbering. We can stave off the pneumonia. Of course you can't question her; don't be ridiculous, man. Even if you could she'd say nothing coherent. She talks all the time about her bag.'

'Her bag?'

'Don't ask me. I'd like to have her mother here. You've identified her, as I understand it.'

218

'Her mother, I think I'm safe in saying, will be here very shortly.'

There was a loud squawk of brakes on the gravel outside the clinic. Castang, knowing that little yellow Alfa-Romeo, said, 'On cue,' in a cute voice that made the doctor glance at him with an awful look; about five cubic centimetres of paraldehyde is what this lot needs all round.

'All right, Colette. The fleet's in at Mobile.'

'Henri,' she rushed into his arms, and fought her way out of them instantly. 'Where's my child?'

'Right here. Sleepy – easy, she's pretty dopey.'

'Mama,' said Rachel. 'I've lost my bag.' And relapsed into sleep.

'Her bag?' said Castang stupidly.

'She must mean her school bag. She didn't have any other bag.'

'What on earth should she be worried about that for?'

The Vicq gendarmerie didn't want to know anything about anything. Since they knew nothing, but had got the child back – and that was the important thing, wasn't it? – they continued to know nothing. It was the brigadier, from Bellac, who drove over in the jeep, and did the detective work.

'Hallo, Castang. My respects, Madame: my felicitations, if you'll allow me. Well . . . it looked like a shot in the water. If we look again, might be in the gold for all that. But they'll deny everything, you know. And we didn't find as much as a hair-ribbon.'

'Good heavens, man,' said Colette hotly, 'she'll recognize them. She'll be able to tell, when she comes out of shock.'

'Madame, forgive me. You're a judge. And even a children's judge. How much credit do you give to eight-year-old witnesses? You must know that she'll say – it will be suggested – anything that is put in her mind to say. Her word, supported by some very circumstantial evidence. Telephone calls! Rabbits! Doesn't mean much. Against theirs. A united front. Not difficult for them. All they've got to do is stick to the same lie, that they don't know nothing, and they're being put upon. Now in the circumstances, Madame,' no, not a rustic Dogberry, this chap, 'there's going to be a lot saying it's a put-up job. Bourgeoisie against country people. Not my pigeon, Madame, but if you'll forgive my saying so we'd be well advised to steer clear of that sort of trap until, or unless, we can find something what can't be accused of any class prejudice, like.'

'She keeps talking about her bag.' Colette's mind was quicker than Castang's.

'Bag?'

'When she was pinched,' said Castang, 'she had with her her school bag.'

'And they got rid of it.' The brigadier's mind was quicker than either. 'They'll have ditched it. Literally. In the ditch.'

The thing was, it was not at all easy to discover where exactly Rachel had been pushed out of a car in the middle of the night with a storm coming on. There were a lot of country roads. And a lot of grass – and weed-grown ditches. Miles and miles of them. A case of dogged does it. But that afternoon – Bernard was there by then, and Richard was there by then, and even Castang had had time for long, gabbling, confused telephone calls to Vera – the gendarmerie, wading step by step through sodden ditches with the weeds waist high, starting from the spot where the farmer found Rachel lying under his vines, found her school bag.

By that time Monsieur Besson, the Procureur de la République, in person, had arrived. With him there, not to speak of laboratory technicians from the P.J., there were fingerprints found on the outside, or the underside if you prefer, of that school bag. Perfectly good fingerprints. Incomplete, being smeared on grained leather, but as damning as anything Poirot ever found.

'My dear man,' said Monsieur Besson to the lieutenant of gendarmerie, 'I've no doubt but that your brigadier, a most able and skilful officer if you will allow me to say so, will take a certain personal satisfaction in arresting this woman. In fact the whole boiling.'

'The boy too?'

'The boy too.' Monsieur Besson, along with Colette and a somewhat incoherent Bernard, had spent an hour by Rachel's bed. 'She says quite clearly that a young man with the aid of rabbits entrapped her into entering the car. There is not the slightest doubt, and I am going to prosecute this in person.'

The moment certainty begins, frustration sets in. Colette felt nothing but lassitude. Our troubles are only just starting, she thought. Why did I ever begin? These things always have roots in a tiny moment of irresponsibility. Why was I so frightened? I reacted frenziedly because I felt under attack.

And presumably the same thing applies to these people. That woman, whom I have only heard but whom Henri has seen – he tells me that she has a small child. A bit smaller than Rachel. . . .

Look at Besson. He's thinking hard, planning ahead. Says he's going to prosecute himself, and to look at him you'd think he was possessed by righteous indignation. Not a bit of it. He'll know how to handle old Jeremiah so that no inconvenient facts come out. Because he knows – or at least he has an informed guess, since Richard has talked to him.

Bernard's thoughts were parallel.

I started this, he told himself gloomily. Come to that I suppose I started the whole thing off with that idiotic and gratuitous squabble over the fruit-trees. Which was only showing off, throwing my weight about, trying to impress Colette with Joséphine's being the bourgeois landed proprietor. She never gave a damn about those lousy cherries. In fact she was happy to let the fellow have them, because he let her have manure for the vines.

But if I hadn't insisted on making a criminal complaint, and dragging the P.J. into it . . . I thought I was being clever, getting the two of them tied together and stuck with it, so that they would realize their responsibility. The result would have been the same, I suppose. The gendarmerie would have found the child, and made the complaint themselves, and there would be a criminal instruction just the same. But there wouldn't be a huddle of magistrates determined to cover up a small disgraceful fact. They can just go blithely ahead ordering psychiatric examinations of this woman and this boy. They won't order any for us. Besson can be relied upon. There are moments of temptation in his own past. Who knows anyhow what little irresponsibilities with other people's wives he may have. . . ?

Castang drove home. He didn't have to arrest anybody. The gendarmerie would do all that. The judge of instruction would go into all the whys and wherefores.

What little grain of torment prompted that woman? Pretty woman too. Could that be something, back in the past, that Bernard . . .? He likes – was it Colette said that, in a snappish moment, or was it that old priss at the office who told me he 'liked kitchen-maids'?

No. Shut your eyes, boy. You're responsible for your own actions, not for those of others.

Your own are quite enough to be going on with.

Rachel had to be found. That was your job, not just your responsibility. I don't think that Richard will say anything. I have a kind of notion that he and Monsieur le Procureur have had their heads together about the whys and the hows.

It was perfectly accurate. Monsieur Richard received him with no sign of fluster. 'I'm glad to hear it,' he said with objective calm. 'It could have been very nasty. You've been rather lucky, haven't you? You can go home now. Give me a written report tomorrow.'

'And by the way, Castang . . . In the future, you'll be a little more careful about your friendships.'

He went home. Vera was asleep, having been up all night too. She woke, of course, and asked whether he wanted anything.

'Well, perhaps there are a couple of things to get straight.'

'Never explain.'

'No, but I think you might have a few false ideas.'

'They're better left untouched you know, however false they are.'

That's it.

Draw a veil over the whole thing.